His hair was grey and clipped short and his neck had as many folds as a concertina. His feet were small, as the feet of fat men often are, and they were in black shiny shoes which were sideways on the carpet and close together and neat and nasty. He wore a dark suit that needed cleaning. I leaned down and buried my fingers in the bottomless fat of his neck. He had an artery in there somewhere, probably, but I couldn't find it and he probably didn't need it any more anyway. Between his bloated knees on the carpet a dark stain had spread and spread—

"MORE THAN JUST DETECTIVE STORIES . . . MARLOWE IS THE SINGULAR RIGHT MAN IN A PLACE GONE DEEPLY AND IRREVOCABLY WRONG."

William Corbett, **Fusion**

Also by Raymond Chandler
Published by Ballantine Books:

KILLER IN THE RAIN

THE LITTLE SISTER

THE LONG GOODBYE

PICKUP ON NOON STREET

PLAYBACK

THE SIMPLE ART OF MURDER

RAYMOND CHANDLER

TROUBLE IS MY BUSINESS

BALLANTINE BOOKS • NEW YORK

The stories in this book appeared in *The Simple Art of Murder*, Houghton Mifflin, 1950. The material in that edition originally appeared in the following magazines: *Black Mask, Dime Detective, Detective Fiction Weekly, The Saturday Evening Post, Atlantic Monthly*, and *The Saturday Review of Literature*.

ISBN 0-345-35494-X

Manufactured in the United States of America

This edition published by arrangement with Houghton Mifflin Company

First Ballantine Books Edition: February 1972
Seventh Printing: October 1987

CONTENTS

INTRODUCTION

SOME literary antiquarian of a rather special type may one day think it worth while to run through the files of the pulp detective magazines which flourished during the late twenties and early thirties, and determine just how and when and by what steps the popular mystery story shed its refined good manners and went native. He will need sharp eyes and an open mind. Pulp paper never dreamed of posterity and most of it must be a dirty brown color by now. And it takes a very open mind indeed to look beyond the unnecessarily gaudy covers, trashy titles and barely acceptable advertisements and recognize the authentic power of a kind of writing that, even at its most mannered and artificial, made most of the fiction of the time taste like a cup of luke-warm consommé at a spinsterish tearoom.

I don't think this power was entirely a matter of violence, although far too many people got killed in these stories and their passing was celebrated with a rather too loving attention to detail. It certainly was not a matter of fine writing, since any attempt at that would have been ruthlessly blue-penciled by the editorial staff. Nor was it because of any great originality of plot or character. Most of the plots were rather ordinary and most of the characters rather primitive types of people. Possibly it was the smell of fear which these stories managed to generate. Their characters lived in a world gone wrong, a world in which, long before the atom bomb, civilization had created the machinery for its own destruction, and was learning to use it with all the moronic delight of a gangster trying out his first machine gun. The law was something to be manipulated for profit and power. The streets were dark with something more than night. The mystery story grew hard and cynical about motive and character, but it was not cynical about the effects it tried to produce nor about its technique of producing them. A few unusual critics recognized this at the time, which was all one had any right to expect. The average critic never recognizes an achievement when it happens. He explains it after it has become respectable.

The emotional basis of the standard detective story was and had always been that murder will out and justice will be done. Its technical basis was the relative insignificance of everything except the final denouement. What led up to that was more or less passagework. The denouement would justify everything. The technical basis of the *Black Mask* type of story on the other hand was that the scene outranked the plot, in the sense that a good plot was one which made good scenes. The ideal mystery was one you would read if the end was missing. We who tried to write it had the same point of view as the film makers. When I first went to work in Hollywood a very intelligent producer told me that you couldn't make a successful motion picture from a mystery story, because the whole point was a disclosure that took a few seconds of screen time while the audience was reaching for its hat. He was wrong, but only because he was thinking of the wrong kind of mystery.

As to the emotional basis of the hard-boiled story, obviously it does not believe that murder will out and justice will be done—unless some very determined individual makes it his business to see that justice is done. The stories were about the men who made that happen. They were apt to be hard men, and what they did, whether they were called police officers, private detectives or newspaper men, was hard, dangerous work. It was work they could always get. There was plenty of it lying around. There still is. Undoubtedly the stories about them had a fantastic element. Such things happened, but not so rapidly, nor to so close-knit a group of people, nor within so narrow a frame of logic. This was inevitable because the demand was for constant action; if you stopped to think you were lost. When in doubt have a man come through a door with a gun in his hand. This could get to be pretty silly, but somehow it didn't seem to matter. A writer who is afraid to overreach himself is as useless as a general who is afraid to be wrong.

As I look back on my own stories it would be absurd if I did not wish they had been better. But if they had been much better they would not have been published. If the formula had been a little less rigid, more of the writing of that time might have survived. Some of us tried pretty hard to break out of the formula, but we usually got caught and sent back. To exceed the limits of a formula without destroying it is the dream of every magazine writer who is not a hopeless hack. There are things in my stories which I might like to change or leave out altogether. To do this may look simple, but if you try, you find you cannot do it at all. You will only destroy what is good without having any noticeable effect on what is bad. You cannot recapture the mood, the state of innocence, much less the animal gusto you had when you had very little else. Everything a writer learns about the art or craft of fiction takes just a little away from his need or desire to write at all. In the end he knows all the tricks and has nothing to say.

As for the literary quality of these exhibits, I am entitled to assume from the imprint of a distinguished publisher that I need not be sickeningly humble. As a writer I have never been able to take myself with that enormous earnestness which is one of the trying characteristics of the craft. And I have been fortunate to escape what has been called "that form of snobbery which can accept the Literature of Entertainment in the Past, but only the Literature of Enlightenment in the Present." Between the one-syllable humors of the comic strip and the anemic subtleties of the litterateurs there is a wide stretch of country, in which the mystery story may or may not be an important landmark. There are those who hate it in all its forms. There are those who like it when it is about nice people ("that charming Mrs. Jones, whoever would have thought she would cut off her husband's head with a meat saw? Such a handsome man, too!"). There are those who think violence and sadism interchangeable terms, and those who regard detective fiction as subliterary on no better grounds than that it does not habitually get itself jammed up with subordinate clauses, tricky punctuation and hypothetical subjunctives. There are those who read it only when they are tired or sick, and, from the number of mystery novels they consume, they must be tired and sick most of the time. There are the aficionados of deduction and the aficionados of sex who can't get it into their hot little heads that the fictional detective is a catalyst, not a Casanova. The former demand a ground plan of Greythorpe Manor, showing the study, the gun room, the main hall and staircase and the passage to that grim little room where the butler polishes the Georgian silver, thin-lipped and silent, hearing the murmur of doom. The latter think the shortest distance between two points is from a blonde to a bed.

No writer can please them all, no writer should try. The stories in this book certainly had no thought of being able to please anyone ten or fifteen years after they were written. The mystery story is a kind of writing that need not dwell in the shadow of the past and owes little if any allegiance to the cult of the classics. It is a good deal more than unlikely that any writer now living will produce a better historical novel than *Henry Esmond,* a better tale of children than *The Golden Age,* a sharper social vignette than *Madame Bovary,* a more graceful and elegant evocation than *The Spoils of Poynton,* a wider and richer canvas than *War and Peace* or *The Brothers Karamazov.* But to devise a more plausible mystery than *The Hound of the Baskervilles* or *The Purloined Letter* should not be too difficult. Nowadays it would be rather more difficult not to. There are no "classics" of crime and detection. Not one. Within its frame of reference, which is the only way it should be judged, a classic is a piece of writing which exhausts the possibilities of its form and can hardly be surpassed. No story or novel of mystery has done that yet. Few have come close. Which is one of the principal reasons why otherwise reasonable people continue to assault the citadel.

RAYMOND CHANDLER.

La Jolla, California
February 15, 1950

TROUBLE IS MY
BUSINESS

1

ANNA HALSEY was about two hundred and forty pounds of middle-aged putty-faced woman in a black tailor-made suit. Her eyes were shiny black shoe buttons, her cheeks were as soft as suet and about the same color. She was sitting behind a black glass desk that looked like Napoleon's tomb and she was smoking a cigarette in a black holder that was not quite as long as a rolled umbrella. She said: "I need a man."

I watched her shake ash from the cigarette to the shiny top of the desk where flakes of it curled and crawled in the draft from an open window.

"I need a man good-looking enough to pick up a dame who has a sense of class, but he's got to be tough enough to swap punches with a power shovel. I need a guy who can act like a bar lizard and backchat like Fred Allen, only better, and get hit on the head with a beer truck and think some cutie in the leg-line topped him with a breadstick."

"It's a cinch," I said. "You need the New York Yankees, Robert Donat, and the Yacht Club Boys."

"You might do," Anna said, "cleaned up a little. Twenty bucks a day and ex's. I haven't brokered a job in years, but this one is out of my line. I'm in the smooth-angles of the detecting business and I make money without getting my can knocked off. Let's see how Gladys likes you."

She reversed the cigarette holder and tipped a key on a large black-and-chromium annunciator box. "Come in and empty Anna's ash tray, honey."

We waited.

3

The door opened and a tall blonde dressed better than the Duchess of Windsor strolled in.

She swayed elegantly across the room, emptied Anna's ash tray, patted her fat cheek, gave me a smooth rippling glance and went out again.

"I think she blushed," Anna said when the door closed. "I guess you still have It."

"She blushed—and I have a dinner date with Darryl Zanuck," I said. "Quit horsing around. What's the story?"

"It's to smear a girl. A redheaded number with bedroom eyes. She's shill for a gambler and she's got her hooks into a rich man's pup."

"What do I do to her?"

Anna sighed. "It's kind of a mean job, Philip, I guess. If she's got a record of any sort, you dig it up and toss it in her face. If she hasn't, which is more likely as she comes from good people, it's kind of up to you. You get an idea once in a while, don't you?"

"I can't remember the last one I had. What gambler and what rich man?"

"Marty Estel."

I started to get up from my chair, then remembered that business had been bad for a month and that I needed the money.

I sat down again.

"You might get into trouble, of course," Anna said. "I never heard of Marty bumping anybody off in the public square at high noon, but he don't play with cigar coupons."

"Trouble is my business," I said. "Twenty-five a day and guarantee of two-fifty, if I pull the job."

"I gotta make a little something for myself," Anna whined.

"O.K. There's plenty of coolie labor around town. Nice to have seen you looking so well. So long, Anna."

I stood up this time. My life wasn't worth much, but

it was worth that much. Marty Estel was supposed to be pretty tough people, with the right helpers and the right protection behind him. His place was out in West Hollywood, on the Strip. He wouldn't pull anything crude, but if he pulled at all, something would pop.

"Sit down, it's a deal," Anna sneered. "I'm a poor old broken-down woman trying to run a high-class detective agency on nothing but fat and bad health, so take my last nickel and laugh at me."

"Who's the girl?" I had sat down again.

"Her name is Harriet Huntress—a swell name for the part too. She lives in the El Milano, nineteen-hundred block on North Sycamore, very high-class. Father went broke back in thirty-one and jumped out of his office window. Mother dead. Kid sister in boarding school back in Connecticut. That might make an angle."

"Who dug up all this?"

"The client got a bunch of photostats of notes the pup had given to Marty. Fifty grand worth. The pup—he's an adopted son to the old man—denied the notes, as kids will. So the client had the photostats experted by a guy named Arbogast, who pretends to be good at that sort of thing. He said O.K. and dug around a bit, but he's too fat to do legwork, like me, and he's off the case now."

"But I could talk to him?"

"I don't know why not." Anna nodded several of her chins.

"This client—does he have a name?"

"Son, you have a treat coming. You can meet him in person—right now."

She tipped the key of her call box again. "Have Mr. Jeeter come in, honey."

"That Gladys," I said, "does she have a steady?"

"You lay off Gladys!" Anna almost screamed at me. "She's worth eighteen grand a year in divorce business to me. Any guy that lays a finger on her, Philip Marlowe, is practically cremated."

"She's got to fall some day," I said. "Why couldn't I catch her?"

The opening door stopped that.

I hadn't seen him in the paneled reception room, so he must have been waiting in a private office. He hadn't enjoyed it. He came in quickly, shut the door quickly, and yanked a thin octagonal platinum watch from his vest and glared at it. He was a tall white-blond type in pin-striped flannel of youthful cut. There was a small pink rosebud in his lapel. He had a keen frozen face, a little pouchy under the eyes, a little thick in the lips. He carried an ebony cane with a silver knob, wore spats and looked a smart sixty, but I gave him close to ten years more. I didn't like him.

"Twenty-six minutes, Miss Halsey," he said icily. "My time happens to be valuable. By regarding it as valuable I have managed to make a great deal of money."

"Well, we're trying to save you some of the money," Anna drawled. She didn't like him either. "Sorry to keep you waiting, Mr. Jeeter, but you wanted to see the operative I selected and I had to send for him."

"He doesn't look the type to me," Mr. Jeeter said, giving me a nasty glance. "I think more of a gentleman—"

"You're not the Jeeter of *Tobacco Road*, are you?" I asked him.

He came slowly towards me and half lifted the stick. His icy eyes tore at me like claws. "So you insult me," he said. "Me—a man in my position."

"Now wait a minute," Anna began.

"Wait a minute nothing," I said. "This party said I was not a gentleman. Maybe that's O.K. for a man in his position, whatever it is—but a man in my position doesn't take a dirty crack from anybody.

He can't afford to. Unless, of course, it wasn't intended."

Mr. Jeeter stiffened and glared at me. He took his watch out again and looked at it. "Twenty-eight minutes," he said. "I apologize, young man. I had no desire to be rude."

"That's swell," I said. "I knew you weren't the Jeeter in *Tobacco Road* all along."

That almost started him again, but he let it go. He wasn't sure how I meant it.

"A question or two while we are together," I said. "Are you willing to give this Huntress girl a little money —for expenses?"

"Not one cent," he barked. "Why should I?"

"It's got to be a sort of custom. Suppose she married him. What would he have?"

"At the moment a thousand dollars a month from a trust fund established by his mother, my late wife." He dipped his head. "When he is twenty-eight years old, far too much money."

"You can't blame the girl for trying," I said. "Not these days. How about Marty Estel? Any settlement there?"

He crumpled his gray gloves with a purple-veined hand. "The debt is uncollectible. It is a gambling debt."

Anna sighed wearily and flicked ash around on her desk.

"Sure," I said. "But gamblers can't afford to let people welsh on them. After all, if your son had won, Marty would have paid *him.*"

"I'm not interested in that," the tall thin man said coldly.

"Yeah, but think of Marty sitting there with fifty grand in notes. Not worth a nickel. How will he sleep nights?"

Mr. Jeeter looked thoughtful. "You mean there is danger of violence?" he suggested, almost suavely.

"That's hard to say. He runs an exclusive place, gets a good movie crowd. He has his own reputation to think of. But he's in a racket and he knows people. Things can happen—a long way off from where Marty is. And Marty is no bathmat. He gets up and walks."

Mr. Jeeter looked at his watch again and it annoyed him. He slammed it back into his vest. "All that is your affair," he snapped. "The district attorney is a personal friend of mine. If this matter seems to be beyond your powers—"

"Yeah," I told him. "But you came slumming down our street just the same. Even if the D.A. is in your vest pocket—along with that watch."

He put his hat on, drew on one glove, tapped the edge of his shoe with his stick, walked to the door and opened it.

"I ask results and I pay for them," he said coldly. "I pay promptly. I even pay generously sometimes, although I am not considered a generous man. I think we all understand one another."

He almost winked then and went on out. The door closed softly against the cushion of air in the door-closer. I looked at Anna and grinned.

"Sweet, isn't he?" she said. "I'd like eight of him for my cocktail set."

I gouged twenty dollars out of her—for expenses.

2

The Arbogast I wanted was John D. Arbogast and he had an office on Sunset near Ivar. I called him up from a phone booth. The voice that answered was fat. It wheezed softly, like the voice of a man who had just won a pie-eating contest.

"Mr. John D. Arbogast?"

"Yeah."

"This is Philip Marlowe, a private detective working on a case you did some experting on. Party named Jeeter."

"Yeah?"

"Can I come up and talk to you about it—after I eat lunch?"

"Yeah." He hung up. I decided he was not a talkative man.

I had lunch and drove out there. It was east of Ivar, an old two-story building faced with brick which had been painted recently. The street floor was stores and a restaurant. The building entrance was the foot of a wide straight stairway to the second floor. On the directory at the bottom I read: John D. Arbogast, Suite 212. I went up the stairs and found myself in a wide straight hall that ran parallel with the street. A man in a smock was standing in an open doorway down to my right. He wore a round mirror strapped to his forehead and pushed back, and his face had a puzzled expression. He went back to his office and shut the door.

I went the other way, about half the distance along the hall. A door on the side away from Sunset was lettered: JOHN D. ARBOGAST, EXAMINER OF QUESTIONED DOCUMENTS. PRIVATE INVESTIGATOR. ENTER. The door opened without resistance onto a small windowless anteroom with a couple of easy chairs, some magazines, two chromium smoking stands. There were two floor lamps and a ceiling fixture, all lighted. A door on the other side of the cheap but thick new rug was lettered: JOHN D. ARBOGAST, EXAMINER OF QUESTIONED DOCUMENTS. PRIVATE.

A buzzer had rung when I opened the outer door and gone on ringing until it closed. Nothing happened. Nobody was in the waiting room. The inner door didn't open. I went over and listened at the panel—no sound of conversation inside. I knocked. That didn't buy me anything either. I tried the knob. It turned, so I opened the door and went in.

This room had two north windows, both curtained at the sides and both shut tight. There was dust on the sills. There was a desk, two filing cases, a carpet which was just a carpet, and walls which were just walls. To the left another door with a glass panel was lettered: JOHN D. ARBOGAST. LABORATORY. PRIVATE.

I had an idea I might be able to remember the name.

The room in which I stood was small. It seemed almost too small even for the pudgy hand that rested on the edge of the desk, motionless, holding a fat pencil like a carpenter's pencil. The hand had a wrist, hairless as a plate. A buttoned shirt cuff, not too clean, came down out of a coat sleeve. The rest of the sleeve dropped over the far edge of the desk out of sight. The desk was less than six feet long, so he couldn't have been a very tall man. The hand and the ends of the sleeves were all I saw of him from where I stood. I went quietly back through the anteroom and fixed its door so that it couldn't be opened from the outside and put out the three lights and went back to the private office. I went around an end of the desk.

He was fat all right, enormously fat, fatter by far than Anna Halsey. His face, what I could see of it, looked about the size of a basket ball. It had a pleasant pinkness, even now. He was kneeling on the floor. He had his large head against the sharp inner corner of the kneehole of the desk, and his left hand was flat on the floor with a piece of yellow paper under it. The fingers were outspread as much as such fat fingers could be, and the yellow paper showed between. He looked as if he were pushing hard on the floor, but he wasn't really. What was holding him up was his own fat. His body was folded down against his enormous thighs, and the thickness and fatness of them held him that way, kneeling, poised solid. It would have taken a couple of good blocking backs to knock him over. That wasn't a very nice idea at the moment, but I had it just the same. I took time out and wiped the back of my neck, although it was not a warm day.

His hair was gray and clipped short and his neck had as many folds as a concertina. His feet were small, as the feet of fat men often are, and they were in black shiny shoes which were sideways on the carpet and close together and neat and nasty. He wore a dark suit that needed cleaning. I leaned down and buried my fingers in the bottomless fat of his neck. He had an artery in there somewhere, probably, but I couldn't find it and he didn't need it any more anyway. Between his bloated knees on the carpet a dark stain had spread and spread—

I knelt in another place and lifted the pudgy fingers that were holding down the piece of yellow paper. They were cool, but not cold, and soft and a little sticky. The paper was from a scratch pad. It would have been very nice if it had had a message on it, but it hadn't. There were vague meaningless marks, not words, not even letters. He had tried to write something after he was shot—perhaps even thought he *was* writing something—but all he managed was some hen scratches.

He had slumped down then, still holding the paper, pinned it to the floor with his fat hand, held on to the fat pencil with his other hand, wedged his torso against his huge thighs, and so died. John D. Arbogast. Examiner of Questioned Documents. Private. Very damned private. He had said "yeah" to me three times over the phone.

And here he was.

I wiped doorknobs with my handkerchief, put off the lights in the anteroom, left the outer door so that it was locked from the outside, left the hallway, left the building and left the neighborhood. So far as I could tell nobody saw me go. So far as I could tell.

3

The El Milano was, as Anna had told me, in the 1900 block on North Sycamore. It was most of the block. I parked fairly near the ornamental forecourt and went along to the pale blue neon sign over the entrance to the basement garage. I walked down a railed ramp into a bright space of glistening cars and cold air. A trim light-colored Negro in a spotless coverall suit with blue cuffs came out of a glass office. His black hair was as smooth as a bandleader's.

"Busy?" I asked him.

"Yes and no, sir."

"I've got a car outside that needs a dusting. About five bucks worth of dusting."

It didn't work. He wasn't the type. His chestnut eyes became thoughtful and remote. "That is a good deal of dusting, sir. May I ask if anything else would be included?"

"A little. Is Miss Harriet Huntress' car in?"

He looked. I saw him look along the glistening row at a canary-yellow convertible which was about as inconspicuous as a privy on the front lawn.

"Yes, sir. It is in."

"I'd like her apartment number and a way to get up there without going through the lobby. I'm a private detective." I showed him a buzzer. He looked at the buzzer. It failed to amuse him.

He smiled the faintest smile I ever saw. "Five dollars is nice money, sir, to a working man. It falls a little short of being nice enough to make me risk my position. About from here to Chicago short, sir. I suggest that you save your five dollars, sir, and try the customary mode of entry."

"You're quite a guy," I said. "What are you going to be when you grow up—a five-foot shelf?"

"I am already grown up, sir. I am thirty-four years old, married happily, and have two children. Good afternoon, sir."

He turned on his heel. "Well, goodbye," I said. "And pardon my whiskey breath. I just got in from Butte."

I went back up along the ramp and wandered along the street to where I should have gone in the first place. I might have known that five bucks and a buzzer wouldn't buy me anything in a place like the El Milano.

The Negro was probably telephoning the office right now.

The building was a huge white stucco affair, Moorish in style, with great fretted lanterns in the forecourt and huge date palms. The entrance was at the inside corner of an L, up marble steps, through an arch framed in California or dishpan mosaic.

A doorman opened the door for me and I went in. The lobby was not quite as big as the Yankee Stadium. It was floored with a pale blue carpet with sponge rubber underneath. It was so soft it made me want to lie down and roll. I waded over to the desk and put an elbow on it and was stared at by a pale thin clerk with one of those mustaches that get stuck under your fingernail. He toyed with it and looked past my shoulder at an Ali Baba oil jar big enough to keep a tiger in.

"Miss Huntress in?"

"Who shall I announce?"

"Mr. Marty Estel."

That didn't take any better than my play in the garage. He leaned on something with his left foot. A blue-and-gilt door opened at the end of the desk and a large sandy-haired man with cigar ash on his vest came out and leaned absently on the end of the desk and stared at the Ali Baba oil jar, as if trying to make up his mind whether it was a spittoon.

The clerk raised his voice. "You are Mr. Marty Estel?"

"From him."

"Isn't that a little different? And what is your name, sir, if one may ask?"

"One may ask," I said. "One may not be told. Such are my orders. Sorry to be stubborn and all that rot."

He didn't like my manner. He didn't like anything about me. "I'm afraid I can't announce you," he said coldly. "Mr. Hawkins, might I have your advice on a matter?"

The sandy-haired man took his eyes off the oil jar and slid along the desk until he was within blackjack range of me.

"Yes, Mr. Gregory?" he yawned.

"Nuts to both of you," I said. "And that includes your lady friends."

Hawkins grinned. "Come into my office, bo. We'll kind of see if we can get you straightened out."

I followed him into the doghole he had come out of. It was large enough for a pint-sized desk, two chairs, a knee-high cuspidor, and an open box of cigars. He placed his rear end against the desk and grinned at me sociably.

"Didn't play it very smooth, did you, bo? I'm the house man here. Spill it."

"Some days I feel like playing smooth," I said, "and some days I feel like playing it like a waffle iron." I got my wallet out and showed him the buzzer and the small photostat of my license behind a celluloid window.

"One of the boys, huh?" He nodded. "You ought to of asked for me in the first place."

"Sure. Only I never heard of you. I want to see

this Huntress frail. She doesn't know me, but I have business with her, and it's not noisy business."

He made a yard and half sideways and cocked his cigar in the other corner of his mouth. He looked at my right eyebrow. "What's the gag? Why try to apple-polish the dinge downstairs? You gettin' any expense money?"

"Could be."

"I'm nice people," he said. "But I gotta protect the guests."

"You're almost out of cigars," I said, looking at the ninety or so in the box. I lifted a couple, smelled them, tucked a folded ten-dollar bill below them and put them back.

"That's cute," he said. "You and me could get along. What you want done?"

"Tell her I'm from Marty Estel. She'll see me."

"It's the job if I get a kickback."

"You won't. I've got important people behind me."

I started to reach for my ten, but he pushed my hand away. "I'll take a chance," he said. He reached for his phone and asked for Suite 814 and began to hum. His humming sounded like a cow being sick. He leaned forward suddenly and his face became a hon-eyed smile. His voice dripped.

"Miss Huntress? This is Hawkins, the house man. Hawkins. Yeah . . . Hawkins. Sure, you meet a lot of people, Miss Huntress. Say, there's a gentleman in my office wanting to see you with a message from Mr. Estel. We can't let him up without your say so, because he don't want to give us no name . . . Yeah, Hawkins, the house detective, Miss Huntress. Yeah, he says you don't know him personal, but he looks O.K. to me . . . O.K. Thanks a lot, Miss Huntress. Serve him right up."

He put the phone down and patted it gently.

"All you needed was some background music," I said.

"You can ride up," he said dreamily. He reached absently into his cigar box and removed the folded bill. "A darb," he said softly. "Every time I think of that dame I have to go out and walk around the block. Let's go."

We went out to the lobby again and Hawkins took me to the elevator and highsigned me in.

As the elevator doors closed I saw him on his way to the entrance, probably for his walk around the block.

The elevator had a carpeted floor and mirrors and indirect lighting. It rose as softly as the mercury in a thermometer. The doors whispered open, I wandered over the moss they used for a hall carpet and came to a door marked 814. I pushed a little button beside it, chimes rang inside and the door opened.

She wore a street dress of pale green wool and a small cockeyed hat that hung on her ear like a butterfly. Her eyes were wide-set and there was thinking room between them. Their color was lapis-lazuli blue and the color of her hair was dusky red, like a fire under control but still dangerous. She was too tall to be cute. She wore plenty of make-up in the right places and the cigarette she was poking at me had a built-on mouthpiece about three inches long. She didn't look hard, but she looked as if she had heard all the answers and remembered the ones she thought she might be able to use sometime.

She looked me over coolly. "Well, what's the message, brown-eyes?"

"I'd have to come in," I said. "I never could talk on my feet."

She laughed disinterestedly and I slid past the end of her cigarette into a long rather narrow room with plenty of nice furniture, plenty of windows, plenty of drapes, plenty of everything. A fire blazed behind a screen, a big log on top of a gas teaser. There was a silk Oriental rug in front of a nice rose davenport in front of the nice fire, and beside that there was Scotch and swish on a tabouret, ice in a bucket, everything to make a man feel at home.

"You'd better have a drink," she said. "You probably can't talk without a glass in your hand."

I sat down and reached for the Scotch. The girl sat in a deep chair and crossed her knees. I thought of Hawkins walking around the block. I could see a little something in his point of view.

"So you're from Marty Estel," she said, refusing a drink.

"Never met him."

"I had an idea to that effect. What's the racket, bum? Marty will love to hear how you used his name."

"I'm shaking in my shoes. What made you let me up?"

"Curiosity. I've been expecting lads like you any day. I never dodge trouble. Some kind of a dick, aren't you?"

I lit a cigarette and nodded. "Private. I have a little deal to propose."

"Propose it." She yawned.

"How much will you take to lay off young Jeeter?"

She yawned again. "You interest me—so little I could hardly tell you."

"Don't scare me to death. Honest, how much are you asking? Or is that an insult?"

She smiled. She had a nice smile. She had lovely teeth. "I'm a bad girl now," she said. "I don't have to ask. They bring it to me, tied up with ribbon."

"The old man's a little tough. They say he draws a lot of water."

"Water doesn't cost much."

I nodded and drank some more of my drink. It was good Scotch. In fact it was perfect. "His idea is you get nothing. You get smeared. You get put in the middle. I can't see it that way."

"But you're working for him."

"Sounds funny, doesn't it? There's probably a smart way to play this, but I just can't think of it at the moment. How much would you take—or would you?"

"How about fifty grand?"

"Fifty grand for you and another fifty for Marty?"

She laughed. "Now, you ought to know Marty wouldn't like me to mix in his business. I was just thinking of my end."

She crossed her legs the other way. I put another lump of ice in my drink.

"I was thinking of five hundred," I said.

"Five hundred what?" She looked puzzled.

"Dollars—not Rolls-Royces."

She laughed heartily. "You amuse me. I ought to tell you to go to hell, but I like brown eyes. Warm brown eyes with flecks of gold in them."

"You're throwing it away. I don't have a nickel."

She smiled and fitted a fresh cigarette between her lips. I went over to light it for her. Her eyes came up and looked into mine. Hers had sparks in them.

"Maybe I have a nickel already," she said softly.

"Maybe that's why he hired the fat boy—so you couldn't make him dance." I sat down again.

"Who hired what fat boy?"

"Old Jeeter hired a fat boy named Arbogast. He was on the case before me. Didn't you know? He got bumped off this afternoon."

I said it quite casually for the shock effect, but she didn't move. The provocative smile didn't leave the corners of her lips. Her eyes didn't change. She made a dim sound with her breath.

"Does it have to have something to do with me?" she asked quietly.

"I don't know. I don't know who murdered him. It was done in his office, around noon or a little later. It may not have anything to do with the Jeeter case.

But it happened pretty pat—just after I had been put on the job and before I got a chance to talk to him."

She nodded. "I see. And you think Marty does things like that. And of course you told the police?"

"Of course I did not."

"You're giving away a little weight there, brother."

"Yeah. But let's get together on a price and it had better be low. Because whatever the cops do to me they'll do plenty to Marty Estel and you when they get the story—if they get it."

"A little spot of blackmail," the girl said coolly. "I think I might call it that. Don't go too far with me, brown-eyes. By the way, do I know your name?"

"Philip Marlowe."

"Then listen, Philip. I was in the Social Register once. My family were nice people. Old man Jeeter ruined my father—all proper and legitimate, the way that kind of heel ruins people—but he ruined him, and my father committed suicide, and my mother died and I've got a kid sister back East in school and perhaps I'm not too damn particular how I get the money to take care of her. And maybe I'm going to take care of old Jeeter one of these days, too—even if I have to marry his son to do it."

"Stepson, adopted son," I said. "No relation at all."

"It'll hurt him just as hard, brother. And the boy will have plenty of the long green in a couple of years. I could do worse—even if he does drink too much."

"You wouldn't say that in front of him, lady."

"No? Take a look behind you, gumshoe. You ought to have the wax taken out of your ears."

I stood up and turned fast. He stood about four feet from me. He had come out of some door and sneaked across the carpet and I had been too busy being clever with nothing on the ball to hear him. He was big, blond, dressed in a rough sporty suit, with a scarf and open-necked shirt. He was red-faced and his eyes glittered and they were not focusing any too well. He was a bit drunk for that early in the day.

"Beat it while you can still walk," he sneered at me. "I heard it. Harry can say anything she likes about me. I like it. Dangle, before I knock your teeth down your throat!"

The girl laughed behind me. I didn't like that. I took a step towards the big blond boy. His eyes blinked. Big as he was, he was a pushover.

"Ruin him, baby," the girl said coldly behind my back. "I love to see these hard numbers bend at the knees.

I looked back at her with a leer. That was a mistake. He was wild, probably, but he could still hit a wall that didn't jump. He hit me while I was looking back over my shoulder. It hurts to be hit that way. He hit me plenty hard, on the back end of the jawbone.

I went over sideways, tried to spread my legs, and slid on the silk rug. I did a nose dive somewhere or other and my head was not as hard as the piece of furniture it smashed into.

For a brief blurred moment I saw his red face sneering down at me in triumph. I think I was a little sorry for him—even then.

Darkness folded down and I went out.

4

When I came to, the light from the windows across the room was hitting me square in the eyes. The back of my head ached. I felt it and it was sticky. I moved around slowly, like a cat in a strange house, got up on my knees and reached for the bottle of Scotch on the tabouret at the end of the davenport. By some miracle I hadn't knocked it over. Falling I had hit my head on the clawlike leg of a chair. That had hurt me a lot more than young Jeeter's haymaker. I could feel the sore place on my jaw all right, but it wasn't important enough to write in my diary.

I got up on my feet, took a swig of the Scotch and looked around. There wasn't anything to see. The room was empty. It was full of silence and the memory of a nice perfume. One of those perfumes you don't notice until they are almost gone, like the last leaf on a tree. I felt my head again, touched the sticky place with my handkerchief, decided it wasn't worth yelling about, and took another drink.

I sat down with the bottle on my knees, listening to traffic noise somewhere, far off. It was a nice room. Miss Harriet Huntress was a nice girl. She knew a few wrong numbers, but who didn't? I should criticize a little thing like that. I took another drink. The level in the bottle was a lot lower now. It was smooth and you hardly noticed it going down. It didn't take half your tonsils with it, like some of the stuff I had to drink. I took some more. My head felt all right now. I felt fine. I felt like singing the Prologue to *Pagliacci*. Yes, she was a nice girl. If she was paying her own rent, she was doing right well. I was for her. She was swell. I used some more of her Scotch.

The bottle was still half full. I shook it gently, stuffed it in my overcoat pocket, put my hat somewhere on my head and left. I made the elevator without hitting the walls on either side of the corridor, floated downstairs, strolled out into the lobby.

Hawkins, the house dick, was leaning on the end of the desk again, staring at the Ali Baba oil jar. The same clerk was nuzzling at the same itsy-bitsy mustache. I smiled at him. He smiled back. Hawkins smiled at me. I smiled back. Everybody was swell.

I made the front door the first time and gave the doorman two bits and floated down the steps and along the walk to the street and my car. The swift California twilight was falling. It was a lovely night. Venus in the west was as bright as a street lamp, as bright as life, as bright as Miss Huntress' eyes, as bright as a bottle of Scotch. That reminded me. I got the square bottle out and tapped it with discretion, corked it, and tucked it away again. There was still enough to get home on.

I crashed five red lights on the way back but my luck was in and nobody pinched me. I parked more or less in front of my apartment house and more or less near the curb. I rode to my floor in the elevator, had a little trouble opening the doors and helped myself out with my bottle. I got the key into my door and un-locked it and stepped inside and found the light switch. I took a little more of my medicine before ex-hausting myself any further. Then I started for the kitchen to get some ice and ginger ale for a real drink.

I thought there was a funny smell in the apartment —nothing I could put a name to offhand—a sort of medicinal smell. I hadn't put it there and it hadn't been there when I went out. But I felt too well to argue about it. I started for the kitchen, got about halfway there.

They came out at me, almost side by side, from the dressing room beside the wall bed—two of them—with guns. The tall one was grinning. He had his hat low on his forehead and he had a wedge-shaped face that ended in a point, like the bottom half of the ace of diamonds. He had dark moist eyes and a nose so bloodless that it might have been made of white wax. His gun was a Colt Woodsman with a long barrel and the front sight filed off. That meant he thought he was good.

The other was a little terrier-like punk with bristly reddish hair and no hat and watery blank eyes and bat ears and small feet in dirty white sneakers. He had an automatic that looked too heavy for him to hold up, but he seemed to like holding it. He breathed openmouthed and noisily and the smell I had noticed came from him in waves—menthol.

"Reach, you bastard," he said.

I put my hands up. There was nothing else to do.

The little one circled around to the side and came at me from the side. "Tell us we can't get away with it," he sneered.

"You can't get away with it," I said.

The tall one kept on grinning loosely and his nose kept on looking as if it was made of white wax. The little one spat on my carpet. "Yah!" He came close to me, leering, and made a pass at my chin with the big gun.

I dodged. Ordinarily that would have been just something which, in the circumstances, I had to take and like. But I was feeling better than ordinary. I was a world-beater. I took them in sets, guns and all. I took the little man around the throat and jerked him hard against my stomach, put a hand over his little gun hand and knocked the gun to the floor. It was easy. Nothing was bad about it but his breath. Blobs of saliva came out on his lips. He spit curses.

The tall man stood and leered and didn't shoot. He didn't move. His eyes looked a little anxious, I thought, but I was too busy to make sure. I went down behind the little punk, still holding him, and got hold of his gun. That was wrong. I ought to have pulled my own.

I threw him away from me and he reeled against a a chair and fell down and began to kick the chair savagely. The tall man laughed.

"It ain't got any firing pin in it," he said.

"Listen," I told him earnestly, "I'm half full of good Scotch and ready to go places and get things done. Don't waste much of my time. What do you boys want?"

"It still ain't got any firing pin in it," Waxnose said. "Try and see. I don't never let Frisky carry a loaded rod. He's too impulsive. You got a nice arm action there, pal. I will say that for you."

Frisky sat up on the floor and spat on the carpet again and laughed. I pointed the muzzle of the big automatic at the floor and squeezed the trigger. It clicked dryly, but from the balance it felt as if it had cartridges in it.

"We don't mean no harm," Waxnose said. "Not this trip. Maybe next trip? Who knows? Maybe you're a guy that will take a hint. Lay off the Jeeter kid is the word. See?"

"No."

"You won't do it?"

"No, I don't see. Who's the Jeeter kid?"

Waxnose was not amused. He waved his long .22 gently. "You oughta get your memory fixed, pal, about the same time you get your door fixed. A pushover that was. Frisky just blew it in with his breath."

"I can understand that," I said.

"Gimme my gat," Frisky yelped. He was up off the floor again, but this time he rushed his partner instead of me.

"Lay off, dummy," the tall one said. "We just got a message for a guy. We don't blast him. Not today."

"Says you!" Frisky snarled and tried to grab the .22 out of Waxnose's hand. Waxnose threw him to one side without trouble but the interlude allowed me to switch the big automatic to my left hand and jerk out my Luger. I showed it to Waxnose. He nodded, but did not seem impressed.

"He ain't got no parents," he said sadly. "I just let him run around with me. Don't pay him no attention unless he bites you. We'll be on our way now. You get the idea. Lay off the Jeeter kid."

"You're looking at a Luger," I said. "Who is the Jeeter kid? And maybe we'll have some cops before you leave."

He smiled wearily. "Mister, I pack this small-bore because I can shoot. If you think you can take me, go to it."

"O.K.," I said. "Do you know anybody named Arbogast?"

"I meet such a lot of people," he said, with another weary smile. "Maybe yes, maybe no. So long, pal. Be pure."

He strolled over to the door, moving a little sideways, so that he had me covered all the time, and I had him covered, and it was just a case of who shot first and straightest, or whether it was worthwhile to shoot at all, or whether I could hit anything with so much nice warm Scotch in me. I let him go. He didn't look like a killer to me, but I could have been wrong.

The little man rushed me again while I wasn't thinking about him. He clawed his big automatic out of my left hand, skipped over to the door, spat on the carpet again, and slipped out. Waxnose backed after him— long sharp face, white nose, pointed chin, weary expression. I wouldn't forget him.

He closed the door softly and I stood there, foolish, holding my gun. I heard the elevator come up and go down again and stop. I still stood there. Marty Estel wouldn't be very likely to hire a couple of comics like that to throw a scare into anybody. I thought about that, but thinking got me nowhere. I remembered the half-bottle of Scotch I had left and went into executive session with it.

An hour and a half later I felt fine, but I still didn't have any ideas. I just felt sleepy.

The jarring of the telephone bell woke me. I had dozed off in the chair, which was a bad mistake, because I woke up with two flannel blankets in my mouth, a splitting headache, a bruise on the back of my head and another on my jaw, neither of them larger than a Yakima apple, but sore for all that. I felt terrible. I felt like an amputated leg.

I crawled over to the telephone and humped myself in a chair beside it and answered it. The voice dripped icicles.

"Mr. Marlowe? This is Mr. Jeeter. I believe we met this morning. I'm afraid I was a little stiff with you."

"I'm a little stiff myself. Your son poked me in the jaw. I mean your stepson, or your adopted son—or whatever he is."

"He is both my stepson and my adopted son. Indeed?" He sounded interested. "And where did you meet him?"

"In Miss Huntress' apartment."

"Oh I see." There had been a sudden thaw. The icicles had melted. "Very interesting. What did Miss Huntress have to say?"

"She liked it. She liked him poking me in the jaw."

"I see. And why did he do that?"

"She had him hid out. He overheard some of our talk. He didn't like it."

"I see. I have been thinking that perhaps some consideration—not large, of course—should be granted to her for her co-operation. That is, if we can secure it."

"Fifty grand is the price."

"I'm afraid I don't—"

"Don't kid me," I snarled. "Fifty thousand dollars. Fifty grand. I offered her five hundred—just for a gag."

"You seem to treat this whole business in a spirit of considerable levity," he snarled back. "I am not accustomed to that sort of thing and I don't like it."

I yawned. I didn't give a damn if school kept in or not. "Listen, Mr. Jeeter, I'm a great guy to horse around, but I have my mind on the job just the same. And there are some very unusual angles to this case. For instance a couple of gunmen just stuck me up in my apartment here and told me to lay off the Jeeter case. I don't see why it should get so tough."

"Good heavens!" He sounded shocked. "I think you

had better come to my house at once and we will discuss matters. I'll send my car for you. Can you come right away?"

"Yeah. But I can drive myself. I—"

"No. I'm sending my car and chauffeur. His name is George; you may rely upon him absolutely. He should be there in about twenty minutes."

"O.K.," I said. "That just gives me time to drink my dinner. Have him park around the corner of Kenmore, facing towards Franklin." I hung up.

When I'd had a hot-and-cold shower and put on some clean clothes I felt more respectable. I had a couple of drinks, small ones for a change, and put a light overcoat on and went down to the street.

The car was there already. I could see it half a block down the side street. It looked like a new market opening. It had a couple of headlamps like the one on the front end of a streamliner, two amber foglights hooked to the front fender, and a couple of sidelights as big as ordinary headlights. I came up beside it and stopped and a man stepped out of the shadows, tossing a cigarette over his shoulder with a neat flip of the wrist. He was tall, broad, dark, wore a peaked cap, a Russian tunic with a Sam Browne belt, shiny leggings and breeches that flared like an English staff major's whipcords.

"Mr. Marlowe?" He touched the peak of his cap with a gloved forefinger.

"Yeah," I said. "At ease. Don't tell me that's old man Jeeter's car."

"One of them." It was a cool voice that could get fresh.

He opened the rear door and I got in and sank down into the cushions and George slid under the wheel and started the big car. It moved away from the curb and around the corner with as much noise as a bill makes in a wallet. We went west. We seemed to be drifting with the current, but we passed everything. We slid through the heart of Hollywood, the west end of it, down to the Strip and along the glitter of that to the cool quiet of Beverly Hills where the bridle path divides the boulevard.

We gave Beverly Hills the swift and climbed along the foothills, saw the distant lights of the university buildings and swung north into Bel-Air. We began to slide up long narrow streets with high walls and no sidewalks and big gates. Lights on mansions glowed politely through the early night. Nothing stirred. There was no sound but the soft purr of the tires on concrete. We swung left again and I caught a sign which read Calvello Drive. Halfway up this George started to swing the car wide to make a left turn in at a pair of twelve-foot wrought-iron gates. Then something happened.

A pair of lights flared suddenly just beyond the gates and a horn screeched and a motor raced. A car charged at us fast. George straightened out with a flick of the wrist, braked the car and slipped off his right glove, all in one motion.

The car came on, the lights swaying. "Damn drunk," George swore over his shoulder.

It could be. Drunks in cars go all kinds of places to drink. It could be. I slid down onto the floor of the car and yanked the Luger from under my arm and reached up to open the catch. I opened the door a little and held it that way, looking over the sill. The headlights hit me in the face and I ducked, then came up again as the beam passed.

The other car jammed to a stop. Its door slammed open and a figure jumped out of it, waving a gun and shouting. I heard the voice and knew.

"Reach, you bastards!" Frisky screamed at us.

George put his left hand on the wheel and I opened my door a little more. The little man in the street was bouncing up and down and yelling. Out of the small dark car from which he had jumped came no sound except the noise of its motor.

"This is a heist!" Frisky yelled. "Out of there and line up, you sons of bitches!"

I kicked my door open and started to get out, the Luger down at my side.

"You asked for it!" the little man yelled.

I dropped—fast. The gun in his hand belched flame. Somebody must have put a firing pin in it. Glass smashed behind my head. Out of the corner of my eye, which oughtn't to have had any corners at that particular moment, I saw George make a movement as smooth as a ripple of water. I brought the Luger up and started to squeeze the trigger, but a shot crashed beside me—George.

I held my fire. It wasn't needed now.

The dark car lurched forward and started down the hill furiously. It roared into the distance while the little man out in the middle of the pavement was still reeling grotesquely in the light reflected from the walls.

There was something dark on his face that spread. His gun bounded along the concrete. His little legs buckled and he plunged sideways and rolled and then, very suddenly, became still.

George said, "Yah!" and sniffed at the muzzle of his revolver.

"Nice shooting." I got out of the car, stood there looking at the little man—a crumpled nothing. The dirty white of his sneakers gleamed a little in the side glare of the car's lights.

George got out beside me. "Why me, brother?"

"I didn't fire. I was watching that pretty hip draw of yours. It was sweeter than honey."

"Thanks, pal. They were after Mister Gerald, of course. I usually ferry him home from the club about this time, full of liquor and bridge losses."

We went over to the little man and looked down at

him. He wasn't anything to see. He was just a little man who was dead, with a big slug in his face and blood on him.

"Turn some of those damn lights off," I growled. "And let's get away from here fast."

"The house is just across the street." George sounded as casual as if he had just shot a nickel in a slot machine instead of a man.

"The Jeeters are out of this, if you like your job. You ought to know that. We'll go back to my place and start all over."

"I get it," he snapped, and jumped back into the big car. He cut the foglights and the sidelights and I got in beside him in the front seat.

We straightened out and started up the hill, over the brow. I looked back at the broken window. It was the small one at the extreme back of the car and it wasn't shatterproof. A large piece was gone from it. They could fit that, if they got around to it, and make some evidence. I didn't think it would matter, but it might.

At the crest of the hill a large limousine passed us going down. Its dome light was on and in the interior, as in a lighted showcase, an elderly couple sat stiffly, taking the royal salute. The man was in evening clothes, with a white scarf and a crush hat. The woman was in furs and diamonds.

George passed them casually, gunned the car and we made a fast right turn into a dark street. "There's a couple of good dinners all shot to hell," he drawled. "and I bet they don't even report it."

"Yeah. Let's get back home and have a drink," I said. "I never really got to like killing people."

5

We sat with some of Miss Harriet Huntress' Scotch in our glasses and looked at each other across the rims. George looked nice with his cap off. His head was clustered over with wavy dark-brown hair and his teeth were very white and clean. He sipped his drink and nibbled a cigarette at the same time. His snappy black eyes had a cool glitter in them.

"Yale?" I asked.

"Dartmouth, if it's any of your business."

"Everything's my business. What's a college education worth these days?"

"Three squares and a uniform," he drawled.

"What kind of guy is young Jeeter?"

"Big blond bruiser, plays a fair game of golf, thinks he's hell with the women, drinks heavy but hasn't sicked up on the rugs so far."

"What kind of guy is old Jeeter?"

"He'd probably give you a dime—if he didn't have a nickel with him."

"Tsk, tsk, you're talking about your boss."

George grinned. "He's so tight his head squeaks when he takes his hat off. I always took chances. Maybe that's why I'm just somebody's driver. This is good Scotch."

I made another drink, which finished the bottle. I sat down again.

"You think those two gunnies were stashed out for Mister Gerald?"

"Why not? I usually drive him home about that time. Didn't today. He had a bad hangover and didn't go out until late. You're a dick, you know what it's all about, don't you?"

"Who told you I was a dick?"

"Nobody but a dick ever asked so goddam many questions."

I shook my head. "Uh-uh. I've asked you just six questions. Your boss has a lot of confidence in you. He must have told you."

The dark man nodded, grinned faintly and sipped. "The whole set-up is pretty obvious," he said. "When the car started to swing for the turn into the driveway these boys went to work. I don't figure they meant to kill anybody, somehow. It was just a scare. Only that little guy was nuts."

I looked at George's eyebrows. They were nice black eyebrows, with a gloss on them like horsehair.

"It doesn't sound like Marty Estel to pick that sort of helpers."

"Sure. Maybe that's why he picked that sort of helpers."

"You're smart. You and I can get along. But shooting that little punk makes it tougher. What will you do about that?"

"Nothing."

"O.K. If they get to you and tie it to your gun, if you still have the gun, which you probably won't, I suppose it will be passed off as an attempted stick-up. There's just one thing."

"What?" George finished his second drink, laid the glass aside, lit a fresh cigarette and smiled.

"It's pretty hard to tell a car from in front—at night. Even with all those lights. It might have been a visitor."

He shrugged and nodded. "But if it's a scare, that would do just as well. Because the family would hear about it and the old man would guess whose boys they were—and why."

"Hell, you really are smart," I said admiringly, and the phone rang.

It was an English-butler voice, very clipped and precise, and it said that if I was Mr. Philip Marlowe, Mr.

Jeeter would like to speak to me. He came on at once, with plenty of frost.

"I must say that you take your time about obeying orders," he barked. "Or hasn't that chauffeur of mine—"

"Yeah, he got here, Mr. Jeeter," I said. "But we ran into a little trouble. George will tell you."

"Young man, when I want something done——"

"Listen, Mr. Jeeter, I've had a hard day. Your son punched me on the jaw and I fell and cut my head open. When I staggered back to my apartment, more dead than alive, I was stuck up by a couple of hard guys with guns who told me to lay off the Jeeter case. I'm doing my best but I'm feeling a little frail, so don't scare me."

"Young man—"

"Listen," I told him earnestly, "if you want to call all the plays in this game, you can carry the ball yourself. Or you can save yourself a lot of money and hire an order taker. I have to do things my way. Any cops visit you tonight?"

"Cops?" he echoed in a sour voice. "You mean policemen?"

"By all means —I mean policemen."

"And why should I see any policemen?" he almost snarled.

"There was a stiff in front of your gates half an hour ago. Stiff meaning dead man. He's quite small. You could sweep him up in a dustpan, if he bothers you."

"My God! Are you serious?"

"Yes. What's more he took a shot at George and me. He recognized the car. He must have been all set for your son, Mr. Jeeter."

A silence with barbs on it. "I thought you said a dead man," Mr. Jeeter's voice said very coldly. "Now you say he shot at you."

"That was while he wasn't dead," I said. "George will tell you. George—"

"You come out here at once!" he yelled at me over the phone. "At once, do you hear? At once!"

"George will tell you," I said softly and hung up.

George looked at me coldly. He stood up and put his cap on. "O.K., pal," he said. "Maybe some day I can put you on to a soft thing." He started for the door.

"It had to be that way. It's up to him. He'll have to decide."

"Nuts," George said, looking back over his shoulder. "Save your breath, shamus. Anything you say to me is just so much noise in the wrong place."

He opened the door, went out, shut it, and I sat there still holding the telephone, with my mouth open and nothing in it but my tongue and a bad taste on that.

I went out to the kitchen and shook the Scotch bottle, but it was still empty. I opened some rye and swallowed a drink and it tasted sour. Something was bothering me. I had a feeling it was going to bother me a lot more before I was through.

They must have missed George by a whisker. I heard the elevator come up again almost as soon as it had stopped going down. Solid steps grew louder along the hallway. A fist hit the door. I went over and opened it.

One was in brown, one in blue, both large, hefty and bored.

The one in brown pushed his hat back on his head with a freckled hand and said: "You Philip Marlowe?"

"Me," I said.

They rode me back into the room without seeming to. The one in blue shut the door. The one in brown palmed a shield and let me catch a glint of the gold and enamel.

"Finlayson, Detective Lieutenant working out of

Central Homicide," he said. "This is Sebold, my partner. We're a couple of swell guys not to get funny with. We hear you're kind of sharp with a gun."

Sebold took his hat off and dusted his salt-and-pepper hair back with the flat of his hand. He drifted noiselessly out to the kitchen.

Finlayson sat down on the edge of a chair and flicked his chin with a thumbnail as square as an ice cube and yellow as a mustard plaster. He was older than Sebold, but not so good-looking. He had the frowsy expression of a veteran cop who hadn't got very far.

I sat down. I said: "How do you mean, sharp with a gun?"

"Shooting people is how I mean."

I lit a cigarette. Sebold came out of the kitchen and went into the dressing room behind the wall bed.

"We understand you're a private-license guy," Finlayson said heavily.

"That's right."

"Give." He held his hand out. I gave him my wallet. He chewed it over and handed it back. "Carry a gun?"

I nodded. He held out his hand for it. Sebold came out of the dressing room. Finlayson sniffed at the Luger, snapped the magazine out, cleared the breech and held the gun so that a little light shone up through the magazine opening into the breech end of the barrel. He looked down the muzzle, squinting. He handed the gun to Sebold. Sebold did the same thing.

"Don't think so," Sebold said. "Clean, but not that clean. Couldn't have been cleaned within the hour. A little dust."

"Right."

Finlayson picked the ejected shell off the carpet, pressed it into the magazine and snapped the magazine back in place. He handed me the gun. I put it back under my arm.

"Been out anywhere tonight?" he asked tersely.

"Don't tell me the plot," I said. "I'm just a bit-player."

"Smart guy," Sebold said dispassionately. He dusted his hair again and opened a desk drawer. "Funny stuff. Good for a column. I like 'em that way—with my blackjack."

Finlayson sighed. "Been out tonight, shamus?"

"Sure. In and out all the time. Why?"

He ignored the question. "Where you been?"

"Out to dinner. Business call or two."

"Where at?"

"I'm sorry, boys. Every business has its private files."

"Had company, too," Sebold said, picking up George's glass and sniffing it. "Recent—within the hour."

"You're not that good," I told him sourly.

"Had a ride in a big Caddy?" Finlayson bored on, taking a deep breath. "Over West L. A. direction?"

"Had a ride in a Chrysler—over Vine Street direction."

"Maybe we better just take him down," Sebold said, looking at his fingernails.

"Maybe you better skip the gang-buster stuff and tell me what's stuck in your nose. I get along with cops—except when they act as if the law is only for citizens."

Finlayson studied me. Nothing I had said made an impression on him. Nothing Sebold said made any impression on him. He had an idea and he was holding it like a sick baby.

"You know a little rat named Frisky Lavon?" he sighed. "Used to be a dummy-chucker, then found out he could bug his way outa raps. Been doing that for say twelve years. Totes a gun and acts simple. But he quit acting tonight at seven-thirty about. Quit cold—with a slug in his head."

"Never heard of him," I said.

"You bumped anybody off tonight?"

"I'd have to look at my notebook."

Sebold leaned forward politely. "Would you care for a smack in the kisser?" he inquired.

Finlayson held his hand out sharply. "Cut it, Ben. Cut it. Listen, Marlowe. Maybe we're going at this wrong. We're not talking about murder. Could have been legitimate. This Frisky Lavon got froze off tonight on Calvello Drive in Bel-Air. Out in the middle of the street. Nobody seen or heard anything. So we kind of want to know."

"All right," I growled. "What makes it my business? And keep that piano tuner out of my hair. He has a nice suit and his nails are clean, but he bears down on his shield too hard."

"Nuts to you," Sebold said.

"We got a funny phone call," Finlayson said. "Which is where you come in. We ain't just throwing our weight around. And we want a forty-five. They ain't sure what kind yet."

"He's smart. He threw it under the bar at Levy's," Sebold sneered.

"I never had a forty-five," I said. "A guy who needs that much gun ought to use a pick."

Finlayson scowled at me and counted his thumbs. Then he took a deep breath and suddenly went human on me. "Sure, I'm just a dumb flatheel," he said. "Anybody could pull my ears off and I wouldn't even notice it. Let's all quit horsing around and talk sense.

"This Frisky was found dead after a no-name phone call to West L.A. police. Found dead outside a big house belonging to a man named Jeeter who owns a string of investment companies. He wouldn't use a guy like Frisky for a penwiper, so there's nothing in that. The servants didn't hear nothing, nor the servants at any of the four houses on the block. Frisky is lying in the street and somebody run over his foot, but what killed him was a forty-five slug smack in his face. West

L. A. ain't hardly started the routine when some guy calls up Central and says to tell Homicide if they want to know who got Frisky Lavon, ask a private eye named Philip Marlowe, complete with address and everything, then a quick hang-up.

"O.K. The guy on the board gives me the dope and I don't know Frisky from a hole in my sock, but I ask Identification and sure enough they have him and just about the time I'm looking it over the flash comes from West L. A. and the description seems to check pretty close. So we get together and it's the same guy all right and the chief of detectives has us drop around here. So we drop around."

"So here you are," I said. "Will you have a drink?"

"Can we search the joint, if we do?"

"Sure. It's a good lead—that phone call, I mean—if you put in about six months on it."

"We already got that idea," Finlayson growled. "A hundred guys could have chilled this little wart, and two-three of them maybe could have thought it was a smart rib to pin it on you. Them two-three is what interests us."

I shook my head.

"No ideas at all, huh?"

"Just for wisecracks," Sebold said.

Finlayson lumbered to his feet. "Well, we gotta look around."

"Maybe we had ought to have brought a search warrant," Sebold said, tickling his upper lip with the end of his tongue.

"I don't *have* to fight this guy, do I?" I asked Finlayson. "I mean, is it all right if I leave him his gag lines and just keep my temper?"

Finlayson looked at the ceiling and said dryly: "His wife left him day before yesterday. He's just trying to compensate, as the fellow says."

Sebold turned white and twisted his knuckles savagely. Then he laughed shortly and got to his feet.

They went at it. Ten minutes of opening and shutting drawers and looking at the backs of shelves and under seat cushions and letting the bed down and peering into the electric refrigerator and the garbage pail fed them up.

They came back and sat down again. "Just a nut," Finlayson said wearily. "Some guy that picked your name outa the directory maybe. Could be anything."

"Now I'll get that drink."

"I don't drink," Sebold snarled.

Finlayson crossed his hands on his stomach. "That don't mean any liquor gets poured in the flowerpot, son."

I got three drinks and put two of them beside Finlayson. He drank half of one of them and looked at the ceiling. "I got another killing, too," he said thoughtfully. "A guy in your racket, Marlowe. A fat guy on Sunset. Name of Arbogast. Ever hear of him?"

"I thought he was a handwriting expert," I said.

"You're talking about police business," Sebold told his partner coldly.

"Sure. Police business that's already in the morning paper. This Arbogast was shot three times with a twenty-two. Target gun. You know any crooks that pack that kind of heat?"

I held my glass tightly and took a long slow swallow. I hadn't thought Waxnose looked dangerous enough, but you never knew.

"I did," I said slowly. "A killer named Al Tessilore. But he's in Folsom. He used a Colt Woodsman."

Finlayson finished the first drink, used the second in about the same time, and stood up. Sebold stood up, still mad.

Finlayson opened the door. "Come on, Ben." They went out.

I heard their steps along the hall, the clang of the elevator once more. A car started just below in the street and growled off into the night.

"Clowns like that don't kill," I said out loud. But it looked as if they did.

I waited fifteen minutes before I went out again. The phone rang while I was waiting, but I didn't answer it.

I drove towards the El Milano and circled around enough to make sure I wasn't followed.

6

The lobby hadn't changed any. The blue carpet still tickled my ankles while I ambled over to the desk, the same pale clerk was handing a key to a couple of horse-faced females in tweeds, and when he saw me he put his weight on his left foot again and the door at the end of the desk popped open and out popped the fat and erotic Hawkins, with what looked like the same cigar stub in his face.

He hustled over and gave me a big warm smile this time, took hold of my arm. "Just the guy I was hoping to see," he chuckled. "Let's us go upstairs a minute."

"What's the matter?"

"Matter?" His smile became broad as the door to a two-car garage. "Nothing ain't the matter. This way."

He pushed me into the elevator and said "Eight" in a fat cheerful voice and up we sailed and out we got and slid along the corridor. Hawkins had a hard hand and knew where to hold an arm. I was interested enough to let him get away with it. He pushed the buzzer beside Miss Huntress' door and Big Ben chimed inside and the door opened and I was looking at a deadpan in a derby hat and a dinner coat. He had his right hand in the side pocket of the coat, and under the derby a pair of scarred eyebrows and under the eyebrows a pair of eyes that had as much expression as the cap on a gas tank.

The mouth moved enough to say: "Yeah?"

"Company for the boss," Hawkins said expansively.

"What company?"

"Let me play too," I said. "Limited liability Company. Gimme the apple."

"Huh?" The eyebrows went this way and that and the jaw came out. "Nobody ain't kiddin' anybody, I hope."

"Now, now, gents—" Hawkins began.

A voice behind the derby-hatted man interrupted him. "What's the matter, Beef?"

"He's in a stew," I said.

"Listen, mugg—"

"Now, now, gents—" as before.

"Ain't nothing the matter," Beef said, throwing his voice over his shoulder as if it were a coil of rope. "The hotel dick got a guy up here and he says he's company."

"Show the company in, Beef." I liked this voice. It was smooth quiet, and you could have cut your name in it with a thirty-pound sledge and a cold chisel.

"Lift the dogs," Beef said, and stood to one side.

We went in. I went first, then Hawkins, then Beef wheeled neatly behind us like a door. We went in so close together that we must have looked like a three-decker sandwich.

Miss Huntress was not in the room. The log in the fireplace had almost stopped smoldering. There was still that smell of sandalwood on the air. With it cigarette smoke blended.

A man stood at the end of the davenport, both hands in the pockets of a blue camel's hair coat with the collar high to a black snap-brim hat. A loose scarf hung outside his coat. He stood motionless, the cigarette in his mouth lisping smoke. He was tall, black-haired, suave, dangerous. He said nothing.

Hawkins ambled over to him. "This is the guy I was telling you about, Mr. Estel," the fat man burbled. "Come in earlier today and said he was from you. Kinda fooled me."

"Give him a ten, Beef."

The derby hat took its left hand from somewhere and there was a bill in it. It pushed the bill at Hawkins. Hawkins took the bill, blushing.

"This ain't necessary, Mr. Estel. Thanks a lot just the same."

"Scram."

"Huh?" Hawkins looked shocked.

"You heard him," Beef said truculently. "Want your fanny out the door first, huh?"

Hawkins drew himself up. "I gotta protect the tenants. You gentlemen know how it is. A man in a job like this."

"Yeah. Scram," Estel said without moving his lips.

Hawkins turned and went out quickly, softly. The door clicked gently shut behind him. Beef looked back at it, then moved behind me.

"See if he's rodded, Beef."

The derby hat saw if I was rodded. He took the Luger and went away from me. Estel looked casually at the Luger, back at me. His eyes held an expression of indifferent dislike.

"Name's Philip Marlowe, eh? A private dick."

"So what?" I said.

"Somebody's goin' to get somebody's face pushed into somebody's floor," Beef said coldly.

"Aw, keep that crap for the boiler room," I told him. "I'm sick of hard guys for this evening. I said 'so what,' and 'so what' is what I said."

Marty Estel looked mildly amused. "Hell, keep your shirt in. I've got to look after my friends, don't I? You know who I am. O.K., I know what you talked to Miss Huntress about. And I know something about you that you don't know I know."

"All right," I said. "This fat slob Hawkins collected ten from me for letting me up here this afternoon—knowing perfectly well who I was—and he has just collected ten from your iron man for slipping me the nasty. Give me back my gun and tell me what makes my business your business."

"Plenty. First off, Harriet's not home. We're waiting for her on account of a thing that happened. I can't wait any longer. Got to go to work at the club. So what did you come after this time?"

"Looking for the Jeeter boy. Somebody shot at his car tonight. From now on he needs somebody to walk behind him."

"You think I play games like that?" Estel asked me coldly.

I walked over to a cabinet and opened it and found a bottle of Scotch. I twisted the cap off, lifted a glass from the tabouret and poured some out. I tasted it. It tasted all right.

I looked around for ice, but there wasn't any. It had all melted long since in the bucket.

"I asked you a question," Estel said gravely.

"I heard it. I'm making my mind up. The answer is, I wouldn't have thought it—no. But it happened. I was there. I was in the car—instead of young Jeeter. His father had sent for me to come to the house to talk things over."

"What things?"

I didn't bother to look surprised. "You hold fifty grand of the boy's paper. That looks bad for you, if anything happens to him."

"I don't figure it that way. Because that way I would lose my dough. The old man won't pay—granted. But I wait a couple of years and I collect from the kid. He

gets his estate out of trust when he's twenty-eight.
Right now he gets a grand a month and he can't even
will anything, because it's still in trust. Savvy?"

"So you wouldn't knock him off," I said, using my
Scotch. "But you might throw a scare into him."

Estel frowned. He discarded his cigarette into a tray
and watched it smoke a moment before he picked it up
again and snubbed it out. He shook his head.

"If you're going to bodyguard him, it would almost
pay me to stand part of your salary, wouldn't it? Almost. A man in my racket can't take care of everything.
He's of age and it's his business who he runs around
with. For instance, women. Any reason why a nice girl
shouldn't cut herself a piece of five million bucks?"

I said: "I think it's a swell idea. What was it you
knew about me that I didn't know you knew?"

He smiled, faintly. "What was it you were waiting to
tell Miss Huntress—the thing that happened?"

He smiled faintly again.

"Listen, Marlowe, there are lots of ways to play any
game. I play mine on the house percentage, because
that's all I need to win. What makes me get tough?"

I rolled a fresh cigarette around in my fingers and
tried to roll it around my glass with two fingers. "Who
said you were tough? I always heard the nicest things
about you."

Marty Estel nodded and looked faintly amused. "I
have sources of information," he said quietly. "When
I have fifty grand invested in a guy, I'm apt to find out
a little about him. Jeeter hired a man named Arbogast
to do a little work. Arbogast was killed in his office
today—with a twenty-two. That could have nothing to
do with Jeeter's business. But there was a tail on you
when you went there and you didn't give it to the law.
Does that make you and me friends?"

I licked the edge of my glass, nodded. "It seems it
does."

"From now on just forget about bothering Harriet, see?"

"O.K."

"So we understand each other real good, now."

"Yeah."

"Well, I'll be going. Give the guy back his Luger, Beef."

The derby hat came over and smacked my gun into my hand hard enough to break a bone.

"Staying?" Estel asked, moving towards the door.

"I guess I'll wait a little while. Until Hawkins comes up to touch me for another ten."

Estel grinned. Beef walked in front of him wooden-faced to the door and opened it. Estel went out. The door closed. The room was silent. I sniffed at the dying perfume of sandalwood and stood motionless, looking around.

Somebody was nuts. I was nuts. Everybody was nuts. None of it fitted together worth a nickel. Marty Estel, as he said, had no good motive for murdering anybody, because that would be the surest way to kill his chances to collect his money. Even if he had a motive for murdering anybody, Waxnose and Frisky didn't seem like the team he would select for the job. I was in bad with the police, I had spent ten dollars of my twenty expense money, and I didn't have enough leverage anywhere to lift a dime off a cigar counter.

I finished my drink, put the glass down, walked up and down the room, smoked a third cigarette, looked at my watch, shrugged and felt disgusted. The inner doors of the suite were closed. I went across to the one out of which young Jeeter must have sneaked that afternoon. Opening it I looked into a bedroom done in ivory and ashes of roses. There was a big double bed with no foot-board, covered with figured brocade. Toilet articles glistened on a built-in dressing table with a panel light. The light was lit. A small lamp on a table beside the door was lit also. A door near the dressing table showed the cool green of bathroom tiles.

I went over and looked in there. Chromium, a glass stall shower, monogrammed towels on a rack, a glass shelf for perfume and bath salts at the foot of the tub, everything nice and refined. Miss Huntress did herself well. I hoped she was paying her own rent. It didn't make any difference to me—I just liked it that way.

I went back towards the living room, stopped in the doorway to take another pleasant look around, and noticed something I ought to have noticed the instant I stepped into the room. I noticed the sharp tang of cordite on the air, almost, but not quite gone. And then I noticed something else.

The bed had been moved over until its head overlapped the edge of a closet door which was not quite closed. The weight of the bed was holding it from opening. I went over there to find out why it wanted to open. I went slowly and about halfway there I noticed that I was holding a gun in my hand.

I leaned against the closet door. It didn't move. I threw more weight against it. It still didn't move. Braced against it I pushed the bed away with my foot, gave ground slowly.

A weight pushed against me hard. I had gone back a foot or so before anything else happened. Then it happened suddenly. He came out—sideways, in a sort of roll. I put some more weight back on the door and held him like that a moment, looking at him.

He was still big, still blond, still dressed in rough sporty material, with scarf and open-necked shirt. But his face wasn't red any more.

I gave ground again and he rolled down the back of the door, turning a little like a swimmer in the surf, thumped the floor and lay there, almost on his back, still looking at me. Light from the bedside lamp glittered on his head. There was a scorched and soggy stain on the rough coat—about where his heart would be. So he wouldn't get that five million after all. And nobody would get anything and Marty Estel wouldn't get his fifty grand. Because young Mister Gerald was dead.

I looked back into the closet where he had been. Its door hung wide open now. There were clothes on racks, feminine clothes, nice clothes. He had been backed in among them, probably with his hands in the air and a gun against his chest. And then he had been shot dead, and whoever did it hadn't been quite quick enough or quite strong enough to get the door shut. Or had been scared and had just yanked the bed over against the door and left it that way.

Something glittered down on the floor. I picked it up. A small automatic, .25 caliber, a woman's purse gun with a beautifully engraved butt inlaid with silver and ivory. I put the gun in my pocket. That seemed a funny thing to do, too.

I didn't touch him. He was as dead as John D. Arbogast and looked a whole lot deader. I left the door open and listened, walked quickly back across the room and into the living room and shut the bedroom door, smearing the knob as I did it.

A lock was being tinkled at with a key. Hawkins was back again, to see what delayed me. He was letting himself in with his passkey.

I was pouring a drink when he came in.

He came well into the room, stopped with his feet planted and surveyed me coldly.

"I seen Estel and his boy leave," he said. "I didn't see you leave. So I come up. I gotta—"

"You gotta protect the guests," I said.

"Yeah. I gotta protect the guests. You can't stay up here, pal. Not without the lady of the house is home."

"But Marty Estel and his hard boy can."

He came a little closer to me. He had a mean look

in his eye. He had always had it, probably, but I noticed it more now.

"You don't want to make nothing of that, do you?" he asked me.

"No. Every man to his own chisel. Have a drink."

"That ain't your liquor."

"Miss Huntress gave me a bottle. We're pals. Marty Estel and I are pals. Everybody is pals. Don't you want to be pals?"

"You ain't trying to kid me, are you?"

"Have a drink and forget it."

I found a glass and poured him one. He took it.

"It's the job if anybody smells it on me," he said.

"Uh-huh."

He drank slowly, rolling it around on his tongue. "Good Scotch."

"Won't be the first time you tasted it, will it?"

He started to get hard again, then relaxed. "Hell, I guess you're just a kidder." He finished the drink, put the glass down, patted his lips with a large and very crumpled handkerchief and sighed.

"O.K.," he said. "But we'll have to leave now."

"All set. I guess she won't be home for a while. You see them go out?"

"Her and the boy friend. Yeah, long time ago."

I nodded. We went towards the door and Hawkins saw me out. He saw me downstairs and off the premises. But he didn't see what was in Miss Huntress' bedroom. I wondered if he would go back up. If he did, the Scotch bottle would probably stop him.

I got into my car and drove off home—to talk to Anna Halsey on the phone. There wasn't any case any more—for us. I parked close to the curb this time. I wasn't feeling gay any more. I rode up in the elevator and unlocked the door and clicked the light on.

Waxnose sat in my best chair, an unlit hand-rolled

brown cigarette between his fingers, his bony knees crossed, and his long Woodsman resting solidly on his leg. He was smiling. It wasn't the nicest smile I ever saw.

"Hi, pal," he drawled. "You still ain't had that door fixed. Kind of shut it, huh?" His voice, for all the drawl, was deadly.

I shut the door, stood looking across the room at him.

"So you killed my pal," he said.

He stood up slowly, came across the room slowly and leaned the .22 against my throat. His smiling thin-lipped mouth seemed as expressionless, for all its smile, as his wax-white nose. He reached quietly under my coat and took the Luger. I might as well leave it home from now on. Everybody in town seemed to be able to take it away from me.

He stepped back across the room and sat down again in the chair.

"Steady does it," he said almost gently. "Park the body, friend. No false moves. No moves at all. You and me are at the jumping-off place. The clock's tickin' and we're waiting to go."

I sat down and stared at him. A curious bird. I moistened my dry lips. "You told me his gun had no firing pin," I said.

"Yeah. He fooled me on that, the little so-and-so. And I told you to lay off the Jeeter kid. That's cold now. It's Frisky I'm thinking about. Crazy, ain't it? Me bothering about a dimwit like that, packin' him around with me, and letting him get hisself bumped off." He sighed and added simply, "He was my kid brother."

"I didn't kill him," I said.

He smiled a little more. He had never stopped smiling. The corners of his mouth just tucked in a little deeper.

"Yeah?"

He slid the safety catch off the Luger, laid it carefully on the arm of the chair at his right, and reached into his pocket. What he brought out made me as cold as an ice bucket.

It was a metal tube, dark and rough-looking, about four inches long and drilled with a lot of small holes. He held his Woodsman in his left hand and began to screw the tube casually on the end of it.

"Silencer," he said. "They're the bunk, I guess you smart guys think. This one ain't the bunk—not for three shots. I oughta know. I made it myself."

I moistened my lips again. "It'll work for one shot," I said. "Then it jams your action. That one looks like cast-iron. It will probably blow your hand off."

He smiled his waxy smile, screwed it on, slowly, lovingly, gave it a last hard turn and sat back relaxed. "Not this baby. She's packed with steel wool and that's good for three shots, like I said. Then you got to repack it. And there ain't enough back pressure to jam the action on this gun. You feel good? I'd like you to feel good."

"I feel swell, you sadistic son of a bitch," I said.

"I'm having you lie down on the bed after a while. You won't feel nothing. I'm kind of fussy about my killings. Frisky didn't feel nothing, I guess. You got him neat."

"You don't see good," I sneered. "The chauffeur got him with a Smith & Wesson forty-four. I didn't even fire."

"Uh-huh."

"O.K., you don't believe me," I said. "What did you kill Arbogast for? There was nothing fussy about that killing. He was just shot at his desk, three times with a twenty-two and he fell down on the floor. What did he ever do to your filthy little brother?"

He jerked the gun up, but his smile held. "You got guts," he said. "Who is this here Arbogast?"

I told him. I told him slowly and carefully, in detail. I told him a lot of things. And he began in some vague way to look worried. His eyes flickered at me, away, back again, restlessly, like a hummingbird.

"I don't know any party named Arbogast, pal," he said slowly. "Never heard of him. And I ain't shot any fat guys today."

"You killed him," I said. "And you killed young Jeeter—in the girl's apartment at the El Milano. He's lying there dead right now. You're working for Marty Estel. He's going to be awfully damn sorry about that kill. Go ahead and make it three in a row."

His face froze. The smile went away at last. His whole face looked waxy now. He opened his mouth and breathed through it, and his breath made a restless worrying sound. I could see the faint glitter of sweat on his forehead, and I could feel the cold from the evaporation of sweat on mine.

Waxnose said very gently: "I ain't killed anybody at all, friend. Not anybody. I wasn't hired to kill people. Until Frisky stopped that slug I didn't have no such ideas. That's straight."

I tried not to stare at the metal tube on the end of the Woodsman.

A flame flickered at the back of his eyes, a small, weak, smoky flame. It seemed to grow larger and clearer. He looked down at the floor between his feet. I looked around at the light switch, but it was too far away. He looked up again. Very slowly he began to unscrew the silencer. He had it loose in his hand. He dropped it back into his pocket, stood up, holding the two guns, one in each hand. Then he had another idea. He sat down again, took all the shells out of the Luger quickly and threw it on the floor after them.

He came towards me softly across the room. "I guess this is your lucky day," he said. "I got to go a place and see a guy."

"I knew all along it was my lucky day. I've been feeling so good."

He moved delicately around me to the door and opened it a foot and started through the narrow opening, smiling again.

"I gotta see a guy," he said very gently, and his tongue moved along his lips.

"Not yet," I said, and jumped.

His gun hand was at the edge of the door, almost beyond the edge. I hit the door hard and he couldn't bring it in quickly enough. He couldn't get out of the way. I pinned him in the doorway, and used all the strength I had. It was a crazy thing. He had given me a break and all I had to do was to stand still and let him go. But I had a guy to see too—and I wanted to see him first.

Waxnose leered at me. He grunted. He fought with his hand beyond the door edge. I shifted and hit his jaw with all I had. It was enough. He went limp. I hit him again. His head bounced against the wood. I heard a light thud beyond the door edge. I hit him a third time. I never hit anything any harder.

I took my weight back from the door then and he slid towards me, blank-eyed, rubber-kneed and I caught him and twisted his empty hands behind him and let him fall. I stood over him panting. I went to the door. His Woodsman lay almost on the sill. I picked it up, dropped it into my pocket—not the pocket that held Miss Huntress' gun. He hadn't even found that.

There he lay on the floor. He was thin, he had no weight, but I panted just the same. In a little while his eyes flickered open and looked up at me.

"Greedy guy," he whispered wearily. "Why did I ever leave Saint Looey?"

I snapped handcuffs on his wrists and pulled him by the shoulders into the dressing room and tied his ankles with a piece of rope. I left him laying on his back, a little sideways, his nose as white as ever, his eyes empty now, his lips moving a little as if he were talking to himself. A funny lad, not all bad, but not so pure I had to weep over him either.

I put my Luger together and left with my three guns. There was nobody outside the apartment house.

7

The Jeeter mansion was on a nine- or ten-acre knoll, a big colonial pile with fat white columns and dormer windows and magnolias and a four-car garage. There was a circular parking space at the top of the driveway with two cars parked in it—one was the big dreadnaught in which I'd ridden and the other a canary-yellow sports convertible I had seen before.

I rang a bell the size of a silver dollar. The door opened and a tall narrow cold-eyed bird in dark clothes looked out at me.

"Mr. Jeeter home? Mr. Jeeter, Senior?"

"May I arsk who is calling?" The accent was a little too thick, like cut Scotch.

"Philip Marlowe. I'm working for him. Maybe I had ought to of gone to the servant's entrance."

He hitched a finger at a wing collar and looked at me without pleasure. "Aw, possibly. You may step in. I shall inform Mr. Jeeter. I believe he is engaged at the moment. Kindly wait 'ere in the 'all."

"The act stinks," I said. "English butlers aren't dropping their h's this year."

"Smart guy, huh?" he snarled, in a voice from not any farther across the Atlantic than Hoboken. "Wait here." He slid away.

I sat down in a carved chair and felt thirsty. After a while the butler came cat-footing back along the hall and jerked his chin at me unpleasantly.

We went along a mile of hallway. At the end it broadened without any doors into a huge sunroom. On the far side of the sunroom the butler opened a wide door and I stepped past him into an oval room with a black-and-silver oval rug, a black marble table in the middle of the rug, stiff high-backed carved chairs against the walls, a huge oval mirror with a rounded-surface that made me look like a pygmy with water on the brain, and in the room three people.

By the door opposite where I came in, George the chauffeur stood stiffly in his neat dark uniform, with his peaked cap in his hand. In the least uncomfortable of the chairs sat Miss Harriet Huntress holding a glass in which there was half a drink. And around the silver margin of the oval rug, Mr. Jeeter, Senior, was trying his legs out in a brisk canter, still under wraps, but mad inside. His face was red and the veins on his nose were distended. His hands were in the pockets of a velvet smoking jacket. He wore a pleated shirt with a black pearl in the bosom, a batwing black tie and one of his patent-leather oxfords was unlaced.

He whirled and yelled at the butler behind me: "Get out and keep those doors shut! And I'm not at home to anybody, understand? Nobody!"

The butler closed the doors. Presumably, he went away. I didn't hear him go.

George gave me a cool one-sided smile and Miss Huntress gave me a bland stare over her glass. "You made a nice comeback," she said demurely.

"You took a chance leaving me alone in your apartment," I told her. "I might have sneaked some of your perfume."

"Well, what do you want?" Jeeter yelled at me. "A nice sort of detective you turned out to be. I put you

on a confidential job and you walk right in on Miss
Huntress and explain the whole thing to her."

"It worked, didn't it?"

He stared. They all stared. "How do you know
that?" he barked.

"I know a nice girl when I see one. She's here telling
you she had an idea she got not to like, and for you
to quit worrying about it. Where's Mister Gerald?"

Old Man Jeeter stopped and gave me a hard level
stare. "I still regard you as incompetent," he said. "My
son is missing."

"I'm not working for you. I'm working for Anna
Halsey. Any complaints you have to make should be
addressed to her. Do I pour my own drink or do you
have a flunky in a purple suit to do it? And what do
you mean, your son is missing?"

"Should I give him the heave, sir?" George asked
quietly.

Jeeter waved his hand at a decanter and siphon and
glasses on the black marble table and started around
the rug again. "Don't be silly," he snapped at George.

George flushed a little, high on his cheekbones. His
mouth looked tough.

I mixed myself a drink and sat down with it and
tasted it and asked again: "What do you mean your son
is missing, Mr. Jeeter?"

"I'm paying you good money," he started to yell at
me, still mad.

"When?"

He stopped dead in his canter and looked at me
again. Miss Huntress laughed lightly. George scowled.

"What do you suppose I mean—my son is missing?"
he snapped. "I should have thought that would be clear
enough even to you. Nobody knows where he is. Miss
Huntress doesn't know. I don't know. No one at any
of the places where he might be known."

"But I'm smarter than they are," I said. "*I* know."

Nobody moved for a long minute. Jeeter stared at me fish-eyed. George stared at me. The girl stared at me. She looked puzzled. The other two just stared.

I looked at her. "Where did you go when you went out, if you're telling?"

Her dark blue eyes were water-clear. "There's no secret about it. We went out together—in a taxi. Gerald had had his driving license suspended for a month. Too many tickets. We went down towards the beach and I had a change of heart, as you guessed. I decided I was just being a chiseler after all. I didn't want Gerald's money really. What I wanted was revenge. On Mr. Jeeter here for ruining my father. Done all legally of course, but done just the same. But I got myself in a spot where I couldn't have my revenge and not look like a cheap chiseler. So I told George to find some other girl to play with. He was sore and we quarreled. I stopped the taxi and got out in Beverly Hills. He went on. I don't know where. Later I went back to the El Milano and got my car out of the garage and came here. To tell Mr. Jeeter to forget the whole thing and not bother to sick sleuths on to me."

"You say you went with him in a taxi," I said. "Why wasn't George driving him, if he couldn't drive himself?"

I stared at her, but I wasn't talking to her. Jeeter answered me, frostily. "George drove me home from the office, of course. At that time Gerald had already gone out. Is there anything important about that?"

I turned to him. "Yeah. There's going to be. Mister Gerald is at the El Milano. Hawkins the house dick told me. He went back there to wait for Miss Huntress and Hawkins let him into her apartment. Hawkins will do you those little favors—for ten bucks. He may be there still and he may not."

I kept on watching them. It was hard to watch all three of them. But they didn't move. They just looked at me.

"Well—I'm glad to hear it," Old Man Jeeter said. "I was afraid he was off somewhere getting drunk."

"No. He's not off anywhere getting drunk," I said. "By the way, among these places you called to see if he was there, you didn't call the El Milano?"

George nodded. "Yes, I did. They said he wasn't there. Looks like this house peeper tipped the phone girl off not to say anything."

"He wouldn't have to do that. She'd just ring the apartment and he wouldn't answer—naturally." I watched old man Jeeter hard then, with a lot of interest. It was going to be hard for him to take that up, but he was going to have to do it.

He did. He licked his lips first. "Why—naturally, if I may ask?" he said coldly.

I put my glass down on the marble table and stood against the wall, with my hands hanging free. I still tried to watch them—all three of them.

"Let's go back over this thing a little," I said. "We're all wise to the situation. I know George is, although he shouldn't be, being just a servant. I know Miss Huntress is. And of course *you* are, Mr. Jeeter. So let's see what we have got. We have a lot of things that don't add up, but I'm smart. I'm going to add them up anyhow. First-off a handful of photostats of notes from Marty Estel. Gerald denies having given these and Mr. Jeeter won't pay them, but he has a handwriting man named Arbogast check the signatures, to see if they look genuine. They do. They are. This Arbogast may have done other things. I don't know. I couldn't ask him. When I went to see him, he was dead—shot three times—as I've since heard—with a twenty-two. No, I didn't tell the police, Mr. Jeeter."

The tall silver-haired man looked horribly shocked. His lean body shook like a bullrush. "Dead?" he whispered. "Murdered?"

I looked at George. George didn't move a muscle. I looked at the girl. She sat quietly, waiting, tight-lipped.

I said: "There's only one reason to suppose his killing had anything to do with Mr. Jeeter's affairs. He was shot with a twenty-two—and there is a man in this case who wears a twenty-two."

I still had their attention. And their silence.

"Why he was shot I haven't the faintest idea. He was not a dangerous man to Miss Huntress or Marty Estel. He was too fat to get around much. My guess is he was a little too smart. He got a simple case of signature identification and he went on from there to find out more than he should. And after he had found out more than he should—he guessed more than he ought—and maybe he even tried a little blackmail. And somebody rubbed him out this afternoon with a twenty-two. O.K., I can stand it. I never knew him.

"So I went over to see Miss Huntress and after a lot of finagling around with this itchy-handed house dick I got to see her and we had a chat, and then Mister Gerald stepped neatly out of hiding and bopped me a nice one on the chin and over I went and hit my head on a chair leg. And when I came out of that the joint was empty. So I went on home.

"And home I found the man with the twenty-two and with him a dimwit called Frisky Lavon, with a bad breath and a very large gun, neither of which matters now as he was shot dead in front of your house tonight, Mr. Jeeter—shot trying to stick up your car. The cops know about that one—they came to see me about it—because the other guy, the one that packs the twenty-two, is the little dimwit's brother and he thought I shot Dimwit and tried to put the bee on me. But it didn't work. That's two killings.

"We now come to the third and most important. I went back to the El Milano because it no longer seemed a good idea for Mister Gerald to be running around casually. He seemed to have a few enemies. It even seemed that he was supposed to be in the car this evening when Frisky Lavon shot at it—but of course that was just a plant."

Old Jeeter drew his white eyebrows together in an expression of puzzlement. George didn't look puzzled. He didn't look anything. He was as wooden-faced as a cigar-store Indian. The girl looked a little white now, a little tense. I plowed on.

"Back at the El Milano I found that Hawkins had let Marty Estel and his bodyguard into Miss Huntress' apartment to wait for her. Marty had something to tell her—that Arbogast had been killed. That made it a good idea for her to lay off young Jeeter for a while— until the cops quieted down anyhow. A thoughtful guy, Marty. A much more thoughtful guy than you would suppose. For instance, he knew about Arbogast and he knew Mr. Jeeter went to Anna Halsey's office this morning and he knew somehow—Anna might have told him herself, I wouldn't put it past her—that I was working on the case now. So he had me tailed to Arbogast's place and away, and he found out later from his cop friends that Arbogast had been murdered, and he knew I hadn't given it out. So he had me there and that made us pals. He went away after telling me this and once more I was left alone in Miss Huntress' apartment. But this time for no reason at all I poked around. And I found young Mister Gerald, in the bedroom, in a closet."

I stepped quickly over to the girl and reached into my pocket and took out the small fancy .25 automatic and laid it down on her knee.

"Ever see this before?"

Her voice had a curious tight sound, but her dark blue eyes looked at me levelly.

"Yes. It's mine."

"You kept it where?"

"In the drawer of a small table beside the bed."

"Sure about that?"

She thought. Neither of the two men stirred.

George began to twitch the corner of his mouth. She shook her head suddenly, sideways.

"No. I have an idea now I took it out to show somebody—because I don't know much about guns—and left it lying on the mantel in the living room. In fact, I'm almost sure I did. It was Gerald I showed it to."

"So he might have reached for it there, if anybody tried to make a wrong play at him?"

She nodded, troubled. "What do you mean—he's in the closet?" she asked in a small quick voice.

"You know. Everybody in this room knows what I mean. They know that I showed you that gun for a purpose." I stepped away from her and faced George and his boss. "He's dead, of course. Shot through the heart—probably with this gun. It was left there with him. That's why it would be left."

The old man took a step and stopped and braced himself against the table. I wasn't sure whether he had turned white or whether he had been white already. He stared stonily at the girl. He said very slowly, between his teeth: "You damned murderess!"

"Couldn't it have been suicide?" I sneered.

He turned his head enough to look at me. I could see that the idea interested him. He half nodded.

"No," I said. "It couldn't have been suicide."

He didn't like that so well. His face congested with blood and the veins on his nose thickened. The girl touched the gun lying on her knee, then put her hand loosely around the butt. I saw her thumb slide very gently towards the safety catch. She didn't know much about guns, but she knew that much.

"It couldn't be suicide." I said again, very slowly. "As an isolated event—maybe. But not with all the other stuff that's been happening. Arbogast, the stick-up down on Calvello Drive outside this house, the thugs planted in my apartment, the job with the twenty-two."

I reached into my pocket again and pulled out Wax-nose's Woodsman. I held it carelessly on the flat of my left hand. "And curiously enough, I don't think it was *this* twenty-two—although this happens to be the gunman's twenty-two. Yeah, I have the gunman, too. He's tied up in my apartment. He came back to knock me off, but I talked him out of it. I'm a swell talker."

"Except that you overdo it," the girl said coolly, and lifted the gun a little.

"It's obvious who killed him, Miss Huntress," I said. "It's simply a matter of motive and opportunity. Marty Estel didn't, and didn't have it done. That would spoil his chances to get his fifty grand. Frisky Lavon's pal didn't, regardless of who he was working for, and I don't think he was working for Marty Estel. He couldn't have got into the El Milano to do the job, and certainly not into Miss Huntress' apartment. Whoever did it had something to gain by it and an opportunity to get to the place where it was done. Well, who had something to gain? Gerald had five million coming to him in two years out of a trust fund. He couldn't will it until he got it. So if he died, his natural heir got it. Who's his natural heir? You'd be surprised. Did you know that in the state of California and some others, but not in all, a man can by his own act become a natural heir? Just by adopting somebody who has money and no heirs!"

George moved then. His movement was once more as smooth as a ripple of water. The Smith & Wesson gleamed dully in his hand, but he didn't fire it. The small automatic in the girl's hand cracked. Blood spurted from George's brown hard hand. The Smith & Wesson dropped to the floor. He cursed. She didn't know much about guns—not very much.

"Of course!" she said grimly. "George could get into the apartment without any trouble, if Gerald was there. He would go in through the garage, a chauffeur in uniform, ride up in the elevator and knock at the door. And when Gerald opened it, George would back him in with that Smith & Wesson. But how did he know Gerald was there?"

I said: "He must have followed your taxi. We don't know where he has been all evening since he left me. He had a car with him. The cops will find out. How much was in it for you, George?"

George held his right wrist with his left hand, held it tightly, and his face was twisted, savage. He said nothing.

"George would back him in with the Smith & Wesson," the girl said wearily. "Then he would see my gun on the mantelpiece. That would be better. He would use that. He would back Gerald into the bedroom, away from the corridor, into the closet, and there, quietly, calmly, he would kill him and drop the gun on the floor."

"George killed Arbogast, too. He killed him with a twenty-two because he knew that Frisky Lavon's brother had a twenty-two, and he knew that because he had hired Frisky and his brother to put over a big scare on Gerald—so that when he was murdered it would look as if Marty Estel had had it done. That was why I was brought out here tonight in the Jeeter car—so that the two thugs who had been warned and planted could pull their act and maybe knock me off, if I got too tough. Only George likes to kill people. He made a neat shot at Frisky. He hit him in the face. It was so good a shot

I think he meant it to be a miss. How about it, George?"

Silence.

I looked at old Jeeter at last. I had been expecting him to pull a gun himself, but he hadn't. He just stood there, openmouthed, appalled, leaning against the black marble table, shaking.

"My God!" he whispered. "My God!"

"You don't have one—except money."

A door squeaked behind me. I whirled, but I needn't have bothered. A hard voice, about as English as Amos and Andy, said: "Put 'em up, bud."

The butler, the very English butler, stood there in the doorway, a gun in his hand, tight-lipped. The girl turned her wrist and shot him just kind of casually, in the shoulder or something. He squealed like a stuck pig.

"Go away, you're intruding," she said coldly.

He ran. We heard his steps running.

"He's going to fall," she said.

I was wearing my Luger in my right hand now, a little late in the season, as usual. I came around with it. Old Man Jeeter was holding on to the table, his face gray as a paving block. His knees were giving. George stood cynically, holding a handkerchief around his bleeding wrist, watching him.

"Let him fall," I said. "Down is where he belongs."

He fell. His head twisted. His mouth went slack. He hit the carpet on his side and rolled a little and his knees came up. His mouth drooled a little. His skin turned violet.

"Go call the law, angel," I said. "I'll watch them now."

"All right," she said standing up. "But you certainly need a lot of help in your private-detecting business, Mr. Marlowe."

8

I HAD been in there for a solid hour, alone. There was the scarred desk in the middle, another against the wall, a brass spittoon on a mat, a police loudspeaker box on the wall, three squashed flies, a smell of cold cigars and old clothes. There were two hard armchairs with felt pads and two hard straight chairs without pads. The electric-light fixture had been dusted about Coolidge's first term.

The door opened with a jerk and Finlayson and Sebold came in. Sebold looked as spruce and nasty as ever, but Finlayson looked older, more worn, mousier. He held a sheaf of papers in his hand. He sat down across the desk from me and gave me a hard bleak stare.

"Guys like you get in a lot of trouble," Finlayson said sourly. Sebold sat down against the wall and tilted his hat over his eyes and yawned and looked at his new stainless-steel wrist watch.

"Trouble is my business," I said. "How else would I made a nickel?"

"We oughta throw you in the can for all this cover-up stuff. How much you making on this one?"

"I was working for Anna Halsey who was working for old man Jeeter. I guess I made a bad debt."

Sebold smiled his blackjack smile at me. Finlayson lit a cigar and licked at a tear on the side of it and pasted it down, but it leaked smoke just the same when he drew on it. He pushed papers across the desk at me.

"Sign three copies."

I signed three copies.

He took them back, yawned and rumpled his old gray head. "The old man's had a stroke," he said. "No dice there. Probably won't know what time it is when he comes out. This George Hasterman, this chauffeur guy, he just laughs at us. Too bad he got pinked. I'd like to wrastle him a bit."

"He's tough," I said.

"Yeah. O.K., you can beat it for now."

I got up and nodded to them and went to the door. "Well, good night, boys."

Neither of them spoke to me.

I went out, along the corridor and down in the night elevator to the City Hall lobby. I went out the Spring Street side and down the long flight of empty steps and the wind blew cold. I lit a cigarette at the bottom. My car was still out at the Jeeter place. I lifted a foot to start walking to a taxi half a block down across the street. A voice spoke sharply from a parked car.

"Come here a minute."

It was a man's voice, tight, hard. It was Marty Estel's voice. It came from a big sedan with two men in the front seat. I went over there. The rear window was down and Marty Estel leaned a gloved hand on it.

"Get in." He pushed the door open. I got in. I was too tired to argue. "Take it away, Skin."

The car drove west through dark, almost quiet streets, almost clean streets. The night air was not pure but it was cool. We went up over a hill and began to pick up speed.

"What they get?" Estel asked coolly.

"They didn't tell me. They didn't break the chauffeur yet."

"You can't convict a couple million bucks of murder in this man's town." The driver called Skin laughed without turning his head. "Maybe I don't even touch my fifty grand now . . . she likes you."

"Uh-huh. So what?"

"Lay off her."

"What will it get me?"

"It's what it'll get you if you don't."

"Yeah, sure," I said. "Go to hell, will you please. I'm tired." I shut my eyes and leaned in the corner of the car and just like that went to sleep. I can do that sometimes, after a strain.

A hand shaking my shoulder woke me. The car had stopped. I looked out at the front of my apartment house.

"Home," Marty Estel said. "And remember. Lay off her."

"Why the ride home? Just to tell me that?"

"She asked me to look out for you. That's why you're loose. She likes you. I like her. See? You don't want any more trouble."

"Trouble—" I started to say, and stopped. I was tired of that gag for that night. "Thanks for the ride, and apart from that, nuts to you." I turned away and went into the apartment house and up.

The door lock was still loose but nobody waited for me this time. They had taken Waxnose away long since. I left the door open and threw the windows up and I was still sniffing at policemen's cigar butts when the phone rang. It was her voice, cool, a little hard, not touched by anything, almost amused. Well, she'd been through enough to make her that way, probably.

"Hello, brown-eyes. Make it home all right?"

"Your pal Marty brought me home. He told me to lay off you. Thanks with all my heart, if I have any, but don't call me up any more."

"A little scared, Mr. Marlowe?"

"No. Wait for me to call you," I said. "Good night, angel."

"Good night, brown-eyes."

The phone clicked. I put it away and shut the door and pulled the bed down. I undressed and lay on it for a while in the cold air.

Then I got up and had a drink and a shower and went to sleep.

They broke George at last, but not enough. He said there had been a fight over the girl and young Jeeter had grabbed the gun off the mantel and George had fought with him and it had gone off. All of which, of couse, looked possible—in the papers. They never pinned the Arbogast killing on him or on anybody. They never found the gun that did it, but it was not Waxnose's gun. Waxnose disappeared—I never heard where. They didn't touch old man Jeeter, because he never came out of his stroke, except to lie on his back and have nurses and tell people how he hadn't lost a nickel in the depression.

Marty Estel called me up four times to tell me to lay off Harriet Huntress. I felt kind of sorry for the poor guy. He had it bad. I went out with her twice and sat with her twice more at home, drinking her Scotch. It was nice, but I didn't have the money, the clothes, the time or the manners. Then she stopped being at the El Milano and I heard she had gone to New York.

I was glad when she left—even though she didn't bother to tell me goodbye.

FINGER
MAN

1

I GOT AWAY from the Grand Jury a little after four, and then sneaked up the back stairs to Fenweather's office. Fenweather, the D.A., was a man with severe, chiseled features and the gray temples women love. He played with a pen on his desk and said: "I think they believed you. They might even indict Manny Tinnen for the Shannon kill this afternoon. If they do, then is the time you begin to watch your step."

I rolled a cigarette around in my fingers and finally put it in my mouth. "Don't put any men on me, Mr. Fenweather. I know the alleys in this town pretty well, and your men couldn't stay close enough to do me any good."

He looked towards one of the windows. "How well do you know Frank Dorr?" he asked, with his eyes away from me.

"I know he's a big politico, a fixer you have to see if you want to open a gambling hell or a bawdy house— or if you want to sell honest merchandise to the city."

"Right." Fenweather spoke sharply, and brought his head around towards me. Then he lowered his voice. "Having the goods on Tinnen was a surprise to a lot of people. If Frank Dorr had an interest in getting rid of Shannon who was the head of the Board where Dorr's supposed to get his contracts, it's close enough to make him take chances. And I'm told he and Manny Tinnen had dealings. I'd sort of keep an eye on him, if I were you."

I grinned. "I'm just one guy," I said. "Frank Dorr covers a lot of territory. But I'll do what I can."

Fenweather stood up and held his hand across the

desk. He said: "I'll be out of town for a couple of days. I'm leaving tonight, if this indictment comes through. Be careful—and if anything should happen to go wrong, see Bernie Ohls, my chief investigator."

I said: "Sure."

We shook hands and I went out past a tired-looking girl who gave me a tired smile and wound one of her lax curls up on the back of her neck as she looked at me. I got back to my office soon after four-thirty. I stopped outside the door of the little reception room for a moment, looking at it. Then I opened it and went in, and of course there wasn't anybody there.

There was nothing there but an old red davenport, two odd chairs, a bit of carpet, and a library table with a few old magazines on it. The reception room was left open for visitors to come in and sit down and wait—if I had any visitors and they felt like waiting.

I went across and unlocked the door into my private office, lettered *"Philip Marlowe . . . Investigations."*

Lou Harger was sitting on a wooden chair on the side of the desk away from the window. He had bright yellow gloves clamped on the crook of a cane, a green snap-brim hat set too far back on his head. Very smooth black hair showed under the hat and grew too low on the nape of his neck.

"Hello. I've been waiting," he said, and smiled languidly.

" 'Lo, Lou. How did you get in here?"

"The door must have been unlocked. Or maybe I had a key that fitted. Do you mind?"

I went around the desk and sat down in the swivel chair. I put my hat down on the desk, picked up a bull-dog pipe out of an ash tray and began to fill it up.

"It's all right as long as it's you," I said. "I just thought I had a better lock."

He smiled with his full red lips. He was a very good-looking boy. He said: "Are you still doing business, or will you spend the next month in a hotel room drinking liquor with a couple of Headquarters boys?"

"I'm still doing business—if there's any business for me to do."

I lit a pipe, leaned back and stared at his clear olive skin, straight, dark eyebrows.

He put his cane on top of the desk and clasped his yellow gloves on the glass. He moved his lips in and out.

"I have a little something for you. Not a hell of a lot. But there's carfare in it."

I waited.

"I'm making a little play at Las Olindas tonight," he said. "At Canales' place."

"The white smoke?"

"Uh-huh. I think I'm going to be lucky—and I'd like to have a guy with a rod."

I took a fresh pack of cigarettes out of a top drawer and slid them across the desk. Lou picked them up and began to break the pack open.

I said: "What kind of a play?"

He got a cigarette halfway out and stared down at it. There was a little something in his manner I didn't like.

"I've been closed up for a month now. I wasn't makin' the kind of money it takes to stay open in this town. The Headquarters boys have been putting the pressure on since repeal. They have bad dreams when they see themselves trying to live on their pay."

I said: "It doesn't cost any more to operate here than anywhere else. And here you pay it all to one organization. That's something."

Lou Harger jabbed the cigarette in his mouth. "Yeah—Frank Dorr," he snarled. "That fat, bloodsuckin' sonofabitch!"

I didn't say anything. I was way past the age when it's fun to swear at people you can't hurt. I watched Lou light his cigarette with my desk lighter. He went

on, through a puff of smoke: "It's a laugh, in a way.
Canales bought a new wheel—from some grafters in
the sheriff's office. I know Pina, Canales' head croupier,
pretty well. The wheel is one they took away from me.
It's got bugs—and I know the bugs."

"And Canales don't . . . That sounds just like
Canales," I said.

Lou didn't look at me. "He gets a nice crowd down
there," he said. "He has a small dance floor and a five-
piece Mexican band to help the customers relax. They
dance a bit and then go back for another trimming, instead of going away disgusted."

I said: "What do *you* do?"

"I guess you might call it a system," he said softly,
and looked at me under his long lashes.

I looked away from him, looked around the room. It
had a rust-red carpet, five green filing cases in a row
under an advertising calendar, an old costumer in the
corner, a few walnut chairs, net curtains over the windows. The fringe of the curtains was dirty from blowing about in the draft. There was a bar of late sunlight
across my desk and it showed up the dust.

"I get it like this," I said. "You think you have that
roulette wheel tamed and you expect to win enough
money so that Canales will be mad at you. You'd like
to have some protection along—me. I think it's
screwy."

"It's not screwy at all," Lou said. "Any roulette
wheel has a tendency to work in a certain rhythm. If
you know the wheel very well indeed—"

I smiled and shrugged. "Okey, I wouldn't know
about that. I don't know enough roulette. It sounds to
me like you're being a sucker for your own racket, but
I could be wrong. And that's not the point anyway."

"What is?" Lou asked thinly.

"I'm not much stuck on bodyguarding—but maybe
that's not the point either. I take it I'm supposed to

think this play is on the level. Suppose I don't, and walk out on you, and you get in a box? Or suppose I think everything is aces, but Canales don't agree with me and gets nasty."

"That's why I need a guy with a rod," Lou said, without moving a muscle except to speak.

I said evenly: "If I'm tough enough for the job—and I didn't know I was—that still isn't what worries me."

"Forget it," Lou said. "It breaks me up enough to know you're worried."

I smiled a little more and watched his yellow gloves moving around on top of the desk, moving too much. I said slowly: "You're the last guy in the world to be getting expense money that way just now. I'm the last guy to be standing behind you while you do it. That's all."

Lou said: "Yeah." He knocked some ash off his cigarette down on the glass top, bent his head to blow it off. He went on, as if it was a new subject: "Miss Glenn is going with me. She's a tall redhead, a swell looker. She used to model. She's nice people in any kind of a spot and she'll keep Canales from breathing on my neck. So we'll make out. I just thought I'd tell you.

I was silent for a minute, then I said: "You know damn well I just got through telling the Grand Jury it was Manny Tinnen I saw lean out of that car and cut the ropes on Art Shannon's wrists after they pushed him on the roadway, filled with lead."

Lou smiled faintly at me. "That'll make it easier for the grafters on the big time; the fellows who take the contracts and don't appear in the business. They say Shannon was square and kept the Board in line. It was a nasty bump-off."

I shook my head. I didn't want to talk about that. I

said: "Canales has a noseful of junk a lot of the time. And maybe he doesn't go for redheads."

Lou stood up slowly and lifted his cane off the desk. He stared at the tip of one yellow finger. He had an almost sleepy expression. Then he moved towards the door, swinging his cane.

"Well, I'll be seein' you some time," he drawled.

I let him get his hand on the knob before I said: "Don't go away sore, Lou. I'll drop down to Las Olindas, if you have to have me. But I don't want any money for it, and for Pete's sake don't pay any more attention to me than you have to."

He licked his lips softly and didn't quite look at me. "Thanks, keed. I'll be careful as hell."

He went out then and his yellow glove disappeared around the edge of the door.

I sat still for about five minutes and then my pipe got too hot. I put it down, looked at my strap watch, and got up to switch on a small radio in the corner beyond the end of the desk. When the A.C. hum died down the last tinkle of a chime came out of the horn, then a voice was saying: "KLI now brings you its regular early evening broadcast of local news releases. An event of importance this afternoon was the indictment returned late today against Maynard J. Tinnen by the Grand Jury. Tinnen is a well-known City Hall lobbyist and man about town. The indictment, a shock to his many friends, was based almost entirely on the testimony—"

My telephone rang sharply and a girl's cool voice said in my ear: "One moment, please. Mr. Fenweather is calling you."

He came on at once. "Indictment returned. Take care of the boy."

I said I was just getting it over the radio. We talked a short moment and then he hung up, after saying he had to leave at once to catch a plane.

I leaned back in my chair again and listened to the radio without exactly hearing it. I was thinking what a damn fool Lou Harger was and that there wasn't anything I could do to change that.

2

It was a good crowd for a Tuesday but nobody was dancing. Around ten o'clock the little five-piece band got tired of messing around with a rhumba that nobody was paying any attention to. The marimba player dropped his sticks and reached under his chair for a glass. The rest of the boys lit cigarettes and just sat there looking bored.

I leaned sidewise against the bar, which was on the same side of the room as the orchestra stand. I was turning a small glass of tequila around on the top of the bar. All the business was at the center one of the three roulette tables.

The bartender leaned beside me, on his side of the bar.

"The flame-top gal must be pickin' them," he said.

I nodded without looking at him. "She's playing with fistfuls now," I said. "Not even counting it."

The red-haired girl was tall. I could see the burnished copper of her hair between the heads of the people behind her. I could see Lou Harger's sleek head beside hers. Everybody seemed to be playing standing up.

"You don't play?" the bartender asked me.

"Not on Tuesdays. I had some trouble on a Tuesday once."

"Yeah? Do you like that stuff straight, or would I smooth it out for you?"

"Smooth it out with what?" I said. "You got a wood rasp handy?"

He grinned. I drank a little more of the tequila and made a face.

"Did anybody invent this stuff on purpose?"

"I wouldn't know, mister."

"What's the limit over there?"

"I wouldn't know that either. How the boss feels, I guess."

The roulette tables were in a row near the far wall. A low railing of gilt metal joined their ends and the players were outside the railing.

Some kind of a confused wrangle started at the center table. Half a dozen people at the two end tables grabbed their chips up and moved across.

Then a clear, very polite voice, with a slightly foreign accent, spoke out: "If you will just be patient, madame ... Mr. Canales will be here in a minute."

I went across, squeezed near the railing. Two croupiers stood near me with their heads together and their eyes looking sidewise. One moved a rake slowly back and forth beside the idle wheel. They were staring at the red-haired girl.

She wore a high-cut black evening gown. She had fine white shoulders, was something less than beautiful and more than pretty. She was leaning on the edge of the table, in front of the wheel. Her long eyelashes were twitching. There was a big pile of money and chips in front of her.

She spoke monotonously, as if she had said the same thing several times already.

"Get busy and spin that wheel! You take it away fast enough, but you don't like to dish it out."

The croupier in charge smiled a cold, even smile. He was tall, dark, disinterested. "The table can't cover your bet," he said with calm precision. "Mr. Canales, perhaps—" He shrugged neat shoulders.

The girl said: "It's your money, highpockets. Don't you want it back?"

Lou Harger licked his lips beside her, put a hand on her arm, stared at the pile of money with hot eyes. He said gently: "Wait for Canales . . ."

"To hell with Canales! I'm hot—and I want to stay that way."

A door opened at the end of the tables and a very slight, very pale man came into the room. He had straight, lusterless black hair, a high bony forehead, flat, impenetrable eyes. He had a thin mustache that was trimmed in two sharp lines almost at right angles to each other. They came down below the corners of his mouth a full inch. The effect was Oriental. His skin had a thick, glistening pallor.

He slid behind the croupiers, stopped at a corner of the center table, glanced at the red-haired girl and touched the ends of his mustache with two fingers, the nails of which had a purplish tint.

He smiled suddenly, and the instant after it was as though he had never smiled in his life. He spoke in a dull, ironic voice.

"Good evening, Miss Glenn. You must let me send somebody with you when you go home. I'd hate to see any of that money get in the wrong pockets."

The red-haired girl looked at him, not very pleasantly.

"I'm not leaving—unless you're throwing me out."

Canales said: "No? What would you like to do?"

"Bet the wad—dark meat!"

The crowd noise became a deathly silence. There wasn't a whisper of any kind of sound. Harger's face slowly got ivory-white.

Canales' face was without expression. He lifted a hand, delicately, gravely, slipped a large wallet from his dinner jacket and tossed it in front of the tall croupier.

"Ten grand," he said in a voice that was a dull rustle of sound. "That's my limit—always."

The tall croupier picked the wallet up, spread it, drew out two flat packets of crisp bills, riffled them, refolded the wallet and passed it along the edge of the table to Canales.

Canales did not move to take it. Nobody moved, except the croupier.

The girl said: "Put it on the red."

The croupier leaned across the table and very carefully stacked her money and chips. He placed her bet for her on the red diamond. He placed his hand along the curve of the wheel.

"If no one objects," Canales said, without looking at anyone, "this is just the two of us."

Heads moved. Nobody spoke. The croupier spun the wheel and sent the ball skimming in the groove with a light flirt of his left wrist. Then he drew his hands back and placed them in full view on the edge of the table, on top of it.

The red-haired girl's eyes shone and her lips slowly parted.

The ball drifted along the groove, dipped past one of the bright metal diamonds, slid down the flank of the wheel and chattered along the tines beside the numbers. Movement went out of it suddenly, with a dry click. It fell next the double-zero, in red twenty-seven. The wheel was motionless.

The croupier took up his rake and slowly pushed the two packets of bills across, added them to the stake, pushed the whole thing off the field of play.

Canales put his wallet back in his breast pocket, turned and walked slowly back to the door, went through it.

I took my cramped fingers off the top of the railing, and a lot of people broke for the bar.

3

When Lou came up I was sitting at a little tile-top table in a corner, fooling with some more of the tequila. The little orchestra was playing a thin, brittle tango and one couple was maneuvering self-consciously on the dance floor.

Lou had a cream-colored overcoat on, with the collar turned up around a lot of white silk scarf. He had a fine-drawn glistening expression. He had white pigskin gloves this time and he put one of them down on the table and leaned at me.

"Over twenty-two thousand," he said softly. "Boy, what a take!"

I said: "Very nice money, Lou. What kind of car are you driving?"

"See anything wrong with it?"

"The play?" I shrugged, fiddled with my glass. "I'm not wised up on roulette, Lou . . . I saw plenty wrong with your broad's manners."

"She's not a broad," Lou said. His voice got a little worried.

"Okey. She made Canales look like a million. What kind of car?"

"Buick sedan. Nile green, with two spotlights and those little fender lights on rods." His voice was still worried.

I said: "Take it kind of slow through town. Give me a chance to get in the parade."

He moved his glove and went away. The red-haired girl was not in sight anywhere. I looked down at the watch on my wrist. When I looked up again Canales was standing across the table. His eyes looked at me lifelessly above his trick mustache.

"You don't like my place," he said.

"On the contrary."

"You don't come here to play." He was telling me, not asking me.

"Is it compulsory?" I asked dryly.

A very faint smile drifted across his face. He leaned a little down and said: "I think you are a dick. A smart dick."

"Just a shamus," I said. "And not so smart. Don't let my long upper lip fool you. It runs in the family."

Canales wrapped his fingers around the top of a chair, squeezed on it. "Don't come here again—for anything." He spoke very softly, almost dreamily. "I don't like pigeons."

I took the cigarette out of my mouth and looked it over before I looked at him. I said: "I heard you insulted a while back. You took it nicely . . . So we won't count this one."

He had a queer expression for a moment. Then he turned and slid away with a little sway of the shoulders. He put his feet down flat and turned them out a good deal as he walked. His walk, like his face, was a little negroid.

I got up and went out through the big white double doors into a dim lobby, got my hat and coat and put them on. I went out through another pair of double doors onto a wide veranda with scrollwork along the edge of its roof. There was sea fog in the air and the windblown Monterey cypresses in front of the house dripped with it. The grounds sloped gently into the dark for a long distance. Fog hid the ocean.

I had parked the car out on the street, on the other side of the house. I drew my hat down and walked soundlessly on the damp moss that covered the driveway, rounded a corner of the porch, and stopped rigidly.

A man just in front of me was holding a gun—but he didn't see me. He was holding the gun down at his side, pressed against the material of his overcoat, and his big hand made it look quite small. The dim light that reflected from the barrel seemed to come out of the fog, to be part of the fog. He was a big man, and he stood very still, poised on the balls of his feet.

I lifted my right hand very slowly and opened the top two buttons of my coat, reached inside and drew out a long .38 with a six-inch barrel. I eased it into my overcoat pocket.

The man in front of me moved, reached his left hand up to his face. He drew on a cigarette cupped inside his hand and the glow put brief light on a heavy chin, wide, dark nostrils, and a square, aggressive nose, the nose of a fighting man.

Then he dropped the cigarette and stepped on it and a quick, light step made faint noise behind me. I was far too late turning.

Something swished and I went out like a light.

4

When I came to I was cold and wet and had a headache a yard wide. There was a soft bruise behind my right ear that wasn't bleeding. I had been put down with a sap.

I got up off my back and saw that I was a few yards from the driveway, between two trees that were wet with fog. There was some mud on the backs of my shoes. I had been dragged off the path, but not very far.

I went through my pockets. My gun was gone, of course, but that was all—that and the idea that this excursion was all fun.

I nosed around through the fog, didn't find anything

or see anyone, gave up bothering about that, and went along the blank side of the house to a curving line of palm trees and an old type arc light that hissed and flickered over the entrance to a sort of lane where I had stuck the 1925 Marmon touring car I still used for transportation. I got into it after wiping the seat off with a towel, teased the motor alive, and choked it along to a big empty street with disused car tracks in the middle.

I went from there to De Cazens Boulevard, which was the main drag of Las Olindas and was called after the man who built Canales' place long ago. After a while there was town, buildings, dead-looking stores, a service station with a night-bell, and at last a drugstore which was still open.

A dolled-up sedan was parked in front of the drugstore and I parked behind that, got out, and saw that a hatless man was sitting at the counter, talking to a clerk in a blue smock. They seemed to have the world to themselves. I started to go in, then I stopped and took another look at the dolled-up sedan.

It was a Buick and of a color that could have been Nile-green in daylight. It had two spotlights and two little egg-shaped amber lights stuck up on thin nickel rods clamped to the front fenders. The window by the driver's seat was down. I went back to the Marmon and got a flash, reached in and twisted the license holder of the Buick around, put the light on it quickly, then off again.

It was registered to Louis N. Harger.

I got rid of the flash and went into the drugstore. There was a liquor display at one side, and the clerk in the blue smock sold me a pint of Canadian Club, which I took over to the counter and opened. There were ten seats at the counter, but I sat down on the one next to the hatless man. He began to look me over, in the mirror, very carefully.

I got a cup of black coffee two-thirds full and added plenty of the rye. I drank it down and waited for a minute, to let it warm me up. Then I looked the hatless man over.

He was about twenty-eight, a little thin on top, had a healthy red face, fairly honest eyes, dirty hands and looked as if he wasn't making much money. He wore a gray whipcord jacket with metal buttons on it, pants that didn't match.

I said carelessly, in a low voice: "Your bus outside?"

He sat very still. His mouth got small and tight and he had trouble pulling his eyes away from mine, in the mirror.

"My brother's," he said, after a moment.

I said: "Care for a drink? . . . Your brother is an old friend of mine."

He nodded slowly, gulped, moved his hand slowly, but finally got the bottle and curdled his coffee with it. He drank the whole thing down. Then I watched him dig up a crumpled pack of cigarettes, spear his mouth with one, strike a match on the counter, after missing twice on his thumbnail, and inhale with a lot of very poor nonchalance that he knew wasn't going over.

I leaned close to him and said evenly: "This doesn't *have* to be trouble."

He said: "Yeah . . . Wh-what's the beef?"

The clerk sidled towards us. I asked for more coffee. When I got it I stared at the clerk until he went and stood in front of the display window with his back to me. I laced my second cup of coffee and drank some of it. I looked at the clerk's back and said: "The guy the car belongs to doesn't have a brother."

He held himself tightly, but turned towards me. "You think it's a hot car?"

"No."

"You don't think it's a hot car?"

I said: "No. I just want the story."

"You a dick?"

"Uh-huh—but it isn't a shakedown, if that's what worries you."

He drew hard on his cigarette and moved his spoon around in his empty cup.

"I can lose my job over this," he said slowly. "But I needed a hundred bucks. I'm a hack driver."

"I guessed that," I said.

He looked surprised, turned his head and stared at me. "Have another drink and let's get on with it," I said. "Car thieves don't park them on the main drag and then sit around in drugstores."

The clerk came back from the window and hovered near us, busying himself with rubbing a rag on the coffee urn. A heavy silence fell. The clerk put the rag down, went along to the back of the store, behind the partition, and began to whistle aggressively.

The man beside me took some more of the whiskey and drank it, nodding his head wisely at me. "Listen— I brought a fare out and was supposed to wait for him. A guy and a jane come up alongside me in the Buick and the guy offers me a hundred bucks to let him wear my cap and drive my hack into town. I'm to hang around here an hour, then take his heap to the Hotel Carillon on Towne Boulevard. My cab will be there for me. He gives me the hundred bucks."

"What was his story?" I asked.

"He said they'd been to a gambling joint and had some luck for a change. They're afraid of holdups on the way in. They figure there's always spotters watchin' the play."

I took one of his cigarettes and straightened it out in my fingers. "It's a story I can't hurt much," I said. "Could I see your cards?"

He gave them to me. His name was Tom Sneyd and he was a driver for the Green Top Cab Company. I corked my pint, slipped it into my side pocket, and danced a half-dollar on the counter.

The clerk came along and made change. He was almost shaking with curiosity.

"Come on, Tom," I said in front of him. "Let's go get that cab. I don't think you should wait around here any longer."

We went out, and I let the Buick lead me away from the straggling lights of Las Olindas, through a series of small beach towns with little houses built on sandlots close to the ocean, and bigger ones built on the slopes of the hills behind. A window was lit here and there. The tires sang on the moist concrete and the little amber lights on the Buick's fenders peeped back at me from the curves.

At West Cimarron we turned inland, chugged on through Canal City, and met the San Angelo Cut. It took us almost an hour to get to 5640 Towne Boulevard, which is the number of the Hotel Carillon. It is a big, rambling slate-roofed building with a basement garage and a forecourt fountain on which they play a pale green light in the evening.

Green Top Cab No. 469 was parked across the street, on the dark side. I couldn't see where anybody had been shooting into it. Tom Sneyd found his cap in the driver's compartment, climbed eagerly under the wheel.

"Does that fix me up? Can I go now?" His voice was strident with relief.

I told him it was all right with me, and gave him my card. It was twelve minutes past one as he took the corner. I climbed into the Buick and tooled it down the ramp to the garage and left it with a colored boy who was dusting cars in slow motion. I went around to the lobby.

The clerk was an ascetic-looking young man who was reading a volume of *California Appellate De-*

cisions under the switchboard light. He said Lou was not in and had not been in since eleven, when he came on duty. After a short argument about the lateness of the hour and the importance of my visit, he rang Lou's apartment, but there wasn't any answer.

I went out and sat in my Marmon for a few minutes, smoked a cigarette, imbibed a little from my pint of Canadian Club. Then I went back into the Carillon and shut myself in a pay booth. I dialed the *Telegram,* asked for the City Desk, got a man named Von Ballin.

He yelped at me when I told him who I was. "You still walking around? That ought to be a story. I thought Manny Tinnen's friends would have had you laid away in old lavender by this time."

I said: "Can that and listen to this. Do you know a man named Lou Harger? He's a gambler. Had a place that was raided and closed up a month ago."

Von Ballin said he didn't know Lou personally, but he knew who he was.

"Who around your rag would know him real well?"

He thought a moment. "There's a lad named Jerry Cross here," he said, "that's supposed to be an expert on night life. What did you want to know?"

"Where would he go to celebrate," I said. Then I told him some of the story, not too much. I left out the part where I got sapped and the part about the taxi. "He hasn't shown at his hotel," I ended. "I ought to get a line on him."

"Well, if you're a friend of his—"

"Of his—not of his crowd," I said sharply.

Von Ballin stopped to yell at somebody to take a call, then said to me softly, close to the phone: "Come through, boy. Come through."

"All right. But I'm talking to you, not to your sheet. I got sapped and lost my gun outside Canales' joint. Lou and his girl switched his car for a taxi they picked up. Then they dropped out of sight. I don't like it too well. Lou wasn't drunk enough to chase around town with that much dough in his pockets. And if he was, the girl wouldn't let him. She had the practical eye."

"I'll see what I can do," Von Ballin said. "But it don't sound promising. I'll give you a buzz."

I told him I lived at the Merritt Plaza, in case he had forgotten, went out and got into the Marmon again. I drove home and put hot towels on my head for fifteen minutes, then sat around in my pajamas and drank hot whiskey and lemon and called the Carillon every once in a while. At two-thirty Von Ballin called me and said no luck. Lou hadn't been pinched, he wasn't in any of the Receiving Hospitals, and he hadn't shown at any of the clubs Jerry Cross could think of.

At three I called the Carillon for the last time. Then I put my light out and went to sleep.

In the morning it was the same way. I tried to trace the red-haired girl a little. There were twenty-eight people named Glenn in the phone book, and three women among them. One didn't answer, the other two assured me they didn't have red hair. One offered to show me.

I shaved, showered, had breakfast, walked three blocks down the hill to the Condor Building.

Miss Glenn was sitting in my little reception room.

5

I unlocked the other door and she went in and sat in the chair where Lou had sat the afternoon before. I opened some windows, locked the outer door of the reception room, and struck a match for the unlighted cigarette she held in her ungloved and ringless left hand.

She was dressed in a blouse and plaid skirt with a loose coat over them, and a close-fitting hat that was far enough out of style to suggest a run of bad luck. But it hid almost all of her hair. Her skin was without make-up and she looked about thirty and had the set face of exhaustion.

She held her cigarette with a hand that was almost too steady, a hand on guard. I sat down and waited for her to talk.

She stared at the wall over my head and didn't say anything. After a little while I packed my pipe and smoked for a minute. Then I got up and went across to the door that opened into the hallway and picked up a couple of letters that had been pushed through the slot.

I sat down at the desk again, looked them over, read one of them twice, as if I had been alone. While I was doing this I didn't look at her directly or speak to her, but I kept an eye on her all the same. She looked like a lady who was getting nerved for something.

Finally she moved. She opened up a big black patent-leather bag and took out a fat manila envelope, pulled a rubber band off it and sat holding the envelope between the palms of her hands, with her head tilted way back and the cigarette dribbling gray smoke from the corners of her mouth.

She said slowly: "Lou said if I ever got caught in the rain, you were the boy to see. It's raining hard where I am."

I stared at the manila envelope. "Lou is a pretty good friend of mine," I said. "I'd do anything in reason for him. Some things not in reason—like last night. That doesn't mean Lou and I always play the same games."

She dropped her cigarette into the glass bowl of the ash tray and left it to smoke. A dark flame burned suddenly in her eyes, then went out.

"Lou is dead." Her voice was quite toneless.

I reached over with a pencil and stabbed at the hot end of the cigarette until it stopped smoking.

She went on: "A couple of Canales' boys got him in my apartment—with one shot from a small gun that looked like my gun. Mine was gone when I looked for it afterwards. I spent the night there with him dead . . . I had to."

She broke quite suddenly. Her eyes turned up in her head and her head came down and hit the desk. She lay still, with the manila envelope in front of her lax hands.

I jerked a drawer open and brought up a bottle and a glass, poured a stiff one and stepped around with it, heaved her up in her chair. I pushed the edge of the glass hard against her mouth—hard enough to hurt. She struggled and swallowed. Some of it ran down her chin, but life came back into her eyes.

I left the whiskey in front of her and sat down again. The flap of the envelope had come open enough for me to see currency inside, bales of currency.

She began to talk to me in a dreamy sort of voice.

"We got all big bills from the cashier, but makes quite a package at that. There's twenty-two thousand even in the envelope. I kept out a few odd hundreds.

"Lou was worried. He figured it would be pretty easy for Canales to catch up with us. You might be right behind and not be able to do very much about it."

I said: "Canales lost the money in full view of everybody there. It was good advertising—even if it hurt."

She went on exactly as though I had not spoken. "Going through the town we spotted a cab driver sitting in his parked cab and Lou had a brain wave. He offered the boy a C note to let him drive the cab into San Angelo and bring the Buick to the hotel after a while. The boy took us up and we went over on another street and made the switch. We were sorry about ditching you, but Lou said you wouldn't mind. And we might get a chance to flag you.

"Lou didn't go into his hotel. We took another cab over to my place. I live at the Hobart Arms, eight hundred block on South Minter. It's a place where you don't have to answer questions at the desk. We went up to my apartment and put the lights on and two guys with masks came around the half-wall between the living room and the dinette. One was small and thin and the other one was a big slob with a chin that stuck out under his mask like a shelf. Lou made a wrong motion and the big one shot him just the once. The gun just made a flat crack, not very loud, and Lou fell down on the floor and never moved."

I said: "It might be the ones that made a sucker out of me. I haven't told you about that yet."

She didn't seem to hear that either. Her face was white and composed, but as expressionless as plaster. "Maybe I'd better have another finger of the hooch," she said.

I poured us a couple of drinks, and we drank them. She went on: "They went through us, but we didn't have the money. We had stopped at an all-night drugstore and had it weighed and mailed it at a branch post office. They went through the apartment, but of course we had just come in and hadn't had time to hide anything. The big one slammed me down with his fist, and when I woke up again they were gone and I was alone with Lou dead on the floor."

She pointed to a mark on the angle of her jaw. There was something there, but it didn't show much. I moved around in my chair a little and said: "They passed you on the way in. Smart boys would have looked a taxi over on that road. How did they know where to go?"

"I thought that out during the night," Miss Glenn said. "Canales knows where I live. He followed me home once and tried to get me to ask him up."

"Yeah," I said, "but why did they go to your place and how did they get in?"

"That's not hard. There's a ledge just below the windows and a man could edge along it to the fire escape. They probably had other boys covering Lou's hotel. We thought of that chance, but we didn't think about my place being known to them."

"Tell me the rest of it," I said.

"The money was mailed to me," Miss Glenn explained. "Lou was a swell boy, but a girl has to protect herself. That's why I had to stay there last night with Lou dead on the floor. Until the mail came. Then I came over here."

I got up and looked out of the window. A fat girl was pounding a typewriter across the court. I could hear the clack of it. I sat down again, stared at my thumb.

"Did they plant the gun?" I asked.

"Not unless it's under him. I didn't look there."

"They let you off too easy. Maybe it wasn't Canales at all. Did Lou open his heart to you much?"

She shook her head quietly. Her eyes were slate-blue now, and thoughtful, without the blank stare.

"All right," I said. "Just what did you think of having me do about it all?"

She narrowed her eyes a little, then put a hand out and pushed the bulging envelope slowly across the desk.

"I'm no baby and I'm in a jam. But I'm not going to the cleaners just the same. Half of this money is mine, and I want it with a clean getaway. One-half net. If I'd called the law last night, there'd have been a way to chisel me out of it . . . I think Lou would like you to have his half, if you want to play with me."

I said: "It's big money to flash at a private dick, Miss Glenn," and smiled wearily. "You're a little worse off for not calling cops last night. But there's an answer to anything they might say. I think I'd better go over there and see what's broken, if anything."

She leaned forward quickly and said: "Will you take care of the money? . . . Dare you?"

"Sure. I'll pop downstairs and put it in a safe-deposit box. You can hold one of the keys—and we'll talk split later on. I think it would be a swell idea if Canales knew he had to see me, and still sweller if you hid out in a little hotel where I have a friend—at least until I nose around a bit."

She nodded. I put my hat on and put the envelope inside my belt. I went out, telling her there was a gun in the top left-hand drawer, if she felt nervous.

When I got back she didn't seem to have moved. But she said she had phoned Canales' place and left a message for him she thought he would understand.

We went by rather devious ways to the Lorraine, at Brant and Avenue C. Nobody shot at us going over, and as far as I could see we were not trailed.

I shook hands with Jim Dolan, the day clerk at the Lorraine, with a twenty folded in my hand. He put his hand in his pocket and said he would be glad to see that "Miss Thompson" was not bothered.

I left. There was nothing in the noon paper about Lou Harger of the Hobart Arms.

6

The Hobart Arms was just another apartment house, in a block lined with them. It was six stories high and had a buff front. A lot of cars were parked at both curbs all along the block. I drove through slowly and looked things over. The neighborhood didn't have the look of having been excited about anything in the immediate past. It was peaceful and sunny, and the parked cars had a settled look, as if they were right at home.

I circled into an alley with a high board fence on each side and a lot of flimsy garages cutting it. I parked beside one that had a For Rent sign and went between two garbage cans into the concrete yard of the Hobart Arms, along the side to the street. A man was putting golf clubs into the back of a coupe. In the lobby a Filipino was dragging a vacuum cleaner over the rug and a dark Jewess was writing at the switchboard.

I used the automatic elevator and prowled along an upper corridor to the last door on the left. I knocked, waited, knocked again, went in with Miss Glenn's key.

Nobody was dead on the floor.

I looked at myself in the mirror that was the back of a pull-down bed, went across and looked out of a window. There was a ledge below that had once been a coping. It ran along to the fire escape. A blind man could have walked in. I didn't notice anything like footmarks in the dust on it.

There was nothing in the dinette or kitchen except what belonged there. The bedroom had a cheerful carpet and painted gray walls. There was a lot of junk in the corner, around a wastebasket, and a broken comb on the dresser held a few strands of red hair. The closets were empty except for some gin bottles.

I went back to the living room, looked behind the

wall bed, stood around for a minute, left the apartment.

The Filipino in the lobby had made about three yards with the vacuum cleaner. I leaned on the counter beside the switchboard.

"Miss Glenn?"

The dark Jewess said: "Five-two-four," and made a check mark on the laundry list.

"She's not in. Has she been in lately?"

She glanced up at me. "I haven't noticed. What is it—a bill?"

I said I was just a friend, thanked her and went away. That established the fact that there had been no excitement in Miss Glenn's apartment. I went back to the alley and the Marmon.

I hadn't believed it quite the way Miss Glenn told it anyhow.

I crossed Cordova, drove a block and stopped beside a forgotten drugstore that slept behind two giant pepper trees and a dusty, cluttered window. It had a single pay booth in the corner. An old man shuffled towards me wistfully, then went away when he saw what I wanted, lowered a pair of steel spectacles on to the end of his nose and sat down again with his newspaper.

I dropped my nickel, dialed, and a girl's voice said: "Telegrayam!" with a tinny drawl. I asked for Von Ballin.

When I got him and he knew who it was I could here him clearing his throat. Then his voice came close to the phone and said very distinctly: "I've got something for you, but it's bad. I'm sorry as all hell. Your friend Harger is in the morgue. We got a flash about ten minutes ago."

I leaned against the wall of the booth and felt my eyes getting haggard. I said: "What else did you get?"

"Couple of radio cops picked him up in somebody's

front yard or something, in West Cimarron. He was
shot through the heart. It happened last night, but for
some reason they only just put out the identification."

I said: "West Cimarron, huh? . . . Well, that takes
care of that. I'll be in to see you."

I thanked him and hung up, stood for a moment
looking out through the glass at a middle-aged gray-
haired man who had come into the store and was pawing over the magazine rack.

Then I dropped another nickel and dialed the Lorraine, asked for the clerk.

I said: "Get your girl to put me on to the redhead,
will you, Jim?"

I got a cigarette out and lit it, puffed smoke at the
glass of the door. The smoke flattened out against the
glass and swirled about in the close air. Then the line
clicked and the operator's voice said: "Sorry, your party
does not answer."

"Give me Jim again," I said. Then, when he answered, "Can you take time to run up and find out
why she doesn't answer the phone? Maybe she's just
being cagey."

Jim said: "You bet. I'll shoot right up with a key."

Sweat was coming out all over me. I put the receiver
down on a little shelf and jerked the booth door open.
The gray-haired man looked up quickly from the magazines, then scowled and looked at his watch. Smoke
poured out of the booth. After a moment I kicked the
door shut and picked up the receiver again.

Jim's voice seemed to come to me from a long way
off. "She's not here. Maybe she went for a walk."

I said: "Yeah—or maybe it was a ride."

I pronged the receiver and pushed on out of the
booth. The gray-haired stranger slammed a magazine
down so hard that it fell to the floor. He stooped to
pick it up as I went past him. Then he straightened
up just behind me and said quietly, but very firmly:

"Keep the hands down, and quiet. Walk on out to your heap. This is business."

Out of the corner of my eye I could see the old man peeking short-sightedly at us. But there wasn't anything for him to see, even if he could see that far. Something prodded my back. It might have been a finger, but I didn't think it was.

We went out of the store very peacefully.

A long gray car had stopped close behind the Marmon. Its rear door was open and a man with a square face and a crooked mouth was standing with one foot out on the running board. His right hand was behind him, inside the car.

My man's voice said: "Get in your car and drive west. Take this first corner and go about twenty-five, not more."

The narrow street was sunny and quiet and the pepper trees whispered. Traffic threshed by on Cordova a short block away. I shrugged, opened the door of my car and got under the wheel. The gray-haired man got in very quickly beside me, watching my hands. He swung his right hand around, with a snub-nosed gun in it.

"Careful getting your keys out, buddy."

I was careful. As I stepped on the starter a car door slammed behind, there were rapid steps, and someone got into the back seat of the Marmon. I let in the clutch and drove around the corner. In the mirror I could see the gray car making the turn behind. Then it dropped back a little.

I drove west on a street that paralleled Cordova and when we had gone a block and a half a hand came down over my shoulder from behind and took my gun away from me. The gray-haired man rested his short revolver on his leg and felt me over carefully with his free hand. He leaned back satisfied.

"Okey. Drop over to the main drag and snap it up,"

he said. "But that don't mean trying to sideswipe a prowl car, if you lamp one . . . Or if you think it does, try it and see."

I made the two turns, speeded up to thirty-five and held it there. We went through some nice residential districts, and then the landscape began to thin out. When it was quite thin the gray car behind dropped back, turned towards town and disappeared.

"What's the snatch for?" I asked.

The gray-haired man laughed and rubbed his broad red chin. "Just business. The big boy wants to talk to you."

"Canales?"

"Canales—hell! I said the *big boy*."

I watched traffic, what there was of it that far out, and didn't speak for a few minutes. Then I said: "Why didn't you pull it in the apartment, or in the alley?"

"Wanted to make sure you wasn't covered."

"Who's this big boy?"

"Skip that—till we get you there. Anything else?"

"Yes. Can I smoke?"

He held the wheel while I lit up. The man in the back seat hadn't said a word at any time. After a while the gray-haired man made me pull up and move over, and he drove.

"I used to own one of these, six years ago, when I was poor," he said jovially.

I couldn't think of a really good answer to that, so I just let smoke seep down into my lungs and wondered why, if Lou had been killed in West Cimarron, the killers didn't get the money. And if he really had been killed at Miss Glenn's apartment, why somebody had taken the trouble to carry him back to West Cimarron.

7

In twenty minutes we were in the foothills. We went over a hogback, drifted down a long white concrete ribbon, crossed a bridge, went halfway up the next slope and turned off on a gravel road that disappeared around a shoulder of scrub oak and manzanita. Plumes of pampas grass flared on the side of the hill, like jets of water. The wheels crunched on the gravel and skidded on the curves.

We came to a mountain cabin with a wide porch and cemented boulder foundations. The windmill of a generator turned slowly on the crest of a spur a hundred feet behind the cabin. A mountain blue jay flashed across the road, zoomed, banked sharply, and fell out of sight like a stone.

The gray-haired man tooled the car up to the porch, beside a tan colored Lincoln coupe, switched off the igniton and set the Marmon's long parking brake. He took the keys out, folded them carefully in their leather case, put the case away in his pocket.

The man in the back seat got out and held the door beside me open. He had a gun in his hand. I got out. The gray-haired man got out. We all went into the house.

There was a big room with walls of knotted pine, beautifully polished. We went across it walking on Indian rugs and the gray-haired man knocked carefully on a door.

A voice shouted: "What is it?"

The gray-haired man put his face against the door and said: "Beasley—and the guy you wanted to talk to."

The voice inside said to come on in. Beasley opened the door, pushed me through it and shut it behind me.

100

It was another big room with knotted pine walls and Indian rugs on the floor. A driftwood fire hissed and puffed on a stone hearth.

The man who sat behind a flat desk was Frank Dorr, the politico.

He was the kind of man who liked to have a desk in front of him, and shove his fat stomach against it, and fiddle with things on it, and look very wise. He had a fat, muddy face, a thin fringe of white hair that stuck up a little, small sharp eyes, small and very delicate hands.

What I could see of him was dressed in a slovenly gray suit, and there was a large black Persian cat on the desk in front of him. He was scratching the cat's head with one of his little neat hands and the cat was leaning against his hand. Its busy tail flowed over the edge of the desk and fell straight down.

He said: "Sit down," without looking away from the cat.

I sat down in a leather chair with a very low seat. Dorr said: "How do you like it up here? Kind of nice, ain't it? This is Toby, my girl friend. Only girl friend I got. Ain't you, Toby?"

I said: "I like it up here—but I don't like the way I got here."

Dorr raised his head a few inches and looked at me with his mouth slightly open. He had beautiful teeth, but they hadn't grown in his mouth. He said: "I'm a busy man, brother. It was simpler than arguing. Have a drink?"

"Sure I'll have a drink," I said.

He squeezed the cat's head gently between his two palms, then pushed it away from him and put both hands down on the arms of his chair. He shoved hard and his face got a little red and he finally got up on his feet. He waddled across to a built-in cabinet and took out a squat decanter of whiskey and two gold-veined glasses.

"No ice today," he said, waddling back to the desk. "Have to drink it straight."

He poured two drinks, gestured, and I went over and got mine. He sat down again. I sat down with my drink. Dorr lit a long brown cigar, pushed the box two inches in my direction, leaned back and stared at me with complete relaxation.

"You're the guy that fingered Manny Tinnen," he said. "It won't do."

I sipped my whiskey. It was good enough to sip.

"Life gets complicated at times," Dorr went on, in the same even, relaxed voice. "Politics—even when it's a lot of fun—is tough on the nerves. You know me. I'm tough and I get what I want. There ain't a hell of a lot I want any more, but what I want—I want bad. And ain't so damn particular how I get it."

"You have that reputation," I said politely.

Dorr's eyes twinkled. He looked around for the cat, dragged it towards him by the tail, pushed it down on its side and began to rub its stomach. The cat seemed to like it.

Dorr looked at me and said very softly: "You bumped Lou Harger."

"What makes you think so?" I asked, without any particular emphasis.

"You bumped Lou Harger. Maybe he needed the bump—but you gave it to him. He was shot once through the heart, with a thirty-eight. You wear a thirty-eight and you're known to be a fancy shot with it. You were with Harger at Las Olindas last night and saw him win a lot of money. You were supposed to be acting as bodyguard for him, but you got a better idea. You caught up with him and that girl in West Cimarron, slipped Harger the dose and got the money."

I finished my whiskey, got up and poured myself some more of it.

"You made a deal with the girl," Dorr said, "but the deal didn't stick. She got a cute idea. But that don't matter, because the police got your gun along with Harger. And you got the dough."

I said: "Is there a tag out for me?"

"Not till I give the word . . . And the gun hasn't been turned in . . . I got a lot of friends, you know."

I said slowly: "I got sapped outside Canales' place. It served me right. My gun was taken from me. I never caught up with Harger, never saw him again. The girl came to me this morning with the money in an envelope and a story that Harger had been killed in her apartment. That's how I have the money—for safekeeping. I wasn't sure about the girl's story, but her bringing the money carried a lot of weight. And Harger was a friend of mine. I started out to investigate."

"You should have let the cops do that," Dorr said with a grin.

"There was a chance the girl was being framed. Besides there was a possibility I might make a few dollars —legitimately. It has been done, even in San Angelo."

Dorr stuck a finger towards the cat's face and the cat bit it, with an absent expression. Then it pulled away from him, sat down on a corner of the desk and began to lick one toe.

"Twenty-two grand, and the jane passed it over to you to keep," Dorr said. "Ain't that just like a jane?"

"You got the dough," Dorr said. "Harger was killed with your gun. The girl's gone—but I could bring her back. I think she'd make a good witness, if we needed one."

"Was the play at Las Olindas crooked?" I asked.

Dorr finished his drink and curled his lips around his cigar again. "Sure," he said carelessly. "The croupier —a guy named Pina—was in on it. The wheel was wired for the double-zero. The old crap. Copper button on the floor, copper button on Pina's shoe sole, wires up his leg, batteries in his hip pockets. The old crap."

I said: "Canales didn't act as if he knew about it."

Dorr chuckled. "He knew the wheel was wired. He didn't know his head croupier was playin' on the other team."

"I'd hate to be Pina," I said.

Dorr made a negligent motion with his cigar. "He's taken care of . . . The play was careful and quiet. They didn't make any fancy long shots, just even money bets, and they didn't win all the time. They couldn't. No wired wheel is that good."

I shrugged, moved around in my chair. "You know a hell of a lot about it," I said. "Was all this just to get me set for a squeeze?"

He grinned softly: "Hell, no! Some of it just happened—the way the best plants do." He waved his cigar again, and a pale gray tendril of smoke curled past his cunning little eyes. There was a muffled sound of talk in the outside room. "I got connections I got to please—even if I don't like all their capers," he added simply.

"Like Manny Tinnen?" I said. "He was around City Hall a lot, knew too much. Okey, Mister Dorr. Just what do you figure on having me do for you? Commit suicide?"

He laughed. His fat shoulders shook cheerfully. He put one of his small hands out with the palm towards me. "I wouldn't think of that," he said dryly, "and the other way's better business. The way public opinion is about the Shannon kill. I ain't sure that louse of a D.A. wouldn't convict Tinnen without you—if he could sell the folks the idea you'd been knocked off to button your mouth."

I got up out of my chair, went over and leaned on the desk, leaned across it towards Dorr.

He said: "No funny business!" a little sharply and breathlessly. His hand went to a drawer and got it half open. His movements with his hands were very quick in contrast with the movements of his body.

I smiled down at the hand and he took it away from the drawer. I saw a gun just inside the drawer.

I said: "I've already talked to the Grand Jury."

Dorr leaned back and smiled at me. "Guys make mistakes," he said. "Even smart private dicks . . . You could have a change of heart—and put it in writing."

I said very softly. "No. I'd be under a perjury rap—which I couldn't beat. I'd rather be under a murder rap—which I can beat. Especially as Fenweather will *want* me to beat it. He won't want to spoil me as a witness. The Tinnen case is too important to him."

Dorr said evenly: "Then you'll have to try and beat it, brother. And after you get through beating it there'll still be enough mud on your neck so no jury'll convict Manny on your say-so alone."

I put my hand out slowly and scratched the cat's ear. "What about the twenty-two grand?"

"It *could* be all yours, if you want to play. After all, it ain't my money . . . If Manny gets clear, I might add a little something that *is* my money."

I tickled the cat under its chin. It began to purr. I picked it up and held it gently in my arms.

"Who did kill Lou Harger, Dorr?" I asked, not looking at him.

He shook his head. I looked at him, smiling. "Swell cat you have," I said.

Dorr licked his lips. "I think the little bastard likes you," he grinned. He looked pleased at the idea.

I nodded—and threw the cat in his face.

He yelped, but his hands came up to catch the cat. The cat twisted neatly in the air and landed with both front paws working. One of them split Dorr's cheek like a banana peel. He yelled very loudly.

I had the gun out of the drawer and the muzzle of it into the back of Dorr's neck when Beasley and the square-faced man dodged in.

For an instant there was a sort of tableau. Then the cat tore itself loose from Dorr's arms, shot to the floor and went under the desk. Beasley raised his snub-nosed gun, but he didn't look as if he was certain what he meant to do with it.

I shoved the muzzle of mine hard into Dorr's neck and said: "Frankie gets it first, boys . . . And that's not a gag."

Dorr grunted in front of me. "Take it easy," he growled to his hoods. He took a handkerchief from his breast pocket and began to dab at his split and bleeding cheek with it. The man with the crooked mouth began to sidle along the wall.

I said: "Don't get the idea I'm enjoying this, but I'm not fooling either. You heels stay put."

The man with the crooked mouth stopped sidling and gave me a nasty leer. He kept his hands low.

Dorr half turned his head and tried to talk over his shoulder to me. I couldn't see enough of his face to get any expression, but he didn't seem scared. He said: "This won't get you anything. I could have you knocked off easy enough, if that was what I wanted. Now where are you? You can't shoot anybody without getting in a worse jam than if you did what I asked you to. It looks like a stalemate to me."

I thought that over for a moment while Beasley looked at me quite pleasantly, as though it was all just routine to him. There was nothing pleasant about the other man. I listened hard, but the rest of the house seemed to be quite silent.

Dorr edged forward from the gun and said: "Well?"

I said: "I'm going out. I have a gun and it looks like a gun that I could hit somebody with, if I have to. I don't want to very much, and if you'll have Beasley

throw my keys over and the other one turn back the
gun he took from me, I'll forget about the snatch."

Dorr moved his arms in the lazy beginning of a
shrug. "Then what?"

"Figure out your deal a little closer," I said. "If you
get enough protection behind me, I might throw in with
you . . . And if you're as tough as you think you are,
a few hours won't cut any ice one way or the other."

"It's an idea," Dorr said and chuckled. Then to
Beasley: "Keep your rod to yourself and give him his
keys. Also his gun—the one you got today."

Beasley sighed and very carefully inserted a hand
into his pants. He tossed my leather keycase across the
room near the end of the desk. The man with the twisted
mouth put his hand up, edged it inside his side pocket
and I eased down behind Dorr's back, while he did it.
He came out with my gun, let it fall to the floor and
kicked it away from him.

I came out from behind Dorr's back, got my keys and
the gun up from the floor, moved sidewise towards the
door of the room. Dorr watched with an empty stare
that meant nothing. Beasley followed me around with
his body and stepped away from the door as I neared it.
The other man had trouble holding himself quiet.

I got to the door and reversed a key that was in it.
Dorr said dreamily: "You're just like one of those rubber balls on the end of an elastic. The farther you get
away, the suddener you'll bounce back."

I said: "The elastic might be a little rotten," and went
through the door, turned the key in it and braced myself
for shots that didn't come. As a bluff, mine was thinner
than the gold on a week-end wedding ring. It worked
because Dorr let it, and that was all.

I got out of the house, got the Marmon started and
wrangled it around and sent it skidding past the shoulder of the hill and so on down to the highway. There
was no sound of anything coming after me.

When I reached the concrete highway bridge it was a little past two o'clock, and I drove with one hand for a while and wiped the sweat off the back of my neck.

8

The morgue was at the end of a long and bright and silent corridor that branched off from behind the main lobby of the County Building. The corridor ended in two doors and a blank wall faced with marble. One door had "Inquest Room" lettered on a glass panel behind which there was no light. The other opened into a small, cheerful office.

A man with gander-blue eyes and rust-colored hair parted in the exact center of his head was pawing over some printed forms at a table. He looked up, looked me over, and then suddenly smiled.

I said: "Hello, Landon . . . Remember the Shelby case?"

The bright blue eyes twinkled. He got up and came around the table with his hand out. "Sure. What can we do—" He broke off suddenly and snapped his fingers. "Hell! You're the guy that put the bee on that hot rod."

I tossed a butt through the open door into the corridor. "That's not why I'm here," I said. "Anyhow not this time. There's a fellow named Louis Harger . . . picked up shot last night or this morning, in West Cimarron, as I get it. Could I take a look-see?"

"They can't stop you," Landon said.

He led the way through a door on the far side of his office into a place that was all white paint and white enamel and glass and bright light. Against one wall was a double tier of large bins with glass windows in them. Through the peepholes showed bundles in white sheeting, and, further back, frosted pipes.

A body covered with a sheet lay on a table that was

high at the head and sloped down to the foot. Landon pulled the sheet down casually from a man's dead, placid, yellowish face. Long black hair lay loosely on a small pillow, with the dankness of water still in it. The eyes were half open and stared incuriously at the ceiling.

I stepped close, looked at the face, Landon pulled the sheet on down and rapped his knuckles on a chest that rang hollowly, like a board. There was a bullet hole over the heart.

"Nice clean shot," he said.

I turned away quickly, got a cigarette out and rolled it around in my fingers. I stared at the floor.

"Who identified him?"

"Stuff in his pockets," Landon said. "We're checking his prints, of course. You know him?"

I said: "Yes."

Landon scratched the base of his chin softly with his thumbnail. We walked back into the office and Landon went behind his table and sat down.

He thumbed over some papers, separated one from the pile and studied it for a moment.

He said: "A sheriff's radio car found him at twelve thirty-five A.M., on the side of the old road out of West Cimarron, a quarter of a mile from where the cutoff starts. That isn't traveled much, but the prowl car takes a slant down it now and then looking for petting parties."

I said: "Can you say how long he had been dead?"

"Not very long. He was still warm, and the nights are cool along there."

I put my unlighted cigarette in my mouth and moved it up and down with my lips. "And I bet you took a long thirty-eight out of him," I said.

"How did you know that?" Landon asked quickly.

"I just guess. It's that sort of hole."

He stared at me with bright, interested eyes. I

thanked him, said I'd be seeing him, went through the door and lit my cigarette in the corridor. I walked back to the elevators and got into one, rode to the seventh floor, then went along another corridor exactly like the one below except that it didn't lead to the morgue. It led to some small, bare offices that were used by the District Attorney's investigators. Halfway along I opened a door and went into one of them.

Bernie Ohls was sitting humped loosely at a desk placed against the wall. He was the chief investigator Fenweather had told me to see, if I got into any kind of a jam. He was a medium-sized bland man with white eyebrows and an outthrust, very deeply cleft chin. There was another desk against the other wall, a couple of hard chairs, a brass spittoon on a rubber mat and very little else.

Ohls nodded casually at me, got out of his chair and fixed the door latch. Then he got a flat tin of little cigars out of his desk, lit one of them, pushed the tin along the desk and stared at me along his nose. I sat down in one of the straight chairs and tilted it back.

Ohls said: "Well?"

"It's Lou Harger," I said. "I thought maybe it wasn't."

"The hell you did. I could have told you it was Harger."

Somebody tried the handle of the door, then knocked. Ohls paid no attention. Whoever it was went away.

I said slowly: "He was killed between eleven-thirty and twelve thirty-five. There was just time for the job to be done where he was found. There wasn't time for it to be done the way the girl said. There wasn't time for me to do it."

Ohls said: "Yeah. Maybe you could prove that. And then maybe you could prove a friend of yours didn't do it with your gun."

I said: "A friend of mine wouldn't be likely to do it with my gun—if he was a friend of mine."

Ohls grunted, smiled sourly at me sidewise. He said: "Most anyone would think that. That's why he might have done it."

I let the legs of my chair settle to the floor. I stared at him.

"Would I come and tell you about the money and the gun—everything that ties me to it?"

Ohls said expressionlessly: "You would—if you knew damn well somebody else had already told it for you."

I said: "Dorr wouldn't lose much time."

I pinched my cigarette out and flipped it towards the brass cuspidor. Then I stood up.

"Okey. There's no tag out for me yet—so I'll go over and tell my story."

Ohls said: "Sit down a minute."

I sat down. He took his little cigar out of his mouth and flung it away from him with a savage gesture. It rolled along the brown linoleum and smoked in the corner. He put his arms down on the desk and drummed with the fingers of both hands. His lower lip came forward and pressed his upper lip back against his teeth.

"Dorr probably knows you're here now," he said. "The only reason you ain't in the tank upstairs is they're not sure but it would be better to knock you off and take a chance. If Fenweather loses the election, I'll be all washed up—if I mess around with you."

I said: "If he convicts Manny Tinnen, he won't lose the election."

Ohls took another of the little cigars out of the box and lit it. He picked his hat off the desk, fingered it a moment, put it on.

"Why'd the redhead give you that song and dance

about the bump in her apartment, the stiff on the floor
—all that hot comedy?"

"They wanted me to go over there. They figured I'd
go to see if a gun was planted—maybe just to check
up on her. That got me away from the busy part of
town. They could tell better if the D.A. had any boys
watching my blind side."

"That's just a guess," Ohls said sourly.

I said: "Sure."

Ohls swung his thick legs around, planted his feet
hard and leaned his hands on his knees. The little cigar
twitched in the corner of his mouth.

"I'd like to get to know some of these guys that let
loose of twenty-two grand just to color up a fairy tale,"
he said nastily.

I stood up again and went past him towards the door.

Ohls said: "What's the hurry?"

I turned around and shrugged, looked at him blank-
ly. "You don't act very interested," I said.

He climbed to his feet, said wearily: "The hack
driver's most likely a dirty little crook. But it might just
be Dorr's lads don't know he rates in this. Let's go get
him while his memory's fresh."

9

The Green Top Garage was on Deviveras, three blocks
east of Main. I pulled the Marmon up in front of a fire-
plug and got out. Ohls slumped in the seat and growled:
"I'll stay here. Maybe I can spot a tail."

I went into a huge echoing garage, in the inner gloom
of which a few brand new paint jobs were splashes of
sudden color. There was a small, dirty, glass-walled
office in the corner and a short man sat there with a
derby hat on the back of his head and a red tie under

his stubbled chin. He was whittling tobacco into the palm of his hand.

I said: "You the dispatcher?"

"Yeah."

"I'm looking for one of your drivers," I said. "Name of Tom Sneyd."

He put down the knife and the plug and began to grind the cut tobacco between his two palms. "What's the beef?" he asked cautiously.

"No beef. I'm a friend of his."

"More friends, huh? . . . He works nights, mister . . . So he's gone I guess. Seventeen twenty-three Renfrew. That's over by Gray Lake."

I said: "Thanks. Phone?"

"No phone."

I pulled a folded city map from an inside pocket and unfolded part of it on the table in front of his nose. He looked annoyed.

"There's a big one on the wall," he growled, and began to pack a short pipe with his tobacco.

"I'm used to this one," I said. I bent over the spread map, looking for Renfrew Street. Then I stopped and looked suddenly at the face of the man in the derby. "You remembered that address damn quick," I said.

He put his pipe in his mouth, bit hard on it, and pushed two quick fingers into the pocket of his open vest.

"Couple other muggs was askin' for it a while back."

I folded the map very quickly and shoved it back into my pocket as I went through the door. I jumped across the sidewalk, slid under the wheel and plunged at the starter.

"We're headed," I told Bernie Ohls. "Two guys got the kid's address there a while back. It might be—"

Ohls grabbed the side of the car and swore as we took the corner on squealing tires. I bent forward over the wheel and drove hard. There was a red light at

Central. I swerved into a corner service station, went through the pumps, popped out on Central and jostled through some traffic to make a right turn east again.

A colored traffic cop blew a whistle at me and then stared hard as if trying to read the license number. I kept on going.

Warehouses, a produce market, a big gas tank, more warehouses, railroad tracks, and two bridges dropped behind us. I beat three traffic signals by a hair and went right through a fourth. Six blocks on I got the siren from a motorcycle cop. Ohls passed me a bronze star and I flashed it out of the car, twisting it so the sun caught it. The siren stopped. The motorcycle kept right behind us for another dozen blocks, then sheered off.

Gray Lake is an artificial reservoir in a cut between two groups of hills, on the east fringe of San Angelo. Narrow but expensively paved streets wind around in the hills, describing elaborate curves along their flanks for the benefit of a few cheap and scattered bungalows.

We plunged up into the hills, reading street signs on the run. The gray silk of the lake dropped away from us and the exhaust of the old Marmon roared between crumbling banks that shed dirt down on the unused sidewalks. Mongrel dogs quartered in the wild grass among the gopher holes.

Renfrew was almost at the top. Where it began there was a small neat bungalow in front of which a child in a diaper and nothing else fumbled around in a wire pen on a patch of lawn. Then there was a stretch without houses. Then there were two houses, then the road dropped, slipped in and out of sharp turns, went between banks high enough to put the whole street in shadow.

Then a gun roared around a bend ahead of us.

Ohls sat up sharply, said: "Oh-oh! That's no rabbit gun," slipped his service pistol out and unlatched the door on his side.

We came out of the turn and saw two more houses on the down side of the hill, with a couple of steep lots between them. A long gray car was slewed across the street in the space between the two houses. Its left front tire was flat and both its front doors were wide open, like the spread ears of an elephant.

A small, dark-faced man was kneeling on both knees in the street beside the open right-hand door. His right arm hung loose from his shoulder and there was blood on the hand that belonged to it. With his other hand he was trying to pick up an automatic from the concrete in front of him.

I skidded the Marmon to a fast stop and Ohls tumbled out.

"Drop that, you!" he yelled.

The man with the limp arm snarled, relaxed, fell back against the running board, and a shot came from behind the car and snapped in the air not very far from my ear. I was out on the road by that time. The gray car was angled enough towards the houses so that I couldn't see any part of its left side except the open door. The shot seemed to come from about there. Ohls put two slugs into the door. I dropped, looked under the car and saw a pair of feet. I shot at them and missed.

About that time there was a thin but very sharp crack from the corner of the nearest house. Glass broke in the gray car. The gun behind it roared and plaster jumped out of the corner of the house wall, above the bushes. Then I saw the upper part of a man's body in the bushes. He was lying downhill on his stomach and he had a light rifle to his shoulder.

He was Tom Sneyd, the taxi driver.

Ohls grunted and charged the gray car. He fired twice more into the door, then dodged down behind the hood. More explosions occurred behind the car. I kicked the wounded man's gun out of his way, slid past him and sneaked a look over the gas tank. But the man behind had had too many angles to figure.

He was a big man in a brown suit and he made a clatter running hard for the lip of the hill between the two bungalows. Ohls' gun roared. The man whirled and snapped a shot without stopping. Ohls was in the open now. I saw his hat jerk off his head. I saw him stand squarely on well-spread feet, steady his pistol as if he was on the police range.

But the big man was already sagging. My bullet had drilled through his neck. Ohls fired at him very carefully and he fell and the sixth and last slug from his gun caught the man in the chest and twisted him around. The side of his head slapped the curb with a sickening crunch.

We walked towards him from opposite ends of the car. Ohls leaned down, heaved the man over on his back. His face in death had a loose, amiable expression, in spite of the blood all over his neck. Ohls began to go through his pockets.

I looked back to see what the other one was doing. He wasn't doing anything but sitting on the running board holding his right arm against his side and grimacing with pain.

Tom Sneyd scrambled up the bank and came towards us.

Ohls said: "It's a guy named Poke Andrews. I've seen him around the poolrooms." He stood up and brushed off his knee. He had some odds and ends in his left hand. "Yeah, Poke Andrews. Gun work by the day, hour or week. I guess there was a livin' in it—for a while."

"It's not the guy that sapped me," I said. "But it's the guy I was looking at when I got sapped. And if the redhead was giving out any truth at all this morning, it's likely the guy that shot Lou Harger."

Ohls nodded, went over and got his hat. There was

a hole in the brim. "I wouldn't be surprised at all," he said, putting his hat on calmly.

Tom Sneyd stood in front of us with his little rifle held rigidly across his chest. He was hatless and coatless, and had sneakers on his feet. His eyes were bright and mad, and he was beginning to shake.

"I knew I'd get them babies!" he crowed. "I knew I'd fix them lousy bastards!" Then he stopped talking and his face began to change color. It got green. He leaned down slowly, dropped his rifle, put both his hands on his bent knees.

Ohls said: "You better go lay down somewhere, buddy. If I'm any judge of color, you're goin' to shoot your cookies."

10

Tom Sneyd was lying on his back on a day bed in the front room of his little bungalow. There was a wet towel across his forehead. A little girl with honey-colored hair was sitting beside him, holding his hand. A young woman with hair a couple of shades darker than the little girl's sat in the corner and looked at Tom Sneyd with tired ecstasy.

It was very hot when we came in. All the windows were shut and all the blinds down. Ohls opened a couple of front windows and sat down beside them, looked out towards the gray car. The dark Mexican was anchored to its steering wheel by his good wrist.

"It was what they said about my little girl," Tom Sneyd said from under the towel. "That's what sent me screwy. They said they'd come back and get her, if I didn't play with them."

Ohls said: "Okey, Tom. Let's have it from the start." He put one of his little cigars in his mouth, looked at Tom Sneyd doubtfully, and didn't light it.

I sat in a very hard Windsor chair and looked down at the cheap, new carpet.

"I was readin' a mag, waiting for time to eat and go to work," Tom Sneyd said carefully. "The little girl opened the door. They come in with guns on us, got us all in here and shut the windows. They pulled down all the blinds but one and the Mex sat by that and kept looking out. He never said a word. The big guy sat on the bed here and made me tell him all about last night —twice. Then he said I was to forget I'd met anybody or come into town with anybody. The rest was okey."

Ohls nodded and said: "What time did you first see this man here?"

"I didn't notice," Tom Sneyd said. "Say eleven-thirty, quarter of twelve. I checked in to the office at one-fifteen, right after I got my hack at the Carillon. It took us a good hour to make town from the beach. We was in the drugstore talkin' say fifteen minutes, maybe longer."

"That figures back to around midnight when you met him," Ohls said.

Tom Sneyd shook his head and the towel fell down over his face. He pushed it back up again.

"Well, no," Tom Sneyd said. "The guy in the drugstore told me he closed up at twelve. He wasn't closing up when we left."

Ohls turned his head and looked at me without expression. He looked back at Tom Sneyd. "Tell us the rest about the two gunnies," he said.

"The big guy said most likely I wouldn't have to talk to anybody about it. If I did and talked right, they'd be back with some dough. If I talked wrong, they'd be back for my little girl."

"Go on," Ohls said. "They're full of crap."

"They went away. When I saw them go on up the street I got screwy. Renfrew is just a pocket—one of them graft jobs. It goes on around the hill half a mile, then stops. There's no way to get off it. So they had to come back this way ... I got my twenty-two, which is all the gun I have, and hid in the bushes. I got the tire with the second shot. I guess they thought it was a blowout. I missed with the next and that put 'em wise. They got guns loose. I got the Mex then, and the big guy ducked behind the car ... That's all there was to it. Then you come along."

Ohls flexed his thick, hard fingers and smiled grimly at the girl in the corner. "Who lives in the next house, Tom?"

"A man named Grandy, a motorman on the interurban. He lives all alone. He's at work now."

"I didn't guess he was home," Ohls grinned. He got up and went over and patted the little girl on the head. "You'll have to come down and make a statement, Tom."

"Sure." Tom Sneyd's voice was tired, listless. "I guess I lose my job, too, for rentin' out the hack last night."

"I ain't so sure about that," Ohls said softly. "Not if your boss likes guys with a few guts to run his hacks."

He patted the little girl on the head again, went towards the door and opened it. I nodded at Tom Sneyd and followed Ohls out of the house. Ohls said quietly: "He don't know about the kill yet. No need to spring it in front of the kid."

We went over to the gray car. We had got some sacks out of the basement and spread them over the late Andrews, weighted them down with stones. Ohls glanced that way and said absently: "I got to get to where there's a phone pretty quick."

He leaned on the door of the car and looked in at the Mexican. The Mexican sat with his head back and his eyes half-closed and a drawn expression on his brown face. His left wrist was shackled to the spider of the wheel.

"What's your name?" Ohls snapped at him.

"Luis Cadena," the Mexican said it in a soft voice without opening his eyes any wider.

"Which one of you heels scratched the guy at West Cimarron last night?"

"No understand, señor," the Mexican said purringly.

"Don't go dumb on me, spig," Ohls said dispassionately. "It gets me sore." He leaned on the window and rolled his little cigar around in his mouth.

The Mexican looked faintly amused and at the same time very tired. The blood on his right hand had dried black.

Ohls said: "Andrews scratched the guy in a taxi at West Cimarron. There was a girl along. We got the girl. You have a lousy chance to prove you weren't in on it."

Light flickered and died behind the Mexican's half-open eyes. He smiled with a glint of small white teeth.

Ohls said: "What did he do with the gun?"

"No understand, señor."

Ohls said: "He's tough. When they get tough it scares me."

He walked away from the car and scuffed some loose dirt from the sidewalk beside the sacks that draped the dead man. His toe gradually uncovered the contractor's stencil in the cement. He read it out loud: "Dorr Paving and Construction Company, San Angelo. It's a wonder the fat louse wouldn't stay in his own racket."

I stood beside Ohls and looked down the hill between the two houses. Sudden flashes of light darted from the windshields of cars going along the boulevard that fringed Gray Lake, far below.

Ohls said: "Well?"

I said: "The killers knew about the taxi—maybe—and the girl friend reached town with the swag. So it wasn't Canales' job. Canales isn't the boy to let anybody play around with twenty-two grand of his money. The redhead was in on the kill, and it was done for a reason."

Ohls grinned. "Sure. It was done so you could be framed for it."

I said: "It's a shame how little account some folks take of human life—or twenty-two grand. Harger was knocked off so I could be framed and the dough was passed to me to make the frame tighter."

"Maybe they thought you'd highball," Ohls grunted. "That would sew you up right."

I rolled a cigarette around in my fingers. "That would have been a little too dumb, even for me. What do we do now? Wait till the moon comes up so we can sing— or go down the hill and tell some more little white lies?"

Ohls spat on one of Poke Andrews' sacks. He said gruffly: "This is county land here. I could take all this mess over to the sub-station at Solano and keep it hush-hush for a while. The hack driver would be tickled to death to keep it under the hat. And I've gone far enough so I'd like to get the Mex in the goldfish room with me personal."

"I'd like it that way too," I said. "I guess you can't hold it down there for long, but you might hold it down long enough for me to see a fat boy about a cat."

11

It was late afternoon when I got back to the hotel. The clerk handed me a slip which read: "Please phone F. D. as soon as possible."

I went upstairs and drank some liquor that was in the bottom of a bottle. Then I phoned down for another pint, scraped my chin, changed clothes and looked up Frank Dorr's number in the book. He lived in a beautiful old house on Greenview Park Crescent.

I made myself a tall smooth one with a tinkle and sat down in an easy chair with the phone at my elbow. I got a maid first. Then I got a man who spoke Mister Dorr's name as though he thought it might blow up in his mouth. After him I got a voice with a lot of silk in it. Then I got a long silence and at the end of the silence I got Frank Dorr himself. He sounded glad to hear from me.

He said: "I've been thinking about our talk this morning, and I have a better idea. Drop out and see me . . . And you might bring that money along. You just have time to get it out of the bank."

I said: "Yeah. The safe-deposit closes at six. But it's not your money."

I heard him chuckle. "Don't be foolish. It's all marked, and I wouldn't want to have to accuse you of stealing it."

I thought that over, and didn't believe it—about the currency being marked. I took a drink out of my glass and said: "I *might* be willing to turn it over to the party I got it from—in your presence."

He said: "Well—I told you that party left town. But I'll see what I can do. No tricks, please."

I said of course no tricks, and hung up. I finished my drink, called Von Ballin of the *Telegram*. He said the sheriff's people didn't seem to have any ideas about Lou Harger—or give a damn. He was a little sore that I still wouldn't let him use my story. I could tell from the way he talked that he hadn't got the doings over near Gray Lake.

I called Ohls, couldn't reach him.

I mixed myself another drink, swallowed half of it and began to feel it too much. I put my hat on, changed my mind about the other half of my drink, went down to my car. The early evening traffic was thick with householders riding home to dinner. I wasn't sure whether two cars tailed me or just one. At any rate nobody tried to catch up and throw a pineapple in my lap.

The house was a square two-storied place of old red brick, with beautiful grounds and a red brick wall with a white stone coping around them. A shiny black limousine was parked under the porte-cochère at the side. I followed a red-flagged walk up over two terraces, and a pale wisp of a man in a cutaway coat let me into a wide, silent hall with dark old furniture and a glimpse of garden at the end. He led me along that and along another hall at right angles and ushered me softly into a paneled study that was dimly lit against the gathering dusk. He went away, leaving me alone.

The end of the room was mostly open french windows, through which a brass-colored sky showed behind a line of quiet trees. In front of the trees a sprinkler swung slowly on a patch of velvety lawn that was already dark. There were large dim oils on the walls, a huge black desk with books across one end, a lot of deep lounging chairs, a heavy soft rug that went from wall to wall. There was a faint smell of good cigars and beyond that somewhere a smell of garden flowers and moist earth. The door opened and a youngish man in nose-glasses came in, gave me a slight formal nod, looked around vaguely, and said that Mr. Dorr would be there in a moment. He went out again, and I lit a cigarette.

In a little while the door opened again and Beasley came in, walked past me with a grin and sat down just inside the windows. Then Dorr came in and behind him Miss Glenn.

Dorr had his black cat in his arms and two lovely red scratches, shiny with collodion, down his right cheek. Miss Glenn had on the same clothes I had seen on her in the morning. She looked dark and drawn and spiritless, and she went past me as though she had never seen me before.

Dorr squeezed himself into the high-backed chair behind the desk and put the cat down in front of him.

The cat strolled over to one corner of the desk and began to lick its chest with a long, sweeping, businesslike motion.

Dorr said: "Well, well. Here we are," and chuckled pleasantly.

The man in the cutaway came in with a tray of cocktails, passed them around, put the tray with the shaker down on a low table beside Miss Glenn. He went out again, closing the door as if he was afraid he might crack it.

We all drank and looked very solemn.

I said: "We're all here but two. I guess we have a quorum."

Dorr said: "What's that?" sharply and put his head to one side.

I said: "Lou Harger's in the morgue and Canales is dodging cops. Otherwise we're all here. All the interested parties."

Miss Glenn made an abrupt movement, then relaxed suddenly and picked at the arm of her chair.

Dorr took two swallows of his cocktail, put the glass aside and folded his small neat hands on the desk. His face looked a little sinister.

"The money," he said coldly. "I'll take charge of it now."

I said: "Not now or any other time. I didn't bring it."

Dorr stared at me and his face got a little red. I looked at Beasley. Beasley had a cigarette in his mouth and his hands in his pockets and the back of his head against the back of his chair. He looked half asleep.

Dorr said softly, meditatively: "Holding out, huh?"

"Yes," I said grimly. "While I have it I'm fairly safe. You overplayed your hand when you let me get my paws on it. I'd be a fool not to hold what advantage it gives me."

Dorr said: "Safe?" with a gently sinister intonation.

I laughed. "Not safe from a frame," I said. "But the last one didn't click so well . . . Not safe from being gun-walked again. But that's going to be harder next time too . . . But fairly safe from being shot in the back and having you sue my estate for the dough."

Dorr stroked the cat and looked at me under his eyebrows.

"Let's get a couple of more important things straightened out," I said. "Who takes the rap for Lou Harger?"

"What makes you so sure *you* don't?" Dorr asked nastily.

"My alibi's been polished up. I didn't know how good it was until I knew how close Lou's death could be timed. I'm clear now . . . regardless of who turns in what gun with what fairy tale . . . And the lads that were sent to scotch my alibi ran into some trouble."

Dorr said: "That so?" without any apparent emotion.

"A thug named Andrews and a Mexican calling himself Luis Cadena. I daresay you've heard of them."

"I don't know such people," Dorr said sharply.

"Then it won't upset you to hear Andrews got very dead, and the law has Cadena."

"Certainly not," Dorr said. "They were from Canales. Canales had Harger killed."

I said: "So that's your new idea. I think it's lousy."

I leaned over and slipped my empty glass under my chair. Miss Glenn turned her head towards me and spoke very gravely, as if it was very important to the future of the race for me to believe what she said: "Of course—*of course* Canales had Lou killed . . . At least, the men he sent after us killed Lou."

I nodded politely. "What for? A packet of money they didn't get? They wouldn't have killed him. They'd have brought him in, brought both of you in. You arranged for that kill, and the taxi stunt was to sidetrack me, not to fool Canales' boys."

She put her hand out quickly. Her eyes were shimmering. I went ahead.

"I wasn't very bright, but I didn't figure on anything so flossy. Who the hell would? Canales had no motive to gun Lou, unless it got back the money he had been gypped out of. Supposing he could know that quick he *had* been gypped."

Dorr was licking his lips and quivering his chins and looking from one of us to the other with his small tight eyes. Miss Glenn said drearily: "Lou knew all about the play. He planned it with the croupier, Pina. Pina wanted some getaway money, wanted to move on to Havana. Of course Canales would have got wise, but not too soon, if I hadn't got noisy and tough. *I* got Lou killed—but not the way you mean."

I dropped an inch of ash off a cigarette I had forgotten all about. "All right," I said grimly. "Canales takes the rap . . . And I suppose you two chiselers think that's all I care about . . . Where was Lou going to be when Canales was *supposed* to find out he'd been gypped?"

"He was going to be gone," Miss Glenn said tonelessly. "A damn long way off. And I was going to be gone with him."

I said: "Nerts! You seem to forget *I* know *why* Lou was killed."

Beasley sat up in his chair and moved his right hand rather delicately towards his left shoulder. "This wise guy bother you, chief?"

Dorr said: "Not yet. Let him rant."

I moved so that I faced a little more towards Beasley. The sky had gone dark outside and the sprinkler had been turned off. A damp feeling came slowly into the room. Dorr opened a cedarwood box and put a long brown cigar in his mouth, bit the end off with a dry snap of his false teeth. There was the harsh noise of a match striking, then the slow, rather labored puffing of his breath in the cigar.

He said slowly, through a cloud of smoke: "Let's forget all this and make a deal about that money . . . Manny Tinnen hung himself in his cell this afternoon."

Miss Glenn stood up suddenly, pushing her arms straight down at her sides. Then she sank slowly down into the chair again, sat motionless. I said: "Did he have any help?" Then I made a sudden, sharp movement—and stopped.

Beasley jerked a swift glance at me, but I wasn't looking at Beasley. There was a shadow outside one of the windows—a lighter shadow than the dark lawn and darker trees. There was a hollow, bitter, coughing plop; a thin spray of whitish smoke in the window.

Beasley jerked, rose halfway to his feet, then fell on his face with one arm doubled under him.

Canales stepped through the windows, past Beasley's body, came three steps further, and stood silent, with a long, black, small-calibered gun in his hand, the larger tube of a silencer flaring from the end of it.

"Be very still," he said. "I am a fair shot—even with this elephant gun."

His face was so white that it was almost luminous. His dark eyes were all smoke-gray iris, without pupils.

"Sound carries well at night, out of open windows," he said tonelessly.

Dorr put both his hands down on the desk and began to pat it. The black cat put its body very low, drifted down over the end of the desk and went under a chair. Miss Glenn turned her head towards Canales very slowly, as if some kind of mechanism moved it.

Canales said: "Perhaps you have a buzzer on that desk. If the door of the room opens, I shoot. It will give me a lot of pleasure to see blood come out of your fat neck."

I moved the fingers of my right hand two inches on

the arm of my chair. The silenced gun swayed towards me and I stopped moving my fingers. Canales smiled very briefly under his angular mustache.

"You are a smart dick," he said. "I thought I had you right. But there are things about you I like."

I didn't say anything. Canales looked back at Dorr. He said very precisely: "I have been bled by your organization for a long time. But this is something else again. Last night I was cheated out of some money. But this is trivial too. I am wanted for the murder of this Harger. A man named Cadena has been made to confess that I hired him ... That is just a little too much fix."

Dorr swayed gently over his desk, put his elbows down hard on it, held his face in his small hands and began to shake. His cigar was smoking on the floor.

Canales said: "I would like to get my money back, and I would like to get clear of this rap—but most of all I would like you to say something—so I can shoot you with your mouth open and see blood come out of it."

Beasley's body stirred on the carpet. His hands groped a little. Dorr's eyes were agony trying not to look at him. Canales was rapt and blind in his act by this time. I moved my fingers a little more on the arm of my chair. But I had a long way to go.

Canales said: "Pina has talked to me. I saw to that. You killed Harger. Because he was a secret witness against Manny Tinnen. The D.A. kept the secret, and the dick here kept it. But Harger could not keep it himself. He told his broad—and the broad told you ... So the killing was arranged, in a way to throw suspicion with a motive on me. First on this dick, and if that wouldn't hold, on me."

There was silence. I wanted to say something, but I couldn't get anything out. I didn't think anybody but Canales would ever again say anything.

Canales said: "You fixed Pina to let Harger and his

girl win my money. It was not hard—because I don't play my wheels crooked."

Dorr had stopped shaking. His face lifted, stone-white, and turned towards Canales, slowly, like the face of a man about to have an epileptic fit. Beasley was up on one elbow. His eyes were almost shut but a gun was laboring upwards in his hand.

Canales leaned forward and began to smile. His trigger finger whitened at the exact moment Beasley's gun began to pulse and roar.

Canales arched his back until his body was a rigid curve. He fell stiffly forward, hit the edge of the desk and slid along it to the floor, without lifting his hands.

Beasley dropped his gun and fell down on his face again. His body got soft and his fingers moved fitfully, then were still.

I got motion into my legs, stood up and went to kick Canales' gun under the desk—senselessly. Doing this I saw that Canales had fired at least once, because Frank Dorr had no right eye.

He sat still and quiet with his chin on his chest and a nice touch of melancholy on the good side of his face.

The door of the room came open and the secretary with the nose-glasses slid in pop-eyed. He staggered back against the door, closing it again. I could hear his rapid breathing across the room.

He gasped: "Is—is anything wrong?"

I thought that very funny, even then. Then I realized that he might be short-sighted and from where he stood Frank Dorr looked natural enough. The rest of it could have been just routine to Dorr's help.

I said: "Yes—but we'll take care of it. Stay out of here."

He said: "Yes, sir," and went out again. That surprised me so much that my mouth fell open. I went down the room and bent over the gray-haired Beasley.

He was unconscious, but had a fair pulse. He was bleeding from the side, slowly.

Miss Glenn was standing up and looked almost as dopy as Canales had looked. She was talking to me quickly, in a brittle, very distinct voice: "I didn't know Lou was to be killed, but I couldn't have done anything about it anyway. They burned me with a branding iron —just for a sample of what I'd get. Look!"

I looked. She tore her dress down in front and there was a hideous burn on her chest almost between her two breasts.

I said: "Okey, sister. That's nasty medicine. But we've got to have some law here now and an ambulance for Beasley."

I pushed past her towards the telephone, shook her hand off my arm when she grabbed at me. She went on talking to my back in a thin, desperate voice.

"I thought they'd just hold Lou out of the way until after the trial. But they dragged him out of the cab and shot him without a word. Then the little one drove the taxi into town and the big one brought me up into the hills to a shack. Dorr was there. He told me how you had to be framed. He promised me the money, if I went through with it, and torture till I died, if I let them down."

It occurred to me that I was turning my back too much to people. I swung around, got the telephone in my hands, still on the hook, and put my gun down on the desk.

"Listen! Give me a break," she said wildly. "Dorr framed it all with Pina, the croupier. Pina was one of the gang that got Shannon where they could fix him. I didn't—"

I said: "Sure—that's all right. Take it easy."

The room, the whole house seemed very still, as if a lot of people were hunched outside the door, listening.

"It wasn't a bad idea," I said, as if I had all the time in the world. "Lou was just a white chip to Frank Dorr. The play he figured put us both out as witnesses. But it was too elaborate, took in too many people. That sort always blows up in your face."

"Lou was getting out of the state," she said, clutching at her dress. "He was scared. He thought the roulette trick was some kind of a pay-off to him."

I said: "Yeah," lifted the phone and asked for police headquarters.

The room door came open again then and the secretary barged in with a gun. A uniformed chauffeur was behind him with another gun.

I said very loudly into the phone: "This is Frank Dorr's house. There's been a killing . . ."

The secretary and the chauffeur dodged out again. I heard running in the hall. I clicked the phone, called the *Telegram* office and got Von Ballin. When I got through giving him the flash Miss Glenn was gone out of the window into the dark garden.

I didn't go after her. I didn't mind very much if she got away.

I tried to get Ohls, but they said he was still down at Solano. And by that time the night was full of sirens.

I had a little trouble but not too much. Fenweather pulled too much weight. Not all of the story came out, but enough so that the City Hall boys in the two-hundred-dollar suits had their left elbows in front of their faces for some time.

Pina was picked up in Salt Lake City. He broke and implicated four others of Manny Tinnen's gang. Two of them were killed resisting arrest, the other two got life without parole.

Miss Glenn made a clean getaway and was never heard of again. I think that's about all, except that I had to turn the twenty-two grand over to the Public Administrator. He allowed me two hundred dollars fee and nine dollars and twenty cents mileage. Sometimes I wonder what he did with the rest of it.

GOLDFISH

1

I WASN'T DOING any work that day, just catching up
on my foot-dangling. A warm gusty breeze was blowing
in at the office window and the soot from the Mansion
House Hotel oil burners across the alley was rolling
across the glass top of my desk in tiny particles, like
pollen drifting over a vacant lot.

I was just thinking about going to lunch when Kathy
Horne came in.

She was a tall, seedy, sad-eyed blonde who had once
been a policewoman and had lost her job when she married a cheap little check bouncer named Johnny Horne,
to reform him. She hadn't reformed him, but she was
waiting for him to come out so she could try again. In
the meantime she ran the cigar counter at the Mansion House, and watched the grifters go by in a haze of
nickel cigar smoke. And once in a while lent one of
them ten dollars to get out of town. She was just that
soft. She sat down and opened her big shiny bag and
got out a package of cigarettes and lit one with my
desk lighter. She blew a plume of smoke, wrinkled her
nose at it.

"Did you ever hear of the Leander pearls?" she
asked. "Gosh, that blue serge shines. You must have
money in the bank, the clothes you wear."

"No," I said, "to both your ideas. I never heard of
the Leander pearls and don't have any money in the
bank."

"Then you'd like to make yourself a cut of twenty-
five grand maybe."

I lit one of her cigarettes. She got up and shut the

135

window, saying: "I get enough of that hotel smell on the job."

She sat down again, went on: "It's nineteen years ago. They had the guy in Leavenworth fifteen and it's four since they let him out. A big lumberman from up north named Sol Leander bought them for his wife—the pearls, I mean—just two of them. They cost two hundred grand."

"It must have taken a hand truck to move them," I said.

"I see you don't know a lot about pearls," Kathy Horne said. "It's not just size. Anyhow they're worth more today and the twenty-five-grand reward the Reliance people put out is still good."

"I get it," I said. "Somebody copped them off."

"Now you're getting yourself some oxygen." She dropped her cigarette into a tray and let it smoke, as ladies will. I put it out for her. "That's what the guy was in Leavenworth for, only they never proved he got the pearls. It was a mail-car job. He got himself hidden in the car somehow and up in Wyoming he shot the clerk, cleaned out the registered mail and dropped off. He got to B.C. before he was nailed. But they didn't get any of the stuff—not then. All they got was him. He got life."

"If it's going to be a long story, let's have a drink."

"I never drink until sundown. That way you don't get to be a heel."

"Tough on the Eskimos," I said. "In the summertime anyway."

She watched me get my little flat bottle out. Then she went on: "His name was Sype—Wally Sype. He did it alone. And he wouldn't squawk about the stuff, not a peep. Then after fifteen long years they offered him a pardon, if he would loosen up with the loot. He gave up everything but the pearls."

"Where did he have it?" I asked. "In his hat?"

"Listen, this ain't just a bunch of gag lines, I've had a lead to those marbles."

I shut my mouth with my hand and looked solemn.

"He said he never had the pearls and they must have halfway believed him because they gave him the pardon. Yet the pearls were in the load, registered mail, and they were never seen again."

My throat began to feel a little thick. I didn't say anything.

Kathy Horne went on: "One time in Leavenworth, just one time in all those years, Wally Sype wrapped himself around a can of white shellac and got as tight as a fat lady's girdle. His cell mate was a little man they called Peeler Mardo. He was doing twenty-seven months for splitting twenty-dollar bills. Sype told him he had the pearls buried somewhere in Idaho."

I leaned forward a little.

"Beginning to get to you, eh?" she said. "Well, get this. Peeler Mardo is rooming at my house and he's a coke hound and he talks in his sleep."

I leaned back again. "Good grief," I said. "And I was practically spending the reward money."

She stared at me coldly. Then her face softened. "All right," she said a little hopelessly. "I know it sounds screwy. All those years gone by and all the smart heads that must have worked on the case, postal men and private agencies and all. And then a cokehead to turn it up. But he's a nice little runt and somehow I believe him. He knows where Sype is."

I said: "Did he talk all this in his sleep?"

"Of course not. But you know me. An old police-woman's got ears. Maybe I was nosy, but I guessed he was an ex-con and I worried about him using the stuff so much. He's the only roomer I've got now and I'd kind of go in by his door and listen to him talking to himself. That way I got enough to brace him. He told me the rest. He wants help to collect."

I leaned forward again. "Where's Sype?"

Kathy Horne smiled, and shook her head. "That's the one thing he wouldn't tell, that and the name Sype is using now. But it's somewhere up north, in or near Olympia, Washington. Peeler saw him up there and found out about him and he says Sype didn't see him."

"What's Peeler doing down here?" I asked.

"Here's where they put the Leavenworth rap on him. You know an old con always goes back to look at the piece of sidewalk he slipped on. But he doesn't have any friends here now."

I lit another cigarette and had another little drink.

"Sype has been out four years, you say. Peeler did twenty-seven months. What's he been doing with all the time since?"

Kathy Horne widened her china-blue eyes pityingly. "Maybe you think there's only one jailhouse he could get into."

"Okey," I said. "Will he talk to me? I guess he wants help to deal with the insurance people, in case there are any pearls and Sype will put them right in Peeler's hand and so on. Is that it?"

Kathy Horne sighed. "Yes, he'll talk to you. He's aching to. He's scared about something. Will you go out now, before he gets junked up for the evening?"

"Sure—if that's what you want."

She took a flat key out of her bag and wrote an address on my pad. She stood up slowly.

"It's a double house. My side's separate. There's a door in between, with the key on my side. That's just in case he won't come to the door."

"Okey," I said. I blew smoke at the ceiling and stared at her.

She went towards the door, stopped, came back. She looked down at the floor.

"I don't rate much in it," she said. "Maybe not anything. But if I could have a grand or two waiting for Johnny when he came out, maybe—"

"Maybe you could hold him straight," I said. "It's a dream, Kathy. It's all a dream. But if it isn't, you cut an even third."

She caught her breath and glared at me to keep from crying. She went towards the door, stopped and came back again.

"That isn't all," she said. "It's the old guy—Sype. He did fifteen years. He paid. Paid hard. Doesn't it make you feel kind of mean?"

I shook my head. "He stole them, didn't he? He killed a man. What does he do for a living?"

"His wife has money," Kathy Horne said. "He just plays around with goldfish."

"Goldfish?" I said. "To hell with him."

She went on out.

2

The last time I had been in the Gray Lake district I had helped a D.A.'s man named Bernie Ohls shoot a gunman named Poke Andrews. But that was higher up the hill, farther away from the lake. This house was on the second level, in a loop the street made rounding a spur of the hill. It stood on a terrace, with a cracked retaining wall in front and several vacant lots behind.

Being originally a double house it had two front doors and two sets of front steps. One of the doors had a sign tacked over the grating that masked the peep window: Ring 1432.

I parked my car and went up right-angle steps, passed between two lines of pinks, went up more steps to the side with the sign. That should be the roomer's side. I rang the bell. Nobody answered it, so I went across to the other door. Nobody answered that one either.

While I was waiting a gray Dodge coupe whished around the curve and a small neat girl in blue looked up at me for a second. I didn't see who else was in the car. I didn't pay much attention. I didn't know it was important.

I took out Kathy Horne's key and let myself into a closed living room that smelled of cedar oil. There was just enough furniture to get by, net curtains, a quiet shaft of sunlight under the drapes in front. There was a tiny breakfast room, a kitchen, a bedroom in the back that was obviously Kathy's, a bathroom, another bedroom in front that seemed to be used as a sewing room. It was this room that had the door cut through to the other side of the house.

I unlocked it and stepped, as it were, through a miror. Everything was backwards, except the furniture. The living room on that side had twin beds, didn't have the look of being lived in.

I went towards the back of the house, past the second bathroom, knocked at the shut door that corresponded to Kathy's bedroom.

No answer. I tried the knob and went in. The little man on the bed was probably Peeler Mardo. I noticed his feet first, because although he had on trousers and a shirt, his feet were bare and hung over the end of the bed. They were tied there by a rope around the ankles.

They had been burned raw on the soles. There was a smell of scorched flesh in spite of the open window. Also a smell of scorched wood. An electric iron on a desk was still connected. I went over and shut it off.

I went back to Kathy Horne's kitchen and found a pint of Brooklyn Scotch in the cooler. I used some of it and breathed deeply for a little while and looked out over the vacant lots. There was a narrow cement walk behind the house and green wooden steps down to the street.

I went back to Peeler Mardo's room. The coat of a brown suit with a red pin stripe hung over a chair with the pockets turned out and what had been in them on the floor.

He was wearing the trousers of the suit, and their pockets were turned out also. Some keys and change and a handkerchief lay on the bed beside him, and a metal box like a woman's compact, from which some glistening white powder had spilled. Cocaine.

He was a little man, not more than five feet four, with thin brown hair and large ears. His eyes had no particular color. They were just eyes, and very wide open and quite dead. His arms were pulled out from him and tied at the wrists by a rope that went under the bed.

I looked him over for bullet or knife wounds, didn't find any. There wasn't a mark on him except his feet. Shock or heart failure or a combination of the two must have done the trick. He was still warm. The gag in his mouth was both warm and wet.

I wiped off everything I had touched, looked out of Kathy's front window for a while before I left the house.

It was three-thirty when I walked into the lobby of the Mansion House, over to the cigar counter in the corner. I leaned on the glass and asked for Camels.

Kathy Horne flicked the pack at me, dropped the change into my outside breast pocket, and gave me her customer's smile.

"Well? You didn't take long," she said, and looked sidewise along her eyes at a drunk who was trying to light a cigar with the old-fashioned flint and steel lighter.

"It's heavy," I told her. "Get set."

She turned away quickly and flipped a pack of paper matches along the glass to the drunk. He fumbled for them, dropped both matches and cigar, scooped them angrily off the floor and went off looking back over his shoulder, as if he expected a kick.

Kathy looked past my head, her eyes cool and empty.

"I'm set," she whispered.

"You cut a full half," I said. "Peeler's out. He's been bumped off—in his bed."

Her eyes twitched. Two fingers curled on the glass near my elbow. A white line showed around her mouth. That was all.

"Listen," I said. "Don't say anything until I'm through. He died of shock. Somebody burned his feet with a cheap electric iron. Not yours, I looked. I'd say he died rather quickly and couldn't have said much. The gag was still in his mouth. When I went out there, frankly, I thought it was all hooey. Now I'm not so sure. If he opened up, we're through, and so is Sype, unless I can find him first. Those workers didn't have any inhibitions at all. If he didn't give up, there's still time."

Her head turned, her set eyes looked towards the revolving door at the lobby entrance. White patches glared in her cheeks.

"What do I do?" she breathed.

I poked at a box of wrapped cigars, dropped her key into it. Her long fingers got it out smoothly, hid it.

"When you get home you find him. You don't know a thing. Leave the pearls out, leave me out. When they check his prints they'll know he had a record and they'll just figure it was something caught up with him."

I broke my cigarettes open and lit one, watched her for a moment. She didn't move an inch.

"Can you face it down?" I asked. "If you can't, now's the time to speak."

"Of course." Her eyebrows arched. "Do I look like a torturer?"

"You married a crook," I said grimly.

She flushed, which was what I wanted. "He isn't! He's just a damn fool! Nobody thinks any the worse of me, not even the boys down at Headquarters."

"All right. I like it that way. It's not our murder, after all. And if we talk now, you can say goodbye to any share in any reward—even if one is ever paid."

"Darn tootin'," Kathy Horne said pertly. "Oh, the poor little runt," she almost sobbed.

I patted her arm, grinned as heartily as I could and left the Mansion House.

3

The Reliance Indemnity Company had offices in the Graas Building, three small rooms that looked like nothing at all. They were a big enough outfit to be as shabby as they liked.

The resident manager was named Lutin, a middle-aged bald-headed man with quiet eyes, dainty fingers that caressed a dappled cigar. He sat behind a large, well-dusted desk and stared peacefully at my chin.

"Marlowe, eh? I've heard of you." He touched my card with a shiny little finger. "What's on your mind?"

I rolled a cigarette around in my fingers and lowered my voice. "Remember the Leander pearls?"

His smile was slow, a little bored. "I'm not likely to forget them. They cost this company one hundred and fifty thousand dollars. I was a cocky young adjuster then."

I said: "I've got an idea. It may be all haywire. It very likely is. But I'd like to try it out. Is your twenty-five grand reward still good?"

He chuckled. "Twenty grand, Marlowe. We spent the difference ourselves. You're wasting time."

"It's my time. Twenty it is then. How much co-operation can I get?"

"What kind of co-operation?"

"Can I have a letter identifying me to your other branches? In case I have to go out of the state. In case I need kind words from some local law."

"Which way out of the state?"

I smiled at him. He tapped his cigar on the edge of a tray and smiled back. Neither of our smiles was honest.

"No letter," he said. "New York wouldn't stand for it. We have our own tie-up. But all the co-operation you can use, under the hat. And the twenty grand, if you click. Of course you won't."

I lit my cigarette and leaned back, puffed smoke at the ceiling.

"No? Why not? You never got those marbles. They existed, didn't they?"

"Darn right they existed. And if they still do, they belong to us. But two hundred grand doesn't get buried for twenty years—and then get dug up."

"All right. It's still my own time."

He knocked a little ash off his cigar and looked down his eyes at me. "I like your front," he said, "even if you are crazy. But we're a large organization. Suppose I have you covered from now on. What then?"

"I lose. I'll know I'm covered. I'm too long in the game to miss that. I'll quit, give up what I know to the law, and go home."

"Why would you do that?"

I leaned forward over the desk again. "Because," I said slowly, "the guy that had the lead got bumped off today."

"Oh—oh," Lutin rubbed his nose.

"I didn't bump him off," I added.

We didn't talk any more for a little while. Then Lutin said: "You don't want any letter. You wouldn't even carry it. And after your telling me that you know damn well I won't dare give it you."

I stood up, grinned, started for the door. He got up himself, very fast, ran around the desk and put his small neat hand on my arm.

"Listen, I know you're crazy, but if you do get anything, bring it in through our boys. We need the advertising."

"What the hell do you think I live on?" I growled.

"Twenty-five grand."

"I thought it was twenty."

"Twenty-five. And you're still crazy. Sype never had those pearls. If he had, he'd have made some kind of terms with us many years ago."

"Okay," I said. "You've had plenty of time to make up your mind."

We shook hands, grinned at each other like a couple of wise boys who know they're not kidding anybody, but won't give up trying.

It was a quarter to five when I got back to the office. I had a couple of short drinks and stuffed a pipe and sat down to interview my brains. The phone rang.

A woman's voice said: "Marlowe?" It was a small, tight, cold voice. I didn't know it.

"Yeah."

"Better see Rush Madder. Know him?"

"No," I lied. "Why should I see him?"

There was a sudden tinkling, icy-cold laugh on the wire. "On account of a guy had sore feet," the voice said.

The phone clicked. I put my end of it aside, struck a match and stared at the wall until the flame burned my fingers.

Rush Madder was a shyster in the Quorn Building. An ambulance chaser, a small-time fixer, an alibi builder-upper, anything that smelled a little and paid a little more. I hadn't heard of him in connection with any big operations like burning people's feet.

4

It was getting toward quitting time on lower Spring Street. Taxis were dawdling close to the curb, stenographers were getting an early start home, streetcars were clogging up, and traffic cops were preventing people from making perfectly legal right turns.

The Quorn Building was a narrow front, the color of dried mustard, with a large case of false teeth in the entrance. The directory held the names of painless dentists, people who teach you how to become a letter carrier, just names, and numbers without any names. Rush Madder, Attorney-at-Law, was in Room 619.

I got out of a jolting open-cage elevator, looked at a dirty spittoon on a dirty rubber mat, walked down a corridor that smelled of butts, and tried the knob below the frosted glass panel of 619. The door was locked. I knocked.

A shadow came against the glass and the door was pulled back with a squeak. I was looking at a thick-set man with a soft round chin, heavy black eyebrows, an oily complexion and a Charlie Chan mustache that made his face look fatter than it was.

He put out a couple of nicotined fingers. "Well, well, the old dog catcher himself. The eye that never forgets. Marlowe is the name, I believe?"

I stepped inside and waited for the door to squeak shut. A bare carpetless room paved in brown linoleum, a flat desk and a rolltop at right angles to it, a big green safe that looked as fireproof as a delicatessen bag, two filing cases, three chairs, a built-in closet and washbowl in the corner by the door.

"Well, well, sit down," Madder said. "Glad to see

you." He fussed around behind his desk and adjusted a burst-out seat cushion, sat on it. "Nice of you to drop around. Business?"

I sat down and put a cigarette between my teeth and looked at him. I didn't say a word. I watched him start to sweat. It started up in his hair. Then he grabbed a pencil and made marks on his blotter. Then he looked at me with a quick darting glance, down at his blotter again. He talked—to the blotter.

"Any ideas?" he asked softly.

"About what?"

He didn't look at me. "About how we could do a little business together. Say, in stones."

"Who was the wren?" I asked.

"Huh? What wren?" He still didn't look at me.

"The one that phoned me."

"Did somebody phone you?"

I reached for his telephone, which was the old-fashioned gallows type. I lifted off the receiver and started to dial the number of Police Headquarters, very slowly. I knew he would know that number about as well as he knew his hat.

He reached over and pushed the hook down. "Now, listen," he complained. "You're too fast. What you calling copper for?"

I said slowly: "They want to talk to you. On account of you know a broad that knows a man had sore feet."

"Does it have to be that way?" His collar was too tight now. He yanked at it.

"Not from my side. But if you think I'm going to sit here and let you play with my reflexes, it does."

Madder opened a flat tin of cigarettes and pushed one past his lips with a sound like somebody gutting a fish. His hand shook.

"All right," he said thickly. "All right. Don't get sore."

"Just stop trying to count clouds with me," I growled.

"Talk sense. If you've got a job for me, it's probably too dirty for me to touch. But I'll at least listen."

He nodded. He was comfortable now. He knew I was bluffing. He puffed a pale swirl of smoke and watched it float up.

"That's all right," he said evenly. "I play dumb myself once in a while. The thing is we're wise. Carol saw you go to the house and leave it again. No law came."

"Carol?"

"Carol Donovan. Friend of mine. She called you up."

I nodded. "Go ahead."

He didn't say anything. He just sat there and looked at me owlishly.

I grinned and leaned across the desk a little and said: "Here's what's bothering you. You don't know why I went to the house or why, having gone, I didn't yell police. That's easy. I thought it was a secret."

"We're just kiddng each other," Madder said sourly.

"All right," I said. "Let's talk about pearls. Does that make it any easier?"

His eyes shone. He wanted to let himself get excited, but he didn't. He kept his voice down, said coolly: "Carol picked him up one night, the little guy. A crazy little number, full of snow, but way back in his noodle an idea. He'd talk about pearls, about an old guy up in the northwest or Canada that swiped them a long time ago and still had them. Only he wouldn't say who the old guy was or where he was. Foxy about that. Holding out. I wouldn't know why."

"He wanted to get his feet burned," I said.

Madder's lips shook and another fine sweat showed in his hair.

"I didn't do that," he said thickly.

"You or Carol, what's the odds? The little guy died. They can make murder out of it. You didn't find out what you wanted to know. That's why I'm here. You think I have information you didn't get. Forget it. If I knew enough, I wouldn't be here, and if you knew enough, you wouldn't want me here. Check?"

He grinned, very slowly, as if it hurt him. He struggled up in his chair and dragged a deeper drawer out from the side of his desk, put a nicely molded brown bottle up on the desk, and two striped glasses. He whispered: "Two-way split. You and me. I'm cutting Carol out. She's too damn rough, Marlowe. I've seen hard women, but she's the bluing on armor plate. And you'd never think it to look at her, would you?"

"Have I seen her?"

"I guess so. She says you did."

"Oh, the girl in the Dodge."

He nodded, and poured two good-sized drinks, put the bottle down and stood up. "Water? I like it in mine."

"No," I said, "but why cut me in? I don't know any more than you mentioned. Or very little. Certainly not as much as you must know to go that far."

He leered across the glasses. "I know where I can get fifty grand for the Leander pearls, twice what you could get. I can give you yours and still have mine. You've got the front I need to work in the open. How about the water?"

"No water," I said.

He went across to the built-in wash place and ran the water and came back with his glass half full. He sat down again, grinned, lifted it.

We drank.

5

So far I had only made four mistakes. The first was mixing in at all, even for Kathy Horne's sake. The second was staying mixed after I found Peeler Mardo dead. The third was letting Rush Madder see I knew what he was talking about. The fourth, the whiskey, was the worst.

It tasted funny even on the way down. Then there was that sudden moment of sharp lucidity when I knew, exactly as though I had seen it, that he had switched his drink for a harmless one cached in the closet.

I sat still for a moment, with the empty glass at my fingers' ends, gathering my strength. Madder's face began to get large and moony and vague. A fat smile jerked in and out under his Charlie Chan mustache as he watched me.

I reached back into my hip pocket and pulled out a loosely wadded handkerchief. The small sap inside it didn't seem to show. At least Madder didn't move, after his first grab under the coat.

I stood up and swayed forward drunkenly and smacked him square on the top of the head.

He gagged. He started to get up. I tapped him on the jaw. He became limp and his hand sweeping down from under his coat knocked his glass over on the desk top. I straightened it, stood silent, listening, struggling with a rising wave of nauseous stupor.

I went over to a communicating door and tried the knob. It was locked. I was staggering by now. I dragged an office chair to the entrance door and propped the back of it under the knob. I leaned against the door panting, gritting my teeth, cursing myself. I got handcuffs out and started back towards Madder.

A very pretty black-haired, gray-eyed girl stepped out of the clothes closet and poked a .32 at me.

She wore a blue suit cut with a lot of snap. An inverted saucer of a hat came down in a hard line across her forehead. Shiny black hair showed at the sides. Her eyes were slate-gray, cold, and yet light-hearted. Her face was fresh and young and delicate, and as hard as a chisel.

"All right, Marlowe. Lie down and sleep it off. You're through."

I stumbled towards her waving my sap. She shook her head. When her face moved it got large before my eyes. Its outlines changed and wobbled. The gun in her hand looked like anything from a tunnel to a toothpick.

"Don't be a goof, Marlowe," she said. "A few hours sleep for you, a few hours start for us. Don't make me shoot. I would."

"Damn you," I mumbled. "I believe you would."

"Right as rain, toots. I'm a lady that wants her own way. That's fine. Sit down."

The floor rose up and bumped me. I sat on it as on a raft in a rough sea. I braced myself on flat hands. I could hardly feel the floor. My hands were numb. My whole body was numb.

I tried to stare her down. "Ha-a! L-lady K-killer!" I giggled.

She threw a chilly laugh at me which I only just barely heard. Drums were beating in my head now, war drums from a far-off jungle. Waves of light were moving, and dark shadows and a rustle as of a wind in treetops. I didn't want to lie down. I lay down.

The girl's voice came from very far off, an elfin voice.

"Two-way split, eh? He doesn't like my method, eh? Bless his big soft heart. We'll see about him."

Vaguely as I floated off I seemed to feel a dull jar that might have been a shot. I hoped she had shot Madder, but she hadn't. She had merely helped me on my way out—with my own sap.

When I came around again it was night. Something clacked overhead with a heavy sound. Through the open window beyond the desk yellow light splashed on the high side walls of a building. The thing clacked again and the light went off. An advertising sign on the roof.

I got up off the floor like a man climbing out of thick mud. I waded over to the washbowl, sloshed water on my face, felt the top of my head and winced, waded back to the door and found the light switch.

Strewn papers lay around the desk, broken pencils, envelopes, an empty brown whiskey bottle, cigarette ends and ashes. The débris of hastily emptied drawers. I didn't bother going through any of it. I left the office, rode down to the street in the shuddering elevator, slid into a bar and had a brandy, then got my car and drove on home.

I changed clothes, packed a bag, had some whiskey and answered the telephone. It was about nine-thirty.

Kathy Horne's voice said: "So you're not gone yet. I hoped you wouldn't be."

"Alone?" I asked, still thick in the voice.

"Yes, but I haven't been. The house has been full of coppers for hours. They were very nice, considering. Old grudge of some kind, they figured."

"And the line is likely bugged now," I growled. "Where was I supposed to be going?"

"Well—you know. Your girl told me."

"Little dark girl? Very cool? Name of Carol Donovan?"

"She had your card. Why, wasn't it—"

"I don't have any girl," I said grimly. "And I bet that just very casually, without thinking at all, a name slipped past your lips—the name of a town up north. Did it?"

"Ye-es," Kathy Horne admitted weakly.

I caught the night plane north.

It was a nice trip except that I had a sore head and a raging thirst for ice water.

6

The Snoqualmie Hotel in Olympia was on Capitol Way, fronting on the usual square city block of park. I left by the coffee-shop door and walked down a hill to where the last, loneliest reach of Puget Sound died and decomposed against a line of disused wharves. Corded firewood filled the foreground and old men pottered about in the middle of the stacks, or sat on boxes with pipes in their mouths and signs behind their heads reading: "Firewood and Split Kindling. Free Delivery."

Behind them a low cliff rose and the vast pines of the north loomed against a gray-blue sky.

Two of the old men sat on boxes about twenty feet apart, ignoring each other. I drifted near one of them. He wore corduroy pants and what had been a red and black Mackinaw. His felt hat showed the sweat of twenty summers. One of his hands clutched a short black pipe, and with the grimed fingers of the other he slowly, carefully, ecstatically jerked at a long curling hair that grew out of his nose.

I set a box on end, sat down, filled my own pipe, lit it, puffed a cloud of smoke. I waved a hand at the water and said: "You'd never think that ever met the Pacific Ocean."

He looked at me.

I said: "Dead end—quiet, restful, like your town. I like a town like this." He went on looking at me.

"I'll bet," I said, "that a man that's been around a town like this knows everybody in it and in the country near it."

He said: "How much you bet?"

I took a silver dollar out of my pocket. They still had a few up there. The old man looked it over, nodded, suddenly yanked the long hair out of his nose and held it up against the light.

"You'd lose," he said.

I put the dollar down on my knee. "Know anybody around here that keeps a lot of goldfish?" I asked.

He stared at the dollar. The other old man near by was wearing overalls and shoes without any laces. He stared at the dollar. They both spat at the same instant. The first old man said: "Leetle deef." He got up slowly and went over to a shack built of old boards of uneven lengths. He went into it, banged the door.

The second old man threw his axe down pettishly, spat in the direction of the closed door and went off among the stacks of cordwood.

The door of the shack opened, the man in the Mackinaw poked his head out of it.

"Sewer crabs is all," he said, and slammed the door again.

I put my dollar in my pocket and went back up the hill. I figured it would take too long to learn their language.

Capitol Way ran north and south. A dull green streetcar shuttled past on the way to a place called Tumwater. In the distance I could see the government buildings. Northward the street passed two hotels and some stores and branched right and left. Right went to Tacoma and Seattle. Left went over a bridge and out to the Olympic Peninsula.

Beyond this right and left turn the street suddenly became old and shabby, with broken asphalt paving, a Chinese restaurant, a boarded-up movie house, a pawnbroker's establishment. A sign jutting over the dirty sidewalk said "Smoke Shop," and in small letters underneath, as if it hoped nobody was looking, "Pool."

I went in past a rack of gaudy magazines and a cigar showcase that had flies inside it. There was a long wooden counter on the left, a few slot machines, a single pool table. Three kids fiddled with the slot machines and a tall thin man with a long nose and no chin played pool all by himself, with a dead cigar in his face.

I sat on a stool and a hard-eyed bald-headed man behind the counter got up from a chair, wiped his hands on a thick gray apron, showed me a gold tooth.

"A little rye," I said. "Know anybody that keeps goldfish?"

"Yeah," he said. "No."

He poured something behind the counter and shoved a thick glass across.

"Two bits."

I sniffed the stuff, wrinkled my nose. "Was it the rye the 'yeah' was for?"

The bald-headed man held up a large bottle with a label that said something about: "Cream of Dixie Straight Rye Whiskey Guaranteed at Least Four Months Old."

"Okey," I said. "I see it just moved in."

I poured some water in it and drank it. It tasted like a cholera culture. I put a quarter on the counter. The barman showed me a gold tooth on the other side of his face and took hold of the counter with two hard hands and pushed his chin at me.

"What was that crack?" he asked, almost gently.

"I just moved in," I said. "I'm looking for some goldfish for the front window. Goldfish."

The barman said very slowly: "Do I look like a guy would know a guy would have goldfish?" His face was a little white.

The long-nosed man who had been playing himself a round of pool racked his cue and strolled over to the counter beside me and threw a nickel on it.

"Draw me a coke before you wet yourself," he told the barman.

The barman pried himself loose from the counter

with a good deal of effort. I looked down to see if his fingers had made any dents in the wood. He drew a coke, stirred it with a swizzle-stick, dumped it on the bar top, took a deep breath and let it out through his nose, grunted and went away towards a door marked "Toilet."

The long-nosed man lifted his coke and looked into the smeared mirror behind the bar. The left side of his mouth twitched briefly. A dim voice came from it, saying: "How's Peeler?"

I pressed my thumb and forefinger together, put them to my nose, sniffed, shook my head sadly.

"Hitting it high, huh?"

"Yeah," I said. "I didn't catch the name."

"Call me Sunset. I'm always movin' west. Think he'll stay clammed?"

"He'll stay clammed," I said.

"What's your handle?"

"Dodge Willis, El Paso," I said.

"Got a room somewhere?"

"Hotel."

He put his glass down empty. "Let's dangle."

7

We went up to my room and sat down and looked at each other over a couple of glasses of Scotch and ice water. Sunset studied me with his close-set expressionless eyes, a little at a time, but very thoroughly in the end, adding it all up.

I sipped my drink and waited. At last he said in his lipless "stir" voice: "How come Peeler didn't come hisself?"

"For the same reason he didn't stay when he was here."

"Meaning which?"

"Figure it out for yourself," I said.

He nodded, just as though I had said something with a meaning. Then: "What's the top price?"

"Twenty-five grand."

"Nuts." Sunset was emphatic, even rude.

I leaned back and lit a cigarette, puffed smoke at the open window and watched the breeze pick it up and tear it to pieces.

"Listen," Sunset complained. "I don't know you from last Sunday's sports section. You may be all to the silk. I just don't know."

"Why'd you brace me?" I asked.

"You had the word, didn't you?"

This was where I took the dive. I grinned at him. "Yeah. Goldfish was the password. The Smoke Shop was the place."

His lack of expression told me I was right. It was one of those breaks you dream of, but don't handle right even in dreams.

"Well, what's the next angle?" Sunset inquired, sucking a piece of ice out of his glass and chewing on it.

I laughed. "Okey, Sunset, I'm satisfied you're cagey. We could go on like this for weeks. Let's put our cards on the table. Where is the old guy?"

Sunset tightened his lips, moistened them, tightened them again. He set his glass down very slowly and his right hand hung lax on his thigh. I knew I had made a mistake, that Peeler knew where the old guy was, exactly. Therefore I should know.

Nothing in Sunset's voice showed I had made a mistake. He said crossly: "You mean why don't I put my cards on the table and you just sit back and look 'em over. Nix."

"Then how do you like this?" I growled. "Peeler's dead."

One eyebrow twitched, and one corner of his mouth.

His eyes got a little blanker than before, if possible. His voice rasped lightly, like a finger on dry leather.

"How come?"

"Competition you two didn't know about." I leaned back, smiled.

The gun made a soft metallic blue in the sunshine. I hardly saw where it came from. Then the muzzle was round and dark and empty looking at me.

"You're kidding the wrong guy," Sunset said lifelessly. "I ain't no soft spot for chiselers to lie on."

I folded my arms, taking care that my right hand was outside, in view.

"I would be—if I was kidding. I'm not. Peeler played with a girl and she milked him—up to a point. He didn't tell her where to find the old fellow. So she and her top man went to see Peeler where he lived. They used a hot iron on his feet. He died of the shock."

Sunset looked unimpressed. "I got a lot of room in my ears yet," he said.

"So have I," I snarled, suddenly pretending anger. "Just what the hell have you said that means anything —except that you know Peeler?"

He spun his gun on his trigger finger, watched it spin. "Old man Sype's at Westport," he said casually. "That mean anything to you?"

"Yeah. Has he got the marbles?"

"How the hell would I know?" He steadied the gun again, dropped it to his thigh. It wasn't pointing at me now. "Where's this competish you mentioned?"

"I hope I ditched them," I said. "I'm not too sure. Can I put my hands down and take a drink?"

"Yeah, go ahead. How did you cut in?"

"Peeler roomed with the wife of a friend of mine who's in stir. A straight girl, one you can trust. He let her in and she passed it to me—afterwards."

"After the bump? How many cuts your side? My half is set."

I took my drink, shoved the empty glass away. "The hell it is."

The gun lifted an inch, dropped again. "How many altogether?" he snapped.

"Three, now Peeler's out. If we can hold off the competition."

"The feet-toasters? No trouble about that. What they look like?"

"Man named Rush Madder, a shyster down south, fifty, fat, thin down-curving mustache, dark hair thin on top, five-nine, a hundred and eighty, not much guts. The girl, Carol Donovan, black hair, long bob, gray eyes, pretty, small features, twenty-five to -eight, five-two, hundred-twenty, last seen wearing blue, hard as they come. The real iron in the combination."

Sunset nodded indifferently and put his gun away. "We'll soften her, if she pokes her snoot in," he said. "I've got a heap at the house. Let's take the air Westport way and look it over. You might be able to ease in on the goldfish angle. They say he's nuts about them. I'll stay under cover. He's too stir-wise for me. I smell of the bucket."

"Swell," I said heartily. "I'm an old goldfish fancier myself."

Sunset reached for the bottle, poured two fingers of Scotch and put it down. He stood up, twitched his collar straight, then shot his chinless jaw forward as far as it would go.

"But don't make no error, bo. It's goin' to take pressure. It's goin' to mean a run out in the deep woods and some thumb-twisting. Snatch stuff, likely."

"That's okey," I said. "The insurance people are behind us."

Sunset jerked down the points of his vest and rubbed the back of this thin neck. I put my hat on, locked the Scotch in the bag by the chair I'd been sitting in, went over and shut the window.

We started towards the door. Knuckles rattled on it just as I reached for the knob. I gestured Sunset back along the wall. I stared at the door for a moment and then I opened it up.

The two guns came forward almost on the same level, one small—a .32, one a big Smith and Wesson. They couldn't come into the room abreast, so the girl came in first.

"Okey, hot shot," she said dryly. "Ceiling zero. See if you can reach it."

8

I backed slowly into the room. The two visitors bored in on me, either side. I tripped over my bag and fell backwards, hit the floor and rolled on my side groaning.

Sunset said casually: "H'ist 'em folks. Pretty now!"

Two heads jerked away from looking down at me and then I had my gun loose, down at my side. I kept on groaning.

There was a silence. I didn't hear any guns fall. The door of the room was still wide open and Sunset was flattened against the wall more or less behind it.

The girl said between her teeth: "Cover the shamus, Rush—and shut the door. Skinny can't shoot here. Nobody can." Then, in a whisper I barely caught, she added: "Slam it!"

Rush Madder waddled backwards across the room keeping the Smith and Wesson pointed my way. His back was to Sunset and the thought of that made his eyes roll. I could have shot him easily enough, but it wasn't the play. Sunset stood with is feet spread and his tongue showing. Something that could have been a smile wrinkled his flat eyes.

He stared at the girl and she stared at him. Their guns stared at each other.

Rush Madder reached the door, grabbed the edge of it and gave it a hard swing. I knew exactly what was going to happen. As the door slammed the .32 was going to go off. It wouldn't be heard if it went off at the right instant. The explosion would be lost in the slamming of the door.

I reached out and took hold of Carol Donovan's ankle and jerked it hard.

The door slammed. Her gun went off and chipped the ceiling.

She whirled on me kicking. Sunset said in his tight but somewhat penetrating drawl: "If this is it, this is it. Let's go!" The hammer clicked back on his Colt.

Something in his voice steadied Carol Donovan. She relaxed, let her automatic fall to her side and stepped away from me with a vicious look back.

Madder turned the key in the door and leaned against the wood, breathing noisily. His hat had tipped over one ear and the ends of two strips of adhesive showed under the brim.

Nobody moved while I had these thoughts. There was no sound of feet outside in the hall, no alarm. I got up on my knees, slid my gun out of sight, rose on my feet and went over to the window. Nobody down on the sidewalk was staring up at the upper floors of the Snoqualmie Hotel.

I sat on the broad old-fashioned sill and looked faintly embarrassed, as though the minister had said a bad word.

The girl snapped at me: "Is this lug your partner?"

I didn't answer. Her face flushed slowly and her eyes burned. Madder put a hand out and fussed: "Now listen, Carol, now listen here. This sort of act ain't the way—"

"Shut up!"

"Yeah," Madder said in a clogged voice. "Sure."

Sunset looked the girl over lazily for the third or

fourth time. His gun hand rested easily against his hip-bone and his whole attitude was of complete relaxation. Having seen him pull his gun once I hoped the girl wasn't fooled.

He said slowly: "We've heard about you two. What's your offer? I wouldn't listen even, only I can't stand a shooting rap."

The girl said: "There's enough in it for four." Madder nodded his big head vigorously, almost managed a smile.

Sunset glanced at me. I nodded. "Four it is," he sighed.

"But that's the top. We'll go to my place and gargle. I don't like it here."

"We must look simple," the girl said nastily.

"Kill-simple," Sunset drawled. "I've met lots of them. That's why we're going to talk it over. It's not a shooting play."

Carol Donovan slipped a suede bag from under her left arm and tucked her .32 into it. She smiled. She was pretty when she smiled.

"My ante is in," she said quietly. "I'll play. Where is the place?"

"Out Water Street. We'll go in a hack."

"Lead on, sport."

We went out of the room and down in the elevator, four friendly people walking out through a lobby full of antlers and stuffed birds and pressed wildflowers in glass frames. The taxi went out Capitol Way, past the square, past a big red apartment house that was too big for the town except when the Legislature was sitting. Along car tracks past the distant Capitol buildings and the high closed gates of the governor's mansion.

Oak trees bordered the sidewalks. A few largish residences showed behind garden walls. The taxi shot past them and veered on to a road that led towards the tip of the Sound. In a short while a house showed in a narrow clearing between tall trees. Water glistened far back behind the tree trunks. The house had a roofed porch, a small lawn rotten with weeds and overgrown bushes. There was a shed at the end of a dirt driveway and an antique touring car squatted under the shed.

We got out and I paid the taxi. All four of us carefully watched it out of sight. Then Sunset said: "My place is upstairs. There's a schoolteacher lives down below. She ain't home. Let's go up and gargle."

We crossed the lawn to the porch and Sunset threw a door open, pointed up narrow steps.

"Ladies first. Lead on, beautiful. Nobody locks a door in this town."

The girl gave him a cool glance and passed him to go up the stairs. I went next, then Madder, Sunset last.

The single room that made up most of the second floor was dark from the trees, had a dormer window, a wide daybed pushed back under the slope of the roof, a table, some wicker chairs, a small radio and a round black stove in the middle of the floor.

Sunset drifted into a kitchenette and came back with a square bottle and some glasses. He poured drinks, lifted one and left the others on the table.

We helped ourselves and sat down.

Sunset put his drink down in a lump, leaned over to put his glass on the floor and came up with his Colt out.

I heard Madder's gulp in the sudden cold silence. The girl's mouth twitched as if she were going to laugh. Then she leaned forward, holding her glass on top of her bag with her left hand.

Sunset slowly drew his lips into a thin straight line. He said slowly and carefully: "Feet-burners, huh?"

Madder choked, started to spread his fat hands. The Colt flicked at him. He put his hands on his knees and clutched his kneecaps.

"And suckers at that," Sunset went on tiredly. "Burn a guy's feet to make him sing and then walk right into the parlor of one of his pals. You couldn't tie that with Christmas ribbon."

Madder said jerkily: "All r-right. W-what's the p-pay-off?" The girl smiled slightly but she didn't say anything.

Sunset grinned. "Rope," he said softly. "A lot of rope tied in hard knots, with water on it. Then me and my pal trundle off to catch fire-flies—pearls to you—and when we come back—" he stopped, drew his left hand across the front of his throat. "Like the idea?" he glanced at me.

"Yeah, but don't make a song about it," I said. "Where's the rope?"

"Bureau," Sunset answered, and pointed with one ear at the corner.

I started in that direction, by way of the walls. Madder made a sudden thin whimpering noise and his eyes turned up in his head and he fell straight forward off the chair on his face, in a dead faint.

That jarred Sunset. He hadn't expected anything so foolish. His right hand jerked around until the Colt was pointing down at Madder's back.

The girl slipped her hand under her bag. The bag lifted an inch. The gun that was caught there in a trick clip—the gun that Sunset thought was inside the bag—spat and flamed briefly.

Sunset coughed. His Colt boomed and a piece of wood detached itself from the back of the chair Madder had been sitting in. Sunset dropped the Colt and put his chin down on his chest and tried to look at the ceiling. His long legs slid out in front of him and his heels made a rasping sound on the floor. He sat like that limp, his chin on his chest, his eyes looking upward. Dead as a pickled walnut.

I kicked Miss Donovan's chair out from under her

and she banged down on her side in a swirl of silken legs. Her hat went crooked on her head. She yelped. I stood on her hand and then shifted suddenly and kicked her gun clear across the attic.

"Get up."

She got up slowly, backed away from me biting her lip, savage-eyed, suddenly a nasty-faced little brat at bay. She kept on backing until the wall stopped her. Her eyes glittered in a ghastly face.

I glanced down at Madder, went over to a closed door. A bathroom was behind it. I reversed a key and gestured at the girl.

"In."

She walked stiff-legged across the floor and passed in front of me, almost touching me.

"Listen a minute, shamus—"

I pushed her through the door and slammed it and turned the key. It was all right with me if she wanted to jump out of the window. I had seen the windows from below.

I went across to Sunset, felt him, felt the small hard lump of keys on a ring in his pocket, and got them out without quite knocking him off his chair. I didn't look for anything else.

There were car keys on the ring.

I looked at Madder again, noticed that his fingers were as white as snow. I went down the narrow dark stairs to the porch, around to the side of the house and got into the old touring car under the shed. One of the keys on the ring fitted its ignition lock.

The car took a beating before it started up and let me back it down the dirt driveway to the curb. Nothing moved in the house that I saw or heard. The tall pines behind and beside the house stirred their upper branches listlessly and a cold heartless sunlight sneaked through them intermittently as they moved.

I drove back to Capitol Way and downtown again

as fast as I dared, past the square and the Snoqualmie Hotel and over the bridge towards the Pacific Ocean and Westport.

9

An hour's fast driving through thinned-out timberland, interrupted by three stops for water and punctuated by the cough of a head gasket leak, brought me within sound of surf. The broad white road, striped with yellow down the center, swept around the flank of a hill, a distant cluster of buildings loomed up in front of the shine of the ocean, and the road forked. The left fork was signposted: "Westport—9 Miles," and didn't go towards the buildings. It crossed a rusty cantilever bridge and plunged into a region of wind-distorted apple orchards.

Twenty minutes more and I chugged into Westport, a sandy spit of land with scattered frame houses dotted over rising ground behind it. The end of the spit a long narrow pier, and the end of the pier a cluster of sailing boats with half-lowered sails flapping against their single masts. And beyond them a buoyed channel and a long irregular line where the water creamed on a hidden sandbar.

Beyond the sandbar the Pacific rolled over to Japan. This was the last outpost of the coast, the farthest west a man could go and still be on the mainland of the United States. A swell place for an ex-convict to hide out with a couple of somebody else's pearls the size of new potatoes—if he didn't have any enemies.

I pulled up in front of a cottage that had a sign in the front yard: "Luncheons, Teas, Dinners." A small rabbit-faced man with freckles was waving a garden rake at two black chickens. The chickens appeared to be sassing him back. He turned when the engine of Sunset's car coughed itself still.

I got out, went through a wicket gate, pointed to the sign.

"Luncheon ready?"

He threw the rake at the chickens, wiped his hands on his trousers and leered. "The wife put that up," he confided to me in a thin, impish voice. "Ham and eggs is what it means."

"Ham and eggs get along with me," I said.

We went into the house. There were three tables covered with patterned oilcloth, some chromos on the walls, a full-rigged ship in a bottle on the mantel. I sat down. The host went away through a swing door and somebody yelled at him and a sizzling noise was heard from the kitchen. He came back and leaned over my shoulder, put some cutlery and a paper napkin on the oilcloth.

"Too early for apple brandy, ain't it?" he whispered.

I told him how wrong he was. He went away again and came back with glasses and a quart of clear amber fluid. He sat down with me and poured. A rich baritone voice in the kitchen was singing "Chloe," over the sizzling.

We clinked glasses and drank and waited for the heat to crawl up our spines.

"Stranger, ain't you?" the little man asked.

I said I was.

"From Seattle maybe? That's a nice piece of goods you got on."

"Seattle," I agreed.

"We don't git many strangers," he said, looking at my left ear. "Ain't on the way to nowheres. Now before repeal—" he stopped, shifted his sharp woodpecker gaze to my other ear.

"Ah, before repeal," I said with a large gesture, and drank knowingly.

He leaned over and breathed on my chin. "Hell, you could load up in any fish stall on the pier. The stuff come in under catches of crabs and oysters. Hell, Westport was lousy with it. They give the kids cases of Scotch to play with. There wasn't a car in this town that slept in a garage, mister. The garages was full to the roof of Canadian hooch. Hell, they had a coastguard cutter off the pier watchin' the boats unload one day every week. Friday. Always the same day." He winked.

I puffed a cigarette and the sizzling noise and the baritone rendering of "Chloe" went on in the kitchen.

"But hell, you wouldn't be in the liquor business," he said.

"Hell, no. I'm a goldfish buyer," I said.

"Okey," he said sulkily.

I poured us another round of the apple brandy. "This bottle is on me," I said. "And I'm taking a couple more with me."

He brightened up. "What did you say the name was?"

"Marlowe. You think I'm kidding you about the goldfish. I'm not."

"Hell, there ain't a livin' in them little fellers, is there?"

I held my sleeve out. "You said it was a nice piece of goods. Sure there's a living out of the fancy brands. New brands, new types all the time. My information is there's an old guy down here somewhere that has a real collection. Maybe would sell it. Some he'd bred himself."

A large woman with a mustache kicked the swing door open a foot and yelled: "Pick up the ham and eggs!"

My host scuttled across and came back with my food. I ate. He watched me minutely. After a time he suddenly smacked his skinny leg under the table.

"Old Wallace," he chuckled. "Sure, you come to see old Wallace. Hell, we don't know him right well. He don't act neighborly."

He turned around in his chair and pointed out through the sleazy curtains at a distant hill. On top of the hill was a yellow and white house that shone in the sun.

"Hell, that's where he lives. He's got a mess of them. Goldfish, huh? Hell, you could bend me with an eye dropper."

That ended my interest in the little man. I gobbled my food, paid off for it and for three quarts of apple brandy at a dollar a quart, shook hands and went back out to the touring car.

There didn't seem to be any hurry. Rush Madder would come out of his faint, and he would turn the girl loose. But they didn't know anything about Westport. Sunset hadn't mentioned the name in their presence. They didn't know it when they reached Olympia, or they would have gone there at once. And if they had listened outside my room at the hotel, they would have known I wasn't alone. They hadn't acted as if they knew that when they charged in.

I had lots of time. I drove down to the pier and looked it over. It looked tough. There were fish stalls, drinking dives, a tiny honkytonk for the fishermen, a pool room, an arcade of slot machines and smutty peep shows. Bait fish squirmed and darted in big wooden tanks down in the water along the piles. There were loungers and they looked like trouble for anyone that tried to interfere with them. I didn't see any law enforcement around.

I drove back up the hill to the yellow and white house. It stood very much alone, four blocks from the next nearest dwelling. There were flowers in front, a trimmed green lawn, a rock garden. A woman in a brown and white print dress was popping at aphids with a spray gun.

I let my heap stall itself, got out and took my hat off."

"Mister Wallace live here?"

She had a handsome face, quiet, firm-looking. She nodded.

"Would you like to see him?" She had a quiet firm voice, a good accent.

It didn't sound like the voice of a train robber's wife.

I gave her my name, said I'd been hearing about his fish down in the town. I was interested in fancy gold-fish.

She put the spray gun down and went into the house. Bees buzzed around my head, large fuzzy bees that wouldn't mind the cold wind off the sea. Far off like background music the surf pounded on the sandbars. The northern sunshine seemed bleak to me, had no heat in the core of it.

The woman came out of the house and held the door open.

"He's at the top of the stairs," she said, "if you'd like to go up."

I went past a couple of rustic rockers and into the house of the man who had stolen the Leander pearls.

10

Fish tanks were all around the big room, two tiers of them on braced shelves, big oblong tanks with metal frames, some with lights over them and some with lights down in them. Water grasses were festooned in careless patterns behind the algae-coated glass and the water held a ghostly greenish light and through the greenish light moved fish of all the colors of rainbow.

There were long slim fish like golden darts and Japanese Veiltails with fantastic trailing tails, and X-ray fish as transparent as colored glass, tiny guppies half an inch long, calico popeyes spotted like a bride's apron, and big lumbering Chinese Moors with telescope eyes, froglike faces and unnecessary fins, waddling through the green water like fat men going to lunch.

Most of the light came from a big sloping skylight. Under the skylight at a bare wooden table a tall gaunt man stood with a squirming red fish in his left hand, and in his right hand a safety-razor blade backed with adhesive tape.

He looked at me from under wide gray eyebrows. His eyes were sunken, colorless, opaque. I went over beside him and looked down at the fish he was holding.

"Fungus?" I asked.

He nodded slowly. "White fungus." He put the fish down on the table and carefully spread its dorsal fin. The fin was ragged and split and the ragged edges had a mossy white color.

"White fungus," he said, "ain't so bad. I'll trim this feller up and he'll be right as rain. What can I do for you, mister?"

I rolled a cigarette around in my fingers and smiled at him.

"Like people," I said. "The fish, I mean. They get things wrong with them."

He held the fish against the wood and trimmed off the ragged part of the fin. He spread the tail and trimmed that. The fish had stopped squirming.

"Some you can cure," he said, "and some you can't. You can't cure swimming-bladder disease, for instance." He glanced up at me. "This don't hurt him, 'case you think it does," he said. "You can shock a fish to death but you can't hurt it like a person."

He put the razor blade down and dipped a cotton swab in some purplish liquid, painted the cut places.

Then he dipped a finger in a jar of white vaseline and smeared that over. He dropped the fish in a small tank off to one side of the room. The fish swam around peacefully, quite content.

The gaunt man wiped his hands, sat down at the edge of a bench and stared at me with lifeless eyes. He had been good-looking once, a long time ago.

"You interested in fish?" he asked. His voice had the quiet careful murmur of the cell block and the exercise yard.

I shook my head. "Not particularly. That was just an excuse. I came a long way to see you, Mister Sype."

He moistened his lips and went on staring at me. When his voice came again it was tired and soft.

"Wallace is the name, mister."

I puffed a smoke ring and poked my finger through it. "For my job it's got to be Sype."

He leaned forward and dropped his hands between his spread bony knees, clasped them together. Big gnarled hands that had done a lot of hard work in their time. His head tipped up at me and his dead eyes were cold under the shaggy brows. But his voice stayed soft.

"Haven't seen a dick in a year. To talk to. What's your lay?"

"Guess," I said.

His voice got still softer. "Listen, dick. I've got a nice home here, quiet. Nobody bothers me any more. Nobody's got a right to. I got a pardon straight from the White House. I've got the fish to play with and a man gets fond of anything he takes care of. I don't owe the world a nickel. I paid up. My wife's got enough dough for us to live on. All I want is to be let alone, dick." He stopped talking, shook his head once. "You can't burn me up—not any more."

I didn't say anything. I smiled a little and watched him.

"Nobody can touch me," he said. "I got a pardon straight from the President's study. I just want to be let alone."

I shook my head and kept on smiling at him. "That's the one thing you can never have—until you give in."

"Listen," he said softly. "You may be new on this case. It's kind of fresh to you. You want to make a rep for yourself. But me, I've had almost twenty years of it, and so have a lot of other people, some of 'em pretty smart people too. They know I don't have nothing that don't belong to me. Never did have. Somebody else got it."

"The mail clerk," I said. "Sure."

"Listen," he said, still softly. "I did my time. I know all the angles. I know they ain't going to stop wondering —long as anybody's alive that remembers. I know they're going to send some punk out once in a while to kind of stir it up. That's okey. No hard feelings. Now what do I do to get you to go home again?"

I shook my head and stared past his shoulder at the fish drifting in their big silent tanks. I felt tired. The quiet of the house made ghosts in my brain, ghosts of a lot of years ago. A train pounding through the darkness, a stick-up hidden in a mail car, a gun flash, a dead clerk on the floor, a silent drop off at some water tank, a man who had kept a secret for nineteen years—almost kept it.

"You made one mistake," I said slowly. "Remember a fellow named Peeler Mardo?"

He lifted his head. I could see him searching in his memory. The name didn't seem to mean anything to him.

"A fellow you knew in Leavenworth," I said. "A little runt that was in there for splitting twenty-dollar bills and putting phony backs on them."

"Yeah," he said. "I remember."

"You told him you had the pearls," I said.

I could see he didn't believe me. "I must have been kidding him," he said slowly, emptily.

"Maybe. But here's the point. He didn't think so. He was up in this country a while ago with a pal, a guy who called himself Sunset. They saw you somewhere and Peeler recognized you. He got to thinking how he could make himself some jack. But he was a coke hound and he talked in his sleep. A girl got wise and then another girl and a shyster. Peeler got his feet burned and he's dead."

Sype stared at me unblinkingly. The lines at the corners of his mouth deepened.

I waved my cigarette and went on: "We don't know how much he told, but the shyster and a girl are in Olympia. Sunset's in Olympia, only he's dead. They killed him. I wouldn't know if they know where you are or not. But they will sometime, or others like them. You can wear the cops down, if they can't find the pearls and you don't try to sell them. You can wear the insurance company down and even the postal men."

Sype didn't move a muscle. His big knotty hands clenched between his knees didn't move. His dead eyes just stared.

"But you can't wear the chiselers down," I said. "They'll never lay off. There'll always be a couple or three with time enough and money enough and meanness enough to bear down. They'll find out what they want to know some way. They'll snatch your wife or take you out in the woods and give you the works. And you'll have to come through . . . Now I've got a decent, square proposition."

"Which bunch are you?" Sype asked suddenly. "I thought you smelled of dick, but I ain't so sure now."

"Insurance," I said. "Here's the deal. Twenty-five grand reward in all. Five grand to the girl that passed me the info. She got it on the square and she's entitled to that cut. Ten grand to me. I've done all the work and looked into all the guns. Ten grand to you, through me. You couldn't get a nickel direct. Is there anything in it? How does it look?"

"It looks fine," he said gently. "Except for one thing. I don't have no pearls, dick."

I scowled at him. That was my wad. I didn't have any more. I straightened away from the wall and dropped a cigarette end on the wood floor, crushed it out. I turned to go.

He stood up and put a hand out. "Wait a minute," he said gravely, "and I'll prove it to you."

He went across the floor in front of me and out of the room. I stared at the fish and chewed my lip. I heard the sound of a car engine somewhere, not very close. I heard a drawer open and shut, apparently in a nearby room.

Sype came back into the fish room. He had a shiny Colt .45 in his gaunt fist. It looked as long as a man's forearm.

He pointed it at me and said: "I got pearls in this, six of them. Lead pearls. I can comb a fly's whiskers at sixty yards. You ain't no dick. Now get up and blow —and tell your redhot friends I'm ready to shoot their teeth out any day of the week and twice on Sunday."

I didn't move. There was a madness in the man's dead eyes. I didn't dare move.

"That's grandstand stuff," I said slowly. "I can prove I'm a dick. You're an ex-con and it's felony just having that rod. Put it down and talk sense."

The car I had heard seemed to be stopping outside the house. Brakes whined on drums. Feet clattered, up a walk, up steps. Sudden sharp voices, a caught exclamation.

Sype backed across the room until he was between the table and a big twenty- or thirty-gallon tank. He grinned at me, the wide clear grin of a fighter at bay.

"I see your friends kind of caught up with you," he drawled. "Take your gat out and drop it on the floor while you still got time—and breath."

I didn't move. I looked at the wiry hair above his eyes. I looked into his eyes. I knew if I moved—even to do what he told me—he would shoot.

Steps came up the stairs. They were clogged, shuffling steps, with a hint of struggle in them.

Three people came into the room.

11

Mrs. Sype came in first, stiff-legged, her eyes glazed, her arms bent rigidly at the elbows and the hands clawing straight forward at nothing, feeling for something that wasn't there. There was a gun in her back, Carol Donovan's small .32, held efficiently in Carol Donovan's small ruthless hand.

Madder came last. He was drunk, brave from the bottle, flushed and savage. He threw the Smith and Wesson down on me and leered.

Carol Donovan pushed Mrs. Sype aside. The older woman stumbled into the corner and sank down on her knees, blank-eyed.

Sype stared at the Donovan girl. He was rattled because she was a girl and young and pretty. He hadn't been used to the type. Seeing her took the fire out of him. If men had come in he would have shot them to pieces.

The small dark white-faced girl faced him coldly, said in her tight chilled voice: "All right, Dad. Shed the heater. Make it smooth now."

Sype leaned down slowly, not taking his eyes off her. He put his enormous frontier Colt on the floor.

"Kick it away from you, Dad."

Sype kicked it. The gun skidded across the bare boards, over towards the center of the room.

"That's the way, old-timer. You hold on him, Rush, while I unrod the dick."

The two guns swiveled and the hard gray eyes were looking at me now. Madder went a little way towards Sype and pointed his Smith and Wesson at Sype's chest.

The girl smiled, not a nice smile. "Bright boy, eh? You sure stick your neck out all the time, don't you? Made a beef, shamus. Didn't frisk your skinny pal. He had a little map in one shoe."

"I didn't need one," I said smoothly, and grinned at her.

I tried to make the grin appealing, because Mrs. Sype was moving her knees on the floor, and every move took her nearer to Sype's Colt.

"But you're all washed up now, you and your big smile. Hoist the mitts while I get your iron. Up, mister."

She was a girl, about five feet two inches tall, and weighed around a hundred and twenty. Just a girl. I was six feet and a half-inch, weighed one-ninety-five. I put my hands up and hit her on the jaw.

That was crazy, but I had all I could stand of the Donovan-Madder act, the Donovan-Madder guns, the Donovan-Madder tough talk. I hit her on the jaw.

She went back a yard and her popgun went off. A slug burned my ribs. She started to fall. Slowly, like a slow motion picture, she fell. There was something silly about it.

Mrs. Sype got the Colt and shot her in the back.

Madder whirled and the instant he turned Sype rushed him. Madder jumped back and yelled and covered Sype again. Sype stopped cold and the wide crazy grin came back on his gaunt face.

The slug from the Colt knocked the girl forward as though a door had whipped in a high wind. A flurry of blue cloth, something thumped my chest—her head.

I saw her face for a moment as she bounced back, a strange face that I had never seen before.

Then she was a huddled thing on the floor at my feet, small, deadly, extinct, with redness coming out from under her, and the tall quiet woman behind her with the smoking Colt held in both hands.

Madder shot Sype twice. Sype plunged forward still grinning and hit the end of the table. The purplish liquid he had used on the sick fish sprayed up over him. Madder shot him again as he was falling.

I jerked my Luger out and shot Madder in the most painful place I could think of that wasn't likely to be fatal—the back of the knee. He went down exactly as if he had tripped over a hidden wire. I had cuffs on him before he even started to groan.

I kicked guns here and there and went over to Mrs. Sype and took the big Colt out of her hands.

It was very still in the room for a little while. Eddies of smoke drifted towards the skylight, filmy gray, pale in the afternoon sun. I heard the surf booming in the distance. Then I heard a whistling sound close at hand.

It was Sype trying to say something. His wife crawled across to him, still on her knees, huddled beside him. There was blood on his lips and bubbles. He blinked hard, trying to clear his head. He smiled up at her. His whistling voice said very faintly: "The Moors, Hattie— the Moors."

Then his neck went loose and the smile melted off his face. His head rolled to one side on the bare floor.

Mrs. Sype touched him, then got very slowly to her feet and looked at me, calm, dry-eyed.

She said in a low clear voice: "Will you help me carry him to the bed? I don't like him here with these people."

I said: "Sure. What was that he said?"

"I don't know. Some nonsense about his fish, I think."

I lifted Sype's shoulders and she took his feet and we carried him into the bedroom and put him on the bed. She folded his hands on his chest and shut his eyes. She went over and pulled the blinds down.

"That's all, thank you," she said, not looking at me. "The telephone is downstairs."

She sat down in a chair beside the bed and put her head down on the coverlet near Sype's arm.

I went out of the room and shut the door.

12

Madder's leg was bleeding slowly, not dangerously. He stared at me with fear-crazed eyes while I tied a tight handkerchief above his knee. I figured he had a cut tendon and maybe a chipped kneecap. He might walk a little lame when they came to hang him.

I went downstairs and stood on the porch looking at the two cars in front, then down the hill towards the pier. Nobody could have told where the shots came from, unless he happened to be passing. Quite likely nobody had even noticed them. There was probably shooting in the woods around there a good deal.

I went back into the house and looked at the crank telephone on the living-room wall, but didn't touch it yet. Something was bothering me. I lit a cigarette and stared out of the window and a ghost voice said in my ears: "The Moors, Hattie. The Moors."

I went back up to the fish room. Madder was groaning now, thick panting groans. What did I care about a torturer like Madder?

The girl was quite dead. None of the tanks was hit. The fish swam peacefully in their green water, slow and peaceful and easy. They didn't care about Madder either.

The tank with the black Chinese Moors in it was

over in the corner, about ten-gallon size. There were just four of them, big fellows, about four inches body length, coal black all over. Two of them were sucking oxygen on top of the water and two were waddling sluggishly on the bottom. They had thick deep bodies with a lot of spreading tail and high dorsal fins and their bulging telescope eyes that made them look like frogs when they were head towards you.

I watched them fumbling around in the green stuff that was growing in the tank. A couple of red pond snails were window-cleaning. The two on the bottom looked thicker and more sluggish than the two on the top. I wondered why.

There was a long-handled strainer made of woven string lying between two of the tanks. I got it and fished down in the tank, trapped one of the big Moors and lifted it out. I turned it over in the net, looked at its faintly silver belly. I saw something that looked like a suture. I felt the place. There was a hard lump under it.

I pulled the other one off the bottom. Same suture, same hard round lump. I got one of the two that had been sucking air on top. No suture, no hard round lump. It was harder to catch too.

I put it back in the tank. My business was with the other two. I like goldfish as well as the next man, but business is business and crime is crime. I took my coat off and rolled my sleeves up and picked the razor blade backed with adhesive tape off the table.

It was a very messy job. It took about five minutes. Then they lay in the palm of my hand, three-quarters of an inch in diameter, heavy, perfectly round, milky white and shimmering with that inner light no other jewel has. The Leander pearls.

I washed them off, wrapped them in my handkerchief, rolled down my sleeves and put my coat back on. I looked at Madder, at his little pain and fear-tortured eyes, the sweat on his face. I didn't care anything about Madder. He was a killer, a torturer.

I went out of the fish room. The bedroom door was still shut. I went down below and cranked the wall telephone.

"This is the Wallace place at Westport," I said. "There's been an accident. We need a doctor and we'll have to have the police. What can you do?"

The girl said: "I'll try and get you a doctor, Mr. Wallace. It may take a little time though. There's a town marshal at Westport. Will he do?"

"I suppose so," I said and thanked her and hung up. There were points about a country telephone after all.

I lit another cigarette and sat down in one of the rustic rockers on the porch. In a little while there were steps and Mrs. Sype came out of the house. She stood a moment looking off down the hills, then she sat down in the other rocker beside me. Her dry eyes looked at me steadily.

"You're a detective, I suppose," she said slowly, diffidently.

"Yes, I represent the company that insured the Leander pearls."

She looked off into the distance. "I thought he would have peace here," she said. "That nobody would bother him any more. That this place would be a sort of sanctuary."

"He ought not to have tried to keep the pearls."

She turned her head, quickly this time. She looked blank now, then she looked scared.

I reached down in my pocket and got out the wadded handkerchief, opened it up on the palm of my hand. They lay there together on the white linen, two hundred grand worth of murder.

"He could have had his sanctuary," I said. "Nobody wanted to take it away from him. But he wasn't satisfied with that."

She looked slowly, lingeringly at the pearls. Then her lips twitched. Her voice got hoarse.

"Poor Wally," she said. "So you did find them. You're pretty clever, you know. He killed dozens of fish before he learned how to do that trick." She looked up into my face. A little wonder showed at the back of her eyes.

She said: "I always hated the idea. Do you remember the old Bible theory of the scapegoat?"

I shook my head, no.

"The animal on which the sins of a man were laid and then it was driven off into the wilderness. The fish were his scapegoat."

She smiled at me. I didn't smile back.

She said, still smiling faintly: "You see, he once had the pearls, the real ones, and suffering seemed to him to make them his. But he couldn't have had any profit from them, even if he had found them again. It seems some landmark changed, while he was in prison, and he never could find the spot in Idaho where they were buried."

An icy finger was moving slowly up and down my spine. I opened my mouth and something I supposed might be my voice said: "Huh?"

She reached a finger out and touched one of the pearls. I was still holding them out, as if my hand was a shelf nailed to the wall.

"So he got these," she said. "In Seattle. They're hollow, filled with white wax. I forget what they call the process. They look very fine. Of course I never saw any really valuable pearls."

"What did he get them for?" I croaked.

"Don't you see? They were his sin. He had to hide them in the wilderness, this wilderness. He hid them in the fish. And do you know——" she leaned towards me again and her eyes shone. She said very slowly, very earnestly: "Sometimes I think that in the very end, just the last year or so, he actually believed they were the real pearls he was hiding. Does all this mean anything to you?"

I looked down at my pearls. My hand and the handkerchief closed over them slowly.

I said: "I'm a plain man, Mrs. Sype. I guess the scapegoat idea is a bit over my head. I'd say he was just trying to kid himself a bit—like any heavy loser."

She smiled again. She was handsome when she smiled. Then she shrugged quite lightly.

"Of course, you would see it that way. But me—" she spread her hands. "Oh, well, it doesn't matter much now. May I have them for a keepsake?"

"Have them?"

"The—the phony pearls. Surely you don't—"

I stood up. An old Ford roadster without a top was chugging up the hill. A man in it had a big star on his vest. The chatter of the motor was like the chatter of some old angry bald-headed ape in the zoo.

Mrs. Sype was standing beside me, with her hand half out, a thin, beseeching look on her face.

I grinned at her with sudden ferocity.

"Yeah, you were pretty good in there for a while," I said. "I damn near fell for it. And was I cold down the back, lady! But you helped. 'Phony' was a shade out of character for you. Your work with the Colt was fast and kind of ruthless. Most of all Sype's last words queered it. 'The Moors, Hattie—the Moors.' He wouldn't have bothered with that if the stones had been ringers. And he wasn't sappy enough to kid himself all the way."

For a moment her face didn't change at all. Then it did. Something horrible showed in her eyes. She put her lips out and spit at me. Then she slammed into the house.

I tucked twenty-five thousand dollars into my vest pocket. Twelve thousand five hundred for me and twelve thousand five hundred for Kathy Horne. I could see her eyes when I brought her the check, and when she put it in the bank, to wait for Johnny to get paroled from Quentin.

The Ford had pulled up behind the other cars. The man driving spit over the side, yanked his emergency brake on, got out without using the door. He was a big fellow in shirt sleeves.

I went down the steps to meet him.

RED WIND

1

THERE WAS a desert wind blowing that night. It was one of those hot dry Santa Anas that come down through the mountain passes and curl your hair and make your nerves jump and your skin itch. On nights like that every booze party ends in a fight. Meek little wives feel the edge of the carving knife and study their husbands' necks. Anything can happen. You can even get a full glass of beer at a cocktail lounge.

I was getting one in a flossy new place across the street from the apartment house where I lived. It had been open about a week and it wasn't doing any business. The kid behind the bar was in his early twenties and looked as if he had never had a drink in his life.

There was only one other customer, a souse on a bar stool with his back to the door. He had a pile of dimes stacked neatly in front of him, about two dollars' worth. He was drinking straight rye in small glasses and he was all by himself in a world of his own.

I sat farther along the bar and got my glass of beer and said: "You sure cut the clouds off them, buddy. I will say that for you."

"We just opened up," the kid said. "We got to build up trade. Been in before, haven't you, mister?"

"Uh-huh."

"Live around here?"

"In the Berglund Apartments across the street," I said. "And the name is Philip Marlowe."

"Thanks, mister. Mine's Lew Petrolle." He leaned close to me across the polished dark bar. "Know that guy?"

"No."

"He ought to go home, kind of. I ought to call a taxi and send him home. He's doing his next week's drinking too soon."

"A night like this," I said. "Let him alone."

"It's not good for him," the kid said, scowling at me.

"Rye!" the drunk croaked, without looking up. He snapped his fingers so as not to disturb his piles of dimes by banging on the bar.

The kid looked at me and shrugged. "Should I?"

"Whose stomach is it? Not mine."

The kid poured him another straight rye and I think he doctored it with water down behind the bar because when he came up with it he looked as guilty as if he'd kicked his grandmother. The drunk paid no attention. He lifted coins off his pile with the exact care of a crack surgeon operating on a brain tumor.

The kid came back and put more beer in my glass. Outside the wind howled. Every once in a while it blew the stained-glass door open a few inches. It was a heavy door.

The kid said: "I don't like drunks in the first place and in the second place I don't like them getting drunk in here, and in the third place I don't like them in the first place."

"Warner Brothers could use that," I said.

"They did."

Just then we had another customer. A car squeaked to a stop outside and the swinging door came open. A fellow came in who looked a little in a hurry. He held the door and ranged the place quickly with flat, shiny, dark eyes. He was well set up, dark, good-looking in a narrow-faced, tight-lipped way. His clothes were dark and a white handkerchief peeped coyly from his pocket and he looked cool as well as under a tension of some sort. I guessed it was the hot wind. I felt a bit the same myself only not cool.

He looked at the drunk's back. The drunk was playing checkers with his empty glasses. The new customer looked at me, then he looked along the line of half-booths at the other side of the place. They were all empty. He came on in—down past where the drunk sat swaying and muttering to himself—and spoke to the bar kid.

"Seen a lady in here, buddy? Tall, pretty, brown hair, in a print bolero jacket over a blue crêpe silk dress. Wearing a wide-brimmed straw hat with a velvet band." He had a tight voice I didn't like.

"No, sir. Nobody like that's been in," the bar kid said.

"Thanks. Straight Scotch. Make it fast, will you?"

The kid gave it to him and the fellow paid and put the drink down in a gulp and started to go out. He took three or four steps and stopped, facing the drunk. The drunk was grinning. He swept a gun from somewhere so fast that it was just a blur coming out. He held it steady and he didn't look any drunker than I was. The tall dark guy stood quite still and then his head jerked back a little and then he was still again.

A car tore by outside. The drunk's gun was a .22 target automatic, with a large front sight. It made a couple of hard snaps and a little smoke curled—very little.

"So long, Waldo," the drunk said.

Then he put the gun on the barman and me.

The dark guy took a week to fall down. He stumbled, caught himself, waved one arm, stumbled again. His hat fell off, and then he hit the floor with his face. After he hit it he might have been poured concrete for all the fuss he made.

The drunk slid down off the stool and scooped his dimes into a pocket and slid towards the door. He turned sideways, holding the gun across his body. I didn't have a gun. I hadn't thought I needed one to buy a glass of beer. The kid behind the bar didn't move or make the slightest sound.

The drunk felt the door lightly with his shoulder, keeping his eyes on us, then pushed through it backwards. When it was wide a hard gust of air slammed in and lifted the hair of the man on the floor. The drunk said: "Poor Waldo. I bet I made his nose bleed."

The door swung shut. I started to rush it—from long practice in doing the wrong thing. In this case it didn't matter. The car outside let out a roar and when I got onto the sidewalk it was flicking a red smear of tail-light around the nearby corner. I got its license number the way I got my first million.

There were people and cars up and down the block as usual. Nobody acted as if a gun had gone off. The wind was making enough noise to make the hard quick rap of .22 ammunition sound like a slammed door, even if anyone heard it. I went back into the cocktail bar.

The kid hadn't moved, even yet. He just stood with his hands flat on the bar, leaning over a little and looking down at the dark guy's back. The dark guy hadn't moved either. I bent down and felt his neck artery. He wouldn't move—ever.

The kid's face had as much expression as a cut of round steak and was about the same color. His eyes were more angry than shocked.

I lit a cigarette and blew smoke at the ceiling and said shortly: "Get on the phone."

"Maybe he's not dead," the kid said.

"When they use a twenty-two that means they don't make mistakes. Where's the phone?"

"I don't have one. I got enough expenses without that. Boy, can I kick eight hundred bucks in the face!"

"You own this place?"

"I did till this happened."

He pulled his white coat off and his apron and came around the inner end of the bar. "I'm locking this door," he said, taking keys out.

He went out, swung the door to and jiggled the lock from the outside until the bolt clicked into place. I bent down and rolled Waldo over. At first I couldn't even see where the shots went in. Then I could. A couple of tiny holes in his coat, over his heart. There was a little blood on his shirt.

The drunk was everything you could ask—as a killer.

The prowl-car boys came in about eight minutes. The kid, Lew Petrolle, was back behind the bar by then. He had his white coat on again and he was counting his money in the register and putting it in his pocket and making notes in a little book.

I sat at the edge of one of the half-booths and smoked cigarettes and watched Waldo's face get deader and deader. I wondered who the girl in the print coat was, why Waldo had left the engine of his car running outside, why he was in a hurry, whether the drunk had been waiting for him or just happened to be there.

The prowl-car boys came in perspiring. They were the usual large size and one of them had a flower stuck under his cap and his cap on a bit crooked. When he saw the dead man he got rid of the flower and leaned down to feel Waldo's pulse.

"Seems to be dead," he said, and rolled him around a little more. "Oh yeah, I see where they went in. Nice clean work. You two see him get it?"

I said yes. The kid behind the bar said nothing. I told them about it, that the killer seemed to have left in Waldo's car.

The cop yanked Waldo's wallet out, went through it rapidly and whistled. "Plenty jack and no driver's license." He put the wallet away. "O.K., we didn't touch him, see? Just a chance we could find did he have a car and put it on the air."

"The hell you didn't touch him," Lew Patrolle said.

The cop gave him one of those looks. "O.K., pal," he said softly. "We touched him."

The kid picked up a clean highball glass and began to polish it. He polished it all the rest of the time we were there.

In another minute a homicide fast-wagon sirened up and screeched to a stop outside the door and four men came in, two dicks, a photographer and a laboratory man. I didn't know either of the dicks. You can be in the detecting business a long time and not know all the men on a big city force.

One of them was a short, smooth, dark, quiet, smiling man, with curly black hair and soft intelligent eyes. The other was big, raw-boned, long-jawed, with a veined nose and glassy eyes. He looked like a heavy drinker. He looked tough, but he looked as if he thought he was a little tougher than he was. He shooed me into the last booth against the wall and his partner got the kid up front and the bluecoats went out. The fingerprint man and photographer set about their work.

A medical examiner came, stayed just long enough to get sore because there was no phone for him to call the morgue wagon.

The short dick emptied Waldo's pockets and then emptied his wallet and dumped everything into a large handkerchief on a booth table. I saw a lot of currency, keys, cigarettes, another handkerchief, very little else.

The big dick pushed me back into the end of the half-booth. "Give," he said. "I'm Copernik, Detective Lieutenant."

I put my wallet in front of him. He looked at it, went through it, tossed it back, made a note in a book.

"Philip Marlowe, huh? A shamus. You here on business?"

"Drinking business," I said. "I live just across the street in the Berglund."

"Know this kid up front?"

"I've been in here once since he opened up."

"See anything funny about him now?"

"No."

"Takes it too light for a young fellow, don't he? Never mind answering. Just tell the story."

I told it—three times. Once for him to get the outline, once for him to get the details and once for him to see if I had it too pat. At the end he said: "This dame interests me. And the killer called the guy Waldo, yet didn't seem to be anyways sure he would be in. I mean, if Waldo wasn't sure the dame would be here, nobody could be sure Waldo would be here."

"That's pretty deep," I said.

He studied me. I wasn't smiling. "Sounds like a grudge job, don't it? Don't sound planned. No getaway except by accident. A guy don't leave his car unlocked much in this town. And the killer works in front of two good witnesses. I don't like that."

"I don't like being a witness," I said. "The pay's too low."

He grinned. His teeth had a freckled look. "Was the killer drunk really?"

"With that shooting? No."

"Me too. Well, it's a simple job. The guy will have a record and he's left plenty prints. Even if we don't have his mug here we'll make him in hours. He had something on Waldo, but he wasn't meeting Waldo tonight. Waldo just dropped in to ask about a dame he had a date with and had missed connections on. It's a hot night and this wind would kill a girl's face. She'd be apt to drop in somewhere to wait. So the killer feeds Waldo two in the right place and scrams and don't worry about you boys at all. It's that simple."

"Yeah," I said.

"It's so simple it stinks," Copernik said.

He took his felt hat off and tousled up his ratty blond hair and leaned his head on his hands. He had a long mean horse face. He got a handkerchief out and mopped it, and the back of his neck and the back of his hands.

He got a comb out and combed his hair—he looked worse with it combed—and put his hat back on.

"I was just thinking," I said.

"Yeah? What?"

"This Waldo knew just how the girl was dressed. So he must already have been with her tonight."

"So, what? Maybe he had to go to the can. And when he came back she's gone. Maybe she changed her mind about him."

"That's right," I said.

But that wasn't what I was thinking at all. I was thinking that Waldo had described the girl's clothes in a way the ordinary man wouldn't know how to describe them. Printed bolero jacket over blue crêpe silk dress. I didn't even know what a bolero jacket was. And I might have said blue dress or even blue silk dress, but never blue crêpe silk dress.

After a while two men came with a basket. Lew Petrolle was still polishing his glass and talking to the short dark dick.

We all went down to headquarters.

Lew Petrolle was all right when they checked on him. His father had a grape ranch near Antioch in Contra Costa County. He had given Lew a thousand dollars to go into business and Lew had opened the cocktail bar, neon sign and all, on eight hundred flat.

They let him go and told him to keep the bar closed until they were sure they didn't want to do any more printing. He shook hands all around and grinned and said he guessed the killing would be good for business after all, because nobody believed a newspaper account of anything and people would come to him for the story and buy drinks while he was telling it.

"There's a guy won't ever do any worrying," Copernik said, when he was gone. "Over anybody else."

"Poor Waldo," I said. "The prints any good?"

"Kind of smudged," Copernik said sourly. "But we'll

get a classification and teletype it to Washington some time tonight. If it don't click, you'll be in for a day on the steel picture racks downstairs."

I shook hands with him and his partner, whose name was Ybarra, and left. They didn't know who Waldo was yet either. Nothing in his pockets told.

2

I got back to my street about 9 P.M. I looked up and down the block before I went into the Berglund. The cocktail bar was farther down on the other side, dark, with a nose or two against the glass, but no real crowd. People had seen the law and the morgue wagon, but they didn't know what had happened. Except the boys playing pinball games in the drugstore on the corner. They know everything, except how to hold a job.

The wind was still blowing, oven-hot, swirling dust and torn paper up against the walls.

I went into the lobby of the apartment house and rode the automatic elevator up to the fourth floor. I unwound the doors and stepped out and there was a tall girl standing there waiting for the car.

She had brown wavy hair under a wide-brimmed straw hat with a velvet band and loose bow. She had wide blue eyes and eyelashes that didn't quite reach her chin. She wore a blue dress that might have been crêpe silk, simple in lines but not missing any curves. Over it she wore what might have been a print bolero jacket.

I said: "Is that a bolero jacket?"

She gave me a distant glance and made a motion as if to brush a cobweb out of the way.

"Yes. Would you mind—I'm rather in a hurry. I'd like—"

I didn't move. I blocked her off from the elevator. We stared at each other and she flushed very slowly.

"Better not go out on the street in those clothes," I said.

"Why, how dare you—"

The elevator clanked and started down again. I didn't know what she was going to say. Her voice lacked the edgy twang of a beer-parlor frill. It had a soft light sound, like spring rain.

"It's not a make," I said. "You're in trouble. If they come to this floor in the elevator, you have just that much time to get off the hall. First take off the hat and jacket—and snap it up!"

She didn't move. Her face seemed to whiten a little behind the not-too-heavy make-up.

"Cops," I said, "are looking for you. In those clothes. Give me the chance and I'll tell you why."

She turned her head swiftly and looked back along the corridor. With her looks I didn't blame her for trying one more bluff.

"You're impertinent, whoever you are. I'm Mrs. Leroy in Apartment Thirty-one. I can assure—"

"That you're on the wrong floor," I said. "This is the fourth." The elevator had stopped down below. The sound of doors being wrenched open came up the shaft.

"Off!" I rapped. "Now!"

She switched her hat off and slipped out of the bolero jacket, fast. I grabbed them and wadded them into a mess under my arm. I took her elbow and turned her and we were going down the hall.

"I live in Forty-two. The front one across from yours, just a floor up. Take your choice. Once again—I'm not on the make."

She smoothed her hair with that quick gesture, like a bird preening itself. Ten thousand years of practice behind it.

"Mine," she said, and tucked her bag under her arm and strode down the hall fast. The elevator stopped at the floor below. She stopped when it stopped. She turned and faced me.

"The stairs are back by the elevator shaft," I said gently.

"I don't have an apartment," she said.

"I didn't think you had."

"Are they searching for me?"

"Yes, but they won't start gouging the block stone by stone before tomorrow. And then only if they don't make Waldo."

She stared at me. "Waldo?"

"Oh, you don't know Waldo," I said.

She shook her head slowly. The elevator started down in the shaft again. Panic flicked in her blue eyes like a ripple on water.

"No," she said breathlessly, "but take me out of this hall."

We were almost at my door. I jammed the key in and shook the lock around and heaved the door inward. I reached in far enough to switch lights on. She went in past me like a wave. Sandalwood floated on the air, very faint.

I shut the door, threw my hat into a chair and watched her stroll over to a card table on which I had a chess problem set out that I couldn't solve. Once inside, with the door locked, her panic had left her.

"So you're a chess player," she said, in that guarded tone, as if she had come to look at my etchings. I wished she had.

We both stood still then and listened to the distant clang of elevator doors and then steps—going the other way.

I grinned, but with strain, not pleasure, went out into the kitchenette and started to fumble with a couple of glasses and then realized I still had her hat and bolero jacket under my arm. I went into the dressing room behind the wall bed and stuffed them into a drawer, went back out to the kitchenette, dug out some extra-fine Scotch and made a couple of highballs.

When I went in with the drinks she had a gun in her hand. It was a small automatic with a pearl grip. It jumped up at me and her eyes were full of horror.

I stopped, with a glass in each hand, and said: "Maybe this hot wind has got you crazy too. I'm a private detective. I'll prove it if you let me."

She nodded slightly and her face was white. I went over slowly and put a glass down beside her, and went back and set mine down and got a card out that had no bent corners. She was sitting down, smoothing one blue knee with her left hand, and holding the gun on the other. I put the card down beside her drink and sat with mine.

"Never let a guy get that close to you," I said. "Not if you mean business. And your safety catch is on."

She flashed her eyes down, shivered, and put the gun back in her bag. She drank half the drink without stopping, put the glass down hard and picked the card up.

"I don't give many people that liquor," I said. "I can't afford to."

Her lips curled. "I supposed you would want money."

"Huh?"

She didn't say anything. Her hand was close to her bag again.

"Don't forget the safety catch," I said. Her hand stopped. I went on: "This fellow I called Waldo is quite tall, say five-eleven, slim, dark, brown eyes with a lot of glitter. Nose and mouth too thin. Dark suit, white handkerchief showing, and in a hurry to find you. Am I getting anywhere?"

She took her glass again. "So that's Waldo," she said. "Well, what about him?" Her voice seemed to have a slight liquor edge now.

"Well, a funny thing. There's a cocktail bar across

the street . . . Say, where have you been all evening?"

"Sitting in my car," she said coldly, "most of the time."

"Didn't you see a fuss across the street up the block?"

Her eyes tried to say no and missed. Her lips said: "I knew there was some kind of disturbance. I saw policemen and red searchlights. I supposed someone had been hurt."

"Someone was. And this Waldo was looking for you before that. In the cocktail bar. He described you and your clothes."

Her eyes were set like rivets now and had the same amount of expression. Her mouth began to tremble and kept on trembling.

"I was in there," I said, "talking to the kid that runs it. There was nobody in there but a drunk on a stool and the kid and myself. The drunk wasn't paying any attention to anything. Then Waldo came in and asked about you and we said no, we hadn't seen you and he started to leave."

I sipped my drink. I like an effect as well as the next fellow. Her eyes ate me.

"Just started to leave. Then this drunk that wasn't paying any attention to anyone called him Waldo and took a gun out. He shot him twice"—I snapped my fingers twice—"like that. Dead."

She fooled me. She laughed in my face. "So my husband hired you to spy on me," she said. "I might have known the whole thing was an act. You and your Waldo."

I gawked at her.

"I never thought of him as jealous," she snapped. "Not of a man who had been our chauffeur anyhow. A little about Stan, of course—that's natural. But Joseph Coates—"

I made motions in the air. "Lady, one of us has this book open at the wrong page," I grunted. "I don't know anybody named Stan or Joseph Coates. So help me, I didn't even know you had a chauffeur. People around here don't run to them. As for husbands—yeah, we do have a husband once in a while. Not often enough."

She shook her head slowly and her hand stayed near her bag and her blue eyes had glitters in them.

"Not good enough, Mr. Marlowe. No, not nearly good enough. I know you private detectives. You're all rotten. You tricked me into your apartment, if it is your apartment. More likely it's the apartment of some horrible man who will swear anything for a few dollars. Now you're trying to scare me. So you can blackmail me—as well as get money from my husband. All right," she said breathlessly, "how much do I have to pay?"

I put my empty glass aside and leaned back. "Pardon me if I light a cigarette," I said. "My nerves are frayed."

I lit it while she watched me without enough fear for any real guilt to be under it. "So Joseph Coates is his name," I said. "The guy that killed him in the cocktail bar called him Waldo."

She smiled a bit disgustedly, but almost tolerantly. "Don't stall. How much?"

"Why were you trying to meet this Joseph Coates?"

"I was going to buy something he stole from me, of course. Something that's valuable in the ordinary way too. Almost fifteen thousand dollars. The man I loved gave it to me. He's dead. There! He's dead! He died in a burning plane. Now, go back and tell my husband that, you slimy little rat!"

"I'm not little and I'm not a rat," I said.

"You're still slimy. And don't bother about telling my husband. I'll tell him myself. He probably knows anyway."

I grinned. "That's smart. Just what was I supposed to find out?"

She grabbed her glass and finished what was left of her drink. "So he thinks I'm meeting Joseph. Well, perhaps I was. But not to make love. Not with a chauffeur.

Not with a bum I picked off the front step and gave a job to. I don't have to dig down that far, if I want to play around."

"Lady," I said, "you don't indeed."

"Now, I'm going," she said. "You just try and stop me." She snatched the pearl-handled gun out of her bag. I didn't move.

"Why, you nasty little string of nothing," she stormed. "How do I know you're a private detective at all? You might be a crook. This card you gave me doesn't mean anything. Anybody can have cards printed."

"Sure," I said. "And I suppose I'm smart enough to live here two years because you were going to move in today so I could blackmail you for not meeting a man named Joseph Coates who was bumped off across the street under the name of Waldo. Have you got the money to buy this something that cost fifteen grand?"

"Oh! You think you'll hold me up, I suppose!"

"Oh!" I mimicked her, "I'm a stick-up artist now, am I? Lady, will you please either put that gun away or take the safety catch off? It hurts my professional feelings to see a nice gun made a monkey of that way."

"You're a full portion of what I don't like," she said. "Get out of my way."

I didn't move. She didn't move. We were both sitting down—and not even close to each other.

"Let me in on one secret before you go," I pleaded. "What in hell did you take the apartment down on the floor below for? Just to meet a guy down on the street?"

"Stop being silly," she snapped. "I didn't. I lied. It's his apartment."

"Joseph Coates'?"

She nodded sharply.

"Does my description of Waldo sound like Joseph Coates?"

She nodded sharply again.

"All right. That's one fact learned at last. Don't you realize Waldo described your clothes before he was shot —when he was looking for you—that the description was passed on to the police—that the police don't know who Waldo is—and are looking for somebody in those clothes to help tell them? Don't you get that much?"

The gun suddenly started to shake in her hand. She looked down at it, sort of vacantly, slowly put it back in her bag.

"I'm a fool," she whispered, "to be even talking to you." She stared at me for a long time, then pulled in a deep breath. "He told me where he was staying. He didn't seem afraid. I guess blackmailers are like that. He was to meet me on the street, but I was late. It was full of police when I got here. So I went back and sat in my car for a while. Then I came up to Joseph's apartment and knocked. Then I went back to my car and waited again. I came up here three times in all. The last time I walked up a flight to take the elevator. I had already been seen twice on the third floor. I met you. That's all."

"You said something about a husband," I grunted. "Where is he?"

"He's at a meeting."

"Oh, a meeting," I said, nastily.

"My husband's a very important man. He has lots of meetings. He's a hydroelectric engineer. He's been all over the world. I'd have you know—"

"Skip it," I said. "I'll take him to lunch some day and have him tell me himself. Whatever Joseph had on you is dead stock now. Like Joseph."

"He's really dead?" she whispered. "Really?"

"He's dead," I said. "Dead, dead, dead. Lady, he's dead."

She believed it at last. I hadn't thought she ever would somehow. In the silence, the elevator stopped at my floor.

I heard steps coming down the hall. We all have hunches. I put my finger to my lips. She didn't move now. Her face had a frozen look. Her big blue eyes were as black as the shadows below them. The hot wind boomed against the shut windows. Windows have to be shut when a Santa Ana blows, heat or no heat.

The steps that came down the hall were the casual ordinary steps of one man. But they stopped outside my door, and somebody knocked.

I pointed to the dressing room behind the wall bed. She stood up without a sound, her bag clenched against her side. I pointed again, to her glass. She lifted it swiftly, slid across the carpet, through the door, drew the door quietly shut after her.

I didn't know just what I was going to all this trouble for.

The knocking sounded again. The backs of my hands were wet. I creaked my chair and stood up and made a loud yawning sound. Then I went over and opened the door—without a gun. That was a mistake.

3

I didn't know him at first. Perhaps for the opposite reason Waldo hadn't seemed to know him. He'd had a hat on all the time over at the cocktail bar and he didn't have one on now. His hair ended completely and exactly where his hat would start. Above that line was hard white sweatless skin almost as glaring as scar tissue. He wasn't just twenty years older. He was a different man.

But I knew the gun he was holding, the .22 target automatic with the big front sight. And I knew his eyes. Bright, brittle, shallow eyes like the eyes of a lizard.

He was alone. He put the gun against my face very

lightly and said between his teeth: "Yeah, me. Let's go on in."

I backed in just far enough and stopped. Just the way he would want me to, so he could shut the door without moving much. I knew from his eyes that he would want me to do just that.

I wasn't scared. I was paralyzed.

When he had the door shut he backed me some more, slowly, until there was something against the back of my legs. His eyes looked into mine.

"That's a card table," he said. "Some goon here plays chess. You?"

I swallowed. "I don't exactly play it. I just fool around."

"That means two," he said with a kind of hoarse softness, as if some cop had hit him across the windpipe with a blackjack once, in a third-degree session.

"It's a problem," I said. "Not a game. Look at the pieces."

"I wouldn't know."

"Well, I'm alone," I said, and my voice shook just enough.

"It don't make any difference," he said. "I'm washed up anyway. Some nose puts the bulls on me tomorrow, next week, what the hell? I just didn't like your map, pal. And that smug-faced pansy in the bar coat that played left tackle for Fordham or something. To hell with guys like you guys."

I didn't speak or move. The big front sight raked my cheek lightly almost caressingly. The man smiled.

"It's kind of good business too," he said. "Just in case. An old con like me don't make good prints, all I got against me is two witnesses. The hell with it."

"What did Waldo do to you?" I tried to make it sound as if I wanted to know, instead of just not wanting to shake too hard.

"Stooled on a bank job in Michigan and got me four

years. Got himself a nolle prosse. Four years in Michigan ain't no summer cruise. They make you be good in them lifer states."

"How'd you know he'd come in there?" I croaked.

"I didn't. Oh yeah, I was lookin' for him. I was wanting to see him all right. I got a flash of him on the street night before last but I lost him. Up to then I wasn't lookin' for him. Then I was. A cute guy, Waldo. How is he?"

"Dead," I said.

"I'm still good," he chuckled. "Drunk or sober. Well, that don't make no doughnuts for me now. They make me downtown yet?"

I didn't answer him quick enough. He jabbed the gun into my throat and I choked and almost grabbed for it by instinct.

"Naw," he cautioned me softly. "Naw. You ain't that dumb."

I put my hands back, down at my sides, open, the palms towards him. He would want them that way. He hadn't touched me, except with the gun. He didn't seem to care whether I might have one too. He wouldn't—if he just meant the one thing.

He didn't seem to care very much about anything, coming back on that block. Perhaps the hot wind did something to him. It was booming against my shut windows like the surf under a pier.

"They got prints," I said. "I don't know how good."

"They'll be good enough—but not for teletype work. Take 'em airmail time to Washington and back to check 'em right. Tell me why I came here, pal."

"You heard the kid and me talking in the bar. I told him my name, where I lived."

"That's how, pal. I said why." He smiled at me. It was a lousy smile to be the last one you might see.

"Skip it," I said. "The hangman won't ask you to guess why he's there."

"Say, you're tough at that. After you, I visit that kid. I tailed him home from headquarters, but I figure you're the guy to put the bee on first. I tail him home from the city hall, in the rent car Waldo had. From head-quarters, pal. Them funny dicks. You can sit in their laps and they don't know you. Start runnin' for a street-car and they open up with machine guns and bump two pedestrians, a hacker asleep in his cab, and an old scrubwoman on the second floor workin' a mop. And they miss the guy they're after. Them funny lousy dicks."

He twisted the gun muzzle in my neck. His eyes looked madder than before.

"I got time," he said. "Waldo's rent car don't get a report right away. And they don't make Waldo very soon. I know Waldo. Smart he was. A smooth boy, Waldo."

"I'm going to vomit," I said, "if you don't take that gun out of my throat."

He smiled and moved the gun down to my heart. "This about right? Say when."

I must have spoken louder than I meant to. The door of the dressing-room by the wall bed showed a crack of darkness. Then an inch. Then four inches. I saw eyes, but didn't look at them. I stared hard into the bald-headed man's eyes. Very hard. I didn't want him to take his eyes off mine.

"Scared?" he asked softly.

I leaned against his gun and began to shake. I thought he would enjoy seeing me shake. The girl came out through the door. She had her gun in her hand again. I was sorry as hell for her. She'd try to make the door—or scream. Either way it would be cur-tains—for both of us.

"Well, don't take all night about it," I bleated. My voice sounded far away, like a voice on a radio on the other side of a street.

"I like this, pal," he smiled. "I'm like that."

The girl floated in the air, somewhere behind him. Nothing was ever more soundless than the way she moved. It wouldn't do any good though. He wouldn't fool around with her at all. I had known him all my life but I had been looking into his eyes for only five minutes.

"Suppose I yell," I said.

"Yeah, suppose you yell. Go ahead and yell," he said with his killer's smile.

She didn't go near the door. She was right behind him.

"Well—here's where I yell," I said.

As if that was the cue, she jabbed the little gun hard into his short ribs, without a single sound.

He had to react. It was like a knee reflex. His mouth snapped open and both his arms jumped out from his sides and he arched his back just a little. The gun was pointing at my right eye.

I sank and kneed him with all my strength, in the groin.

His chin came down and I hit it. I hit it as if I was driving the last spike on the first transcontinental railroad. I can still feel it when I flex my knuckles.

His gun raked the side of my face but it didn't go off. He was already limp. He writhed down gasping, his left side against the floor. I kicked his right shoulder—hard. The gun jumped away from him, skidded on the carpet, under a chair. I heard the chessmen tinkling on the floor behind me somewhere.

The girl stood over him, looking down. Then her wide dark horrified eyes came up and fastened on mine.

"That buys me," I said. "Anything I have is yours —now and forever."

She didn't hear me. Her eyes were strained open so hard that the whites showed under the vivid blue iris. She backed quickly to the door with her little gun up, felt behind her for the knob and twisted it. She pulled the door open and slipped out.

The door shut.

She was bareheaded and without her bolero jacket.

She had only the gun, and the safety catch on that was still set so that she couldn't fire it.

It was silent in the room then, in spite of the wind. Then I heard him gasping on the floor. His face had a greenish pallor. I moved behind him and pawed him for more guns, and didn't find any. I got a pair of store cuffs out of my desk and pulled his arms in front of him and snapped them on his wrists. They would hold if he didn't shake them too hard.

His eyes measured me for a coffin, in spite of their suffering. He lay in the middle of the floor, still on his left side, a twisted, wizened, bald-headed little guy with drawn-back lips and teeth spotted with cheap silver fillings. His mouth looked like a black pit and his breath came in little waves, choked, stopped, came on again, limping.

I went into the dressing room and opened the drawer of the chest. Her hat and jacket lay there on my shirts. I put them underneath, at the back, and smoothed the shirts over them. Then I went out to the kitchenette and poured a stiff jolt of whiskey and put it down and stood a moment listening to the hot wind howl against the window glass. A garage door banged, and a power-line wire with too much play between the insulators thumped the side of the building with a sound like somebody beating a carpet.

The drink worked on me. I went back into the living room and opened a window. The guy on the floor hadn't smelled her sandalwood, but somebody else might.

I shut the window again, wiped the palms of my hands and used the phone to dial headquarters.

Copernik was still there. His smart-aleck voice said: "Yeah? Marlowe? Don't tell me. I bet you got an idea."

"Make that killer yet?"

"We're not saying, Marlowe. Sorry as all hell and so on. You know how it is."

"O.K. I don't care who he is. Just come and get him off the floor of my apartment."

"Holy Christ!" Then his voice hushed and went down low. "Wait a minute, now. Wait a minute." A long way off I seemed to hear a door shut. Then his voice again. "Shoot," he said softly.

"Handcuffed," I said. "All yours. I had to knee him, but he'll be all right. He came here to eliminate a witness."

Another pause. The voice was full of honey. "Now listen, boy, who else is in this with you?"

"Who else? Nobody. Just me."

"Keep it that way, boy. All quiet. O.K.?"

"Think I want all the bums in the neighborhood in here sightseeing?"

"Take it easy, boy. Easy. Just sit tight and sit still. I'm practically there. No touch nothing. Get me?"

"Yeah." I gave him the address and apartment number again to save him time.

I could see his big bony face glisten. I got the .22 target gun from under the chair and sat holding it until feet hit the hallway outside my door and knuckles did a quiet tattoo on the door panel.

Copernik was alone. He filled the doorway quickly, pushed me back into the room with a tight grin and shut the door. He stood with his back to it, his hand under the left side of his coat. A big hard bony man with flat cruel eyes.

He lowered them slowly and looked at the man on the floor. The man's neck was twitching a little. His eyes moved in short stabs—sick eyes.

"Sure it's the guy?" Copernik's voice was hoarse.

"Positive. Where's Ybarra?"

"Oh, he was busy." He didn't look at me when he said that. "Those your cuffs?"

"Yeah."

"Key."

I tossed it to him. He went down swiftly on one knee beside the killer and took my cuffs off his wrists, tossed them to one side. He got his own off his hip, twisted the bald man's hands behind him and snapped the cuffs on.

"All right, you bastard," the killer said tonelessly.

Copernik grinned and balled his fist and hit the hand-cuffed man in the mouth a terrific blow. His head snapped back almost enough to break his neck. Blood dribbled from the lower corner of his mouth.

"Get a towel," Copernik ordered.

I got a hand towel and gave it to him. Hs stuffed it between the handcuffed man's teeth, viciously, stood up and rubbed his bony fingers through his ratty blond hair.

"All right. Tell it."

I told it—leaving the girl out completely. It sounded a little funny. Copernik watched me, said nothing. He rubbed the side of his veined nose. Then he got his comb out and worked on his hair just as he had done earlier in the evening, in the cocktail bar.

I went over and gave him the gun. He looked at it casually, dropped it into his side pocket. His eyes had something in them and his face moved in a hard bright grin.

I bent down and began picking up my chessmen and dropping them into the box. I put the box on the mantel, straightened out a leg of the card table, played around for a while. All the time Copernik watched me. I wanted him to think something out.

At last he came out with it. "This guy uses a twenty-two," he said. "He uses it because he's good enough to get by with that much gun. That means he's good. He knocks at your door, pokes that gat in your belly, walks you back into the room, says he's here to close your mouth for keeps—and yet you take him. You not having any gun. You take him alone. You're kind of good yourself, pal."

"Listen," I said, and looked at the floor. I picked up

another chessman and twisted it between my fingers. "I was doing a chess problem," I said. "Trying to forget things."

"You got something on your mind, pal," Copernik said softly. "You wouldn't try to fool an old copper, would you, boy?"

"It's a swell pinch and I'm giving it to you," I said. "What the hell more do you want?"

The man on the floor made a vague sound behind the towel. His bald head glistened with sweat.

"What's the matter, pal? You been up to something?" Copernik almost whispered.

I looked at him quickly, looked away again. "All right," I said. "You know damn well I couldn't take him alone. He had the gun on me and he shoots where he looks."

Copernik closed one eye and squinted at me amiably with the other. "Go on, pal. I kind of thought of that too."

I shuffled around a little more, to make it look good. I said, slowly: "There was a kid here who pulled a job over in Boyle Heights, a heist job. It didn't take. A two-bit service station stick-up. I know his family. He's not really bad. He was here trying to beg train money off me. When the knock came he sneaked in—there."

I pointed at the wall bed and the door beside. Copernik's head swiveled slowly, swiveled back. His eyes winked again. "And this kid had a gun," he said.

I nodded. "And he got behind him. That takes guts, Copernik. You've got to give the kid a break. You've got to let him stay out of it."

"Tag out for this kid?" Copernik asked softly.

"Not yet, he says. He's scared there will be."

Copernik smiled. "I'm a homicide man," he said. "I wouldn't know—or care."

I pointed down at the gagged and handcuffed man on the floor. "You took him, didn't you?" I said gently.

Copernik kept on smiling. A big whitish tongue came

out and massaged his thick lower lip. "How'd I do it?" he whispered.

"Get the slugs out of Waldo?"

"Sure. Long twenty-two's. One smashed a rib, one good."

"You're a careful guy. You don't miss any angles. You know anything about me? You dropped in on me to see what guns I had."

Copernik got up and went down on one knee again beside the killer. "Can you hear me, guy?" he asked with his face close to the face of the man on the floor.

The man made some vague sound. Copernik stood up and yawned. "Who the hell cares what he says? Go on, pal."

"You wouldn't expect to find I had anything, but you wanted to look around my place. And while you were mousing around in there"—I pointed to the dressing room—"and me not saying anything, being a little sore, maybe, a knock came on the door. So he came in. So after a while you sneaked out and took him."

"Ah," Copernik grinned widely, with as many teeth as a horse. "You're on, pal. I socked him and I kneed him and I took him. You didn't have no gun and the guy swiveled on me pretty sharp and I left-hooked him down the backstairs. O.K.?"

"O.K.," I said.

"You'll tell it like that downtown?"

"Yeah," I said.

"I'll protect you, pal. Treat me right and I'll always play ball. Forget about that kid. Let me know if he needs a break."

He came over and held out his hand. I shook it. It was as clammy as a dead fish. Clammy hands and the people who own them make me sick.

"There's just one thing," I said. "This partner of yours—Ybarra. Won't he be a bit sore you didn't bring him along on this?"

Copernik tousled his hair and wiped his hatband with a large yellowish silk handkerchief.

"That guinea?" he sneered. "To hell with him!" He came close to me and breathed in my face. "No mistakes, pal—about that story of ours."

His breath was bad. It would be.

4

There were just five of us in the chief-of-detective's office when Copernik laid it before them. A stenographer, the chief, Copernik, myself, Ybarra. Ybarra sat on a chair tilted against the side wall. His hat was down over his eyes but their softness loomed underneath, and the small still smile hung at the corners of the clean-cut Latin lips. He didn't look directly at Copernik. Copernik didn't look at him at all.

Outside in the corridor there had been photos of Copernik shaking hands with me, Copernik with his hat on straight and his gun in his hand and a stern, purposeful look on his face.

They said they knew who Waldo was, but they wouldn't tell me. I didn't believe they knew, because the chief-of-detectives had a morgue photo of Waldo on his desk. A beautiful job, his hair combed, his tie straight, the light hitting his eyes just right to make them glisten. Nobody would have known it was a photo of a dead man with two bullet holes in his heart. He looked like a dance-hall sheik making up his mind whether to take the blonde or the redhead.

It was about midnight when I got home. The apartment door was locked and while I was fumbling for my keys a low voice spoke to me out of the darkness.

All it said was: "Please!" but I knew it. I turned and looked at a dark Cadillac coupe parked just off the loading zone. It had no lights. Light from the street touched the brightness of a woman's eyes.

I went over there. "You're a darn fool," I said.

She said: "Get in."

I climbed in and she started the car and drove it a block and a half along Franklin and turned down Kingsley Drive. The hot wind still burned and blustered. A radio lilted from an open, sheltered side window of an apartment house. There were a lot of parked cars but she found a vacant space behind a small brand-new Packard cabriolet that had the dealer's sticker on the windshield glass. After she'd jockeyed us up to the curb she leaned back in the corner with her gloved hands on the wheel.

She was all in black now, or dark brown, with a small foolish hat. I smelled the sandalwood in her perfume.

"I wasn't very nice to you, was I?" she said.

"All you did was save my life."

"What happened?"

"I called the law and fed a few lies to a cop I don't like and gave him all the credit for the pinch and that was that. That guy you took away from me was the man who killed Waldo."

"You mean—you didn't tell them about me?"

"Lady," I said again, "all you did was save my life. What else do you want done? I'm ready, willing, and I'll try to be able."

She didn't say anything, or move.

"Nobody learned who you are from me," I said. "Incidentally, I don't know myself."

"I'm Mrs. Frank C. Barsaly, Two-twelve Fremont Place, Olympia Two-four-five-nine-six. Is that what you wanted?"

"Thanks," I mumbled, and rolled a dry unlit cigarette around in my fingers. "Why did you come back?" Then I snapped the fingers of my left hand. "The hat and jacket," I said. "I'll go up and get them."

"It's more than that," she said. "I want my pearls." I might have jumped a little. It seemed as if there had been enough without pearls.

A car tore by down the street going twice as fast as it should. A thin bitter cloud of dust lifted in the street lights and whirled and vanished. The girl ran the window up quickly against it.

"All right," I said. "Tell me about the pearls. We have had a murder and a mystery woman and a mad killer and a heroic rescue and a police detective framed into making a false report. Now we will have pearls. All right—feed it to me."

"I was to buy them for five thousand dollars. From the man you call Waldo and I call Joseph Coates. He should have had them."

"No pearls," I said. "I saw what came out of his pockets. A lot of money, but no pearls."

"Could they be hidden in his apartment?"

"Yes," I said. "So far as I know he could have had them hidden anywhere in California except in his pockets. How's Mr. Barsaly this hot night?"

"He's still downtown at his meeting. Otherwise I couldn't have come."

"Well, you could have brought him," I said. "He could have sat in the rumble seat."

"Oh, I don't know," she said. "Frank weighs two hundred pounds and he's pretty solid. I don't think he would like to sit in the rumble seat, Mr. Marlowe."

"What the hell are we talking about anyway?"

She didn't answer. Her gloved hands tapped lightly, provokingly on the rim of the slender wheel. I threw the unlit cigarette out the window, turned a little and took hold of her.

When I let go of her, she pulled as far away from me as she could against the side of the car and rubbed the back of her glove against her mouth. I sat quite still.

We didn't speak for some time. Then she said very slowly: "I meant you to do that. But I wasn't always that way. It's only been since Stan Phillips was killed in his plane. If it hadn't been for that, I'd be Mrs. Phillips now. Stan gave me the pearls. They cost fifteen thousand dollars, he said once. White pearls, forty-one of them, the largest about a third of an inch across. I don't know how many grains. I never had them appraised or showed them to a jeweler, so I don't know those things. But I loved them on Stan's account. I loved Stan. The way you do just the one time. Can you understand?"

"What's your first name?" I asked.

"Lola."

"Go on talking, Lola." I got another dry cigarette out of my pocket and fumbled it between my fingers just to give them something to do.

"They had a simple silver clasp in the shape of a two-bladed propeller. There was one small diamond where the boss would be. I told Frank they were store pearls I had bought myself. He didn't know the difference. It's not so easy to tell, I dare say. You see— Frank is pretty jealous."

In the darkness she came closer to me and her side touched my side. But I didn't move this time. The wind howled and the trees shook. I kept on rolling the cigarette around in my fingers.

"I suppose you've read that story," she said. "About the wife and the real pearls and her telling her husband they were false?"

"I've read it," I said, "Maugham."

"I hired Joseph. My husband was in Argentina at the time. I was pretty lonely."

"*You* should be lonely," I said.

"Joseph and I went driving a good deal. Sometimes we had a drink or two together. But that's all. I don't go around—"

"You told him about the pearls," I said. "And when

your two hundred pounds of beef came back from Argentina and kicked him out—he took the pearls, because he knew they were real. And then offered them back to you for five grand."

"Yes," she said simply. "Of course I didn't want to go to the police. And of course in the circumstance Joseph wasn't afraid of my knowing where he lived."

"Poor Waldo," I said. "I feel kind of sorry for him. It was a hell of a time to run into an old friend that had a down on you."

I struck a match on my shoe sole and lit the cigarette. The tobacco was so dry from the hot wind that it burned like grass. The girl sat quietly beside me, her hands on the wheel again.

"Hell with women—these fliers," I said. "And you're still in love with him, or think you are. Where did you keep the pearls?"

"In a Russian malachite jewelry box on my dressing table. With some other costume jewelry. I had to, if I ever wanted to wear them."

"And they were worth fifteen grand. And you think Joseph might have hidden them in his apartment. Thirty-one, wasn't it?"

"Yes," she said. "I guess it's a lot to ask."

I opened the door and got out of the car. "I've been paid," I said. "I'll go look. The doors in my apartment are not very obstinate. The cops will find out where Waldo lived when they publish his photo, but not tonight, I guess."

"It's awfully sweet of you," she said. "Shall I wait here?"

I stood with a foot on the running board, leaning in, looking at her. I didn't answer her question. I just stood there looking in at the shine of her eyes. Then I shut the car door and walked up the street towards Franklin.

Even with the wind shriveling my face I could still smell the sandalwood in her hair. And feel her lips.

I unlocked the Berglund door, walked through the silent lobby to the elevator, and rode up to Three. Then I soft-footed along the silent corridor and peered down at the sill of Apartment 31. No light. I rapped—the old light, confidential tattoo of the bootlegger with the big smile and the extra-deep hip pockets. No answer. I took the piece of thick hard celluloid that pretended to be a window over the driver's license in my wallet, and eased it between the lock and the jamb, leaning hard on the knob, pushing it toward the hinges. The edge of the celluloid caught the slope of the spring lock and snapped it back with a small brittle sound, like an icicle breaking. The door yielded and I went into near darkness. Street light filtered in and touched a high spot here and there.

I shut the door and snapped the light on and just stood. There was a queer smell in the air. I made it in a moment—the smell of dark-cured tobacco. I prowled over to a smoking stand by the window and looked down at four brown butts—Mexican or South American cigarettes.

Upstairs, on my floor, feet hit the carpet and somebody went into a bathroom. I heard the toilet flush. I went into the bathroom of Apartment 31. A little rubbish, nothing, no place to hide anything. The kitchenette was a longer job, but I only half searched. I knew there were no pearls in that apartment. I knew Waldo had been on his way out and that he was in a hurry and that something was riding him when he turned and took two bullets from an old friend.

I went back to the living room and swung the wall bed and looked past its mirror side into the dressing room for signs of still current occupancy. Swinging the bed farther I was no longer looking for pearls. I was looking at a man.

He was small, middle-aged, iron-gray at the temples, with a very dark skin, dressed in a fawn-colored suit with a wine-colored tie. His neat little brown hands hung limply by his sides. His small feet, in pointed polished shoes, pointed almost at the floor.

He was hanging by a belt around his neck from the metal top of the bed. His tongue stuck out farther than I thought it possible for a tongue to stick out.

He swung a little and I didn't like that, so I pulled the bed shut and he nestled quietly between the two clamped pillows. I didn't touch him yet. I didn't have to touch him to know that he would be cold as ice.

I went around him into the dressing room and used my handkerchief on drawer knobs. The place was stripped clean except for the light litter of a man living alone.

I came out of there and began on the man. No wallet. Waldo would have taken that and ditched it. A flat box of cigarettes, half full, stamped in gold: "Louis Tapia y Cia, Calle de Paysandú, 19, Montevideo." Matches from the Spezia Club. An under-arm holster of dark-grained leather and in it a 9-millimeter Mauser.

The Mauser made him a professional, so I didn't feel so badly. But not a very good professional, or bare hands would not have finished him, with the Mauser— a gun you can blast through a wall with—undrawn in his shoulder holster.

I made a little sense of it, not much. Four of the brown cigarettes had been smoked, so there had been either waiting or discussion. Somewhere along the line Waldo had got the little man by the throat and held him in just the right way to make him pass out in a matter of seconds. The Mauser had been less useful to him than a toothpick. Then Waldo had hung him up by the strap, probably dead already. That would account for haste, cleaning out the apartment, for Waldo's anxiety about the girl. It would account for the car left unlocked outside the cocktail bar.

That is, it would account for these things if Waldo

had killed him, if this was really Waldo's apartment—if I wasn't just being kidded.

I examined some more pockets. In the left trouser one I found a gold penknife, some silver. In the left hip pocket a handkerchief, folded, scented. On the right hip another, unfolded but clean. In the right leg pocket four or five tissue handkerchiefs. A clean little guy. He didn't like to blow his nose on his handkerchief. Under these there was a small new keytainer holding four new keys —car keys. Stamped in gold on the keytainer was: Compliments of R. K. Vogelsang, Inc. "The Packard House."

I put everything as I had found it, swung the bed back, used my handkerchief on knobs and other projections, and flat surfaces, killed the light and poked my nose out the door. The hall was empty. I went down to the street and around the corner to Kingsley Drive. The Cadillac hadn't moved.

I opened the car door and leaned on it. She didn't seem to have moved, either. It was hard to see any expression on her face. Hard to see anything but her eyes and chin, but not hard to smell the sandalwood.

"That perfume," I said, "would drive a deacon nuts ... no pearls."

"Well, thanks for trying," she said in a low, soft vibrant voice. "I guess I can stand it. Shall I . . . Do we ... Or ... ?"

"You go on home now," I said. "And whatever happens you never saw me before. Whatever happens. Just as you may never see me again."

"I'd hate that."

"Good luck, Lola." I shut the car door and stepped back.

The lights blazed on, the motor turned over. Against the wind at the corner the big coupe made a slow contemptuous turn and was gone. I stood there by the vacant space at the curb where it had been.

It was quite dark there now. Windows had become blanks in the apartment where the radio sounded. I stood looking at the back of a Packard cabriolet which seemed to be brand new. I had seen it before—before I went upstairs, in the same place, in front of Lola's car. Parked, dark, silent, with a blue sticker pasted to the right-hand corner of the shiny windshield.

And in my mind I was looking at something else, a set of brand-new car keys in a keytainer stamped: "The Packard House," upstairs, in a dead man's pocket.

I went up to the front of the cabriolet and put a small pocket flash on the blue slip. It was the same dealer all right. Written in ink below his name and slogan was a name and address—Eugénie Kolchenko, 5315 Arvieda Street, West Los Angeles.

It was crazy. I went back up to Apartment 31, jimmied the door as I had done before, stepped in behind the wall bed and took the keytainer from the trousers pocket of the neat brown dangling corpse. I was back down on the street beside the cabriolet in five minutes The keys fitted.

5

It was a small house, near a canyon rim out beyond Sawtelle, with a circle of writhing eucalyptus strees in front of it. Beyond that, on the other side of the street, one of those parties was going on where they come out and smash bottles on the sidewalk with a whoop like Yale making a touchdown against Princeton.

There was a wire fence at my number and some rose trees, and a flagged walk and a garage that was wide open and had no car in it. There was no car in front of the house either. I rang the bell. There was a long wait, then the door opened rather suddenly.

I wasn't the man she had been expecting. I could see

it in her glittering kohl-rimmed eyes. Then I couldn't see anything in them. She just stood and looked at me, a long, lean, hungry brunette, with rouged cheekbones, thick black hair parted in the middle, a mouth made for three-decker sandwiches, coral-and-gold pajamas, sandals—and gilded toenails. Under her ear lobes a couple of miniature temple bells gonged lightly in the breeze. She made a slow disdainful motion with a cigarette in a holder as long as a baseball bat.

"We-el, what ees it, little man? You want sometheeng? You are lost from the bee-ootiful party across the street, hein?"

"Ha-ha," I said. "Quite a party, isn't it? No, I just brought your car home. Lost it, didn't you?"

Across the street somebody had delirium tremens in the front yard and a mixed quartet tore what was left of the night into small strips and did what they could to make the strips miserable. While this was going on the exotic brunette didn't move more than one eyelash.

She wasn't beautiful, she wasn't even pretty, but she looked as if things would happen where she was.

"You have said what?" she got out, at last, in a voice as silky as a burnt crust of toast.

"Your car." I pointed over my shoulder and kept my eyes on her. She was the type that uses a knife.

The long cigarette holder dropped very slowly to her side and the cigarette fell out of it. I stamped it out, and that put me in the hall. She backed away from me and I shut the door.

The hall was like the long hall of a railroad flat. Lamps glowed pinkly in iron brackets. There was a bead curtain at the end, a tiger skin on the floor. The place went with her.

"You're Miss Kolchenko?" I asked, not getting any more action.

"Ye-es. I am Mees Kolchenko. What the 'ell you want?"

She was looking at me now as if I had come to wash the windows, but at an inconvenient time.

I got a card out with my left hand, held it out to her. She read it in my hand, moving her head just enough. "A detective?" she breathed.

"Yeah."

She said something in a spitting language. Then in English: "Come in! Thees damn wind dry up my skeen like so much teesue paper."

"We're in," I said. "I just shut the door. Snap out of it, Nazimova. Who was he? The little guy?"

Beyond the bead curtain a man coughed. She jumped as if she had been stuck with an oyster fork. Then she tried to smile. It wasn't very successful.

"A reward," she said softly. "You weel wait 'ere? Ten dollars it is fair to pay, no?"

"No," I said.

I reached a finger towards her slowly and added: "He's dead."

She jumped about three feet and let out a yell.

A chair creaked harshly. Feet pounded beyond the bead curtain, a large hand plunged into view and snatched it aside, and a big hard-looking blond man was with us. He had a purple robe over his pajamas, his right hand held something in his robe pocket. He stood quite still as soon as he was through the curtain, his feet planted solidly, his jaw out, his colorless eyes like gray ice. He looked like a man who would be hard to take out on an off-tackle play.

"What's the matter, honey?" He had a solid, burring voice, with just the right sappy tone to belong to a guy who would go for a woman with gilded toenails.

"I came about Miss Kolchenko's car," I said.

"Well, you could take your hat off," he said. "Just for a light workout."

I took it off and apologized.

"O.K.," he said, and kept his right hand shoved

down hard in the purple pocket. "So you came about Miss Kolchenko's car. Take it from there."

I pushed past the woman and went closer to him. She shrank back against the wall and flattened her palms against it. Camille in a high-school play. The long holder lay empty at her toes.

When I was six feet from the big man he said easily: "I can hear you from there. Just take it easy. I've got a gun in this pocket and I've had to learn to use one. Now about the car?"

"The man who borrowed it couldn't bring it," I said, and pushed the card I was still holding towards his face. He barely glanced at it. He looked back at me.

"So what?" he said.

"Are you always this tough?" I asked. "Or only when you have your pajamas on?"

"So why couldn't he bring it himself?" he asked. "And skip the mushy talk."

The dark woman made a stuffed sound at my elbow.

"It's all right, honeybunch," the man said. "I'll handle this. Go on."

She slid past both of us and flicked through the bead curtain.

I waited a little while. The big man didn't move a muscle. He didn't look any more bothered than a toad in the sun.

"He couldn't bring it because somebody bumped him off," I said. "Let's see you handle that."

"Yeah?" he said. "Did you bring him with you to prove it?"

"No," I said. "But if you put your tie and crush hat on, I'll take you down and show you."

"Who the hell did you say you were, now?"

"I didn't say. I thought maybe you could read." I held the card at him some more.

"Oh, that's right," he said. "Philip Marlowe, Private

Investigator. Well, well. So I should go with you to look at who, why?"

"Maybe he stole the car," I said.

The big man nodded. "That's a thought. Maybe he did. Who?"

"The little brown guy who had the keys to it in his pocket, and had it parked around the corner from the Berglund Apartments."

He thought that over, without any apparent embarrassment. "You've got something there," he said. "Not much. But a little. I guess this must be the night of the Police Smoker. So you're doing all their work for them."

"Huh?"

"The card says private detective to me," he said. "Have you got some cops outside that were too shy to come in?"

"No, I'm alone."

He grinned. The grin showed white ridges in his tanned skin. "So you find somebody dead and take some keys and find a car and come riding out here—all alone. No cops. Am I right?"

"Correct."

He sighed. "Let's go inside," he said. He yanked the bead curtain aside and made an opening for me to go through. "It might be you have an idea I ought to hear."

I went past him and he turned, keeping his heavy pocket towards me. I hadn't noticed until I got quite close that there were beads of sweat on his face. It might have been the hot wind but I didn't think so.

We were in the living room of the house.

We sat down and looked at each other across a dark floor, on which a few Navajo rugs and a few dark Turkish rugs made a decorating combination with some well-used overstuffed furniture. There was a fireplace, a small baby grand, a Chinese screen, a tall Chinese lantern on a teakwood pedestal, and gold net curtains against lattice windows. The windows to the south were open. A fruit tree with a whitewashed trunk whipped about outside the screen, adding its bit to the noise from across the street.

The big man eased back into a brocaded chair and put his slippered feet on a footstool. He kept his right hand where it had been since I met him—on his gun.

The brunette hung around in the shadows and a bottle gurgled and her temple bells gonged in her ears.

"It's all right, honeybunch," the man said. "It's all under control. Somebody bumped somebody off and this lad thinks we're interested. Just sit down and relax."

The girl tilted her head and poured half a tumbler of whiskey down her throat. She sighed, said, "Goddam," in a casual voice, and curled up on a davenport. It took all of the davenport. She had plenty of legs. Her gilded toenails winked at me from the shadowy corner where she kept herself quiet from then on.

I got a cigarette out without being shot at, lit it and went into my story. It wasn't all true, but some of it was. I told them about the Berglund Apartments and that I had lived there and that Waldo was living there in Apartment 31 on the floor below mine and that I had been keeping an eye on him for business reasons.

"Waldo what?" the blond man put in. "And what business reasons?"

"Mister," I said, "have you no secrets?" He reddened slightly.

I told him about the cocktail lounge across the street from the Berglund and what had happened there. I didn't tell him about the printed bolero jacket or the girl who had worn it. I left her out of the story altogether.

"It was an undercover job—from my angle," I said. "If you know what I mean." He reddened again, bit his teeth. I went on: "I got back from the city hall without telling anybody I knew Waldo. In due time, when I decided they couldn't find out where he lived that night, I took the liberty of examining his apartment."

"Looking for what?" the big man said thickly.

"For some letters. I might mention in passing there was nothing there at all—except a dead man. Strangled and hanging by a belt to the top of the wall bed—well out of sight. A small man, about forty-five, Mexican or South American, well-dressed in a fawn-colored——"

"That's enough," the big man said. "I'll bite, Marlowe. Was it a blackmail job you were on?"

"Yeah. The funny part was this little brown man had plenty of gun under his arm."

"He wouldn't have five hundred bucks in twenties in his pocket, of course? Or are you saying?"

"He wouldn't. But Waldo had over seven hundred in currency when he was killed in the cocktail bar."

"Looks like I underrated this Waldo," the big man said calmly. "He took my guy and his pay-off money, gun and all. Waldo have a gun?"

"Not on him."

"Get us a drink, honeybunch," the big man said. "Yes, I certainly did sell this Waldo person shorter than a bargain-counter shirt."

The brunette unwound her legs and made two drinks with soda and ice. She took herself another gill without trimmings, wound herself back on the davenport. Her big glittering black eyes watched me solemnly.

"Well, here's how," the big man said, lifting his glass in salute. "I haven't murdered anybody, but I've got a divorce suit on my hands from now on. You haven't murdered anybody, the way you tell it, but you laid an egg down at police headquarters. What the hell! Life's a lot of trouble, anyway you look at it. I've still got honeybunch here. She's a white Russian I met in Shanghai. She's safe as a vault and she looks as if she could cut your throat for a nickel. That's what I like about her. You get the glamor without the risk."

"You talk damn foolish," the girl spat him.

"You look O.K. to me," the big man went on ignoring her. "That is, for a keyhole peeper. Is there an out?"

"Yeah. But it will cost a little money."

"I expected that. How much?"

"Say another five hundred."

"Goddam, thees hot wind make me dry like the ashes of love," the Russian girl said bitterly.

"Five hundred might do," the blond man said. "What do I get for it?"

"If I swing it—you get left out of the story. If I don't —you don't pay."

He thought it over. His face looked lined and tired now. The small beads of sweat twinkled in his short blond hair.

"This murder will make you talk," he grumbled. "The second one, I mean. And I don't have what I was going to buy. And if it's a hush, I'd rather buy it direct."

"Who was the little brown man?" I asked.

"Name's Leon Valesanos, a Uruguayan. Another of my importations. I'm in a business that takes me a lot of places. He was working in the Spezzia Club in Chiseltown—you know, the strip of Sunset next to Beverly Hills. Working on roulette, I think. I gave him the five hundred to go down to this—this Waldo—and buy back some bills for stuff Miss Kolchenko had charged to my account and delivered here. That wasn't bright, was it? I had them in my briefcase and this Waldo got a chance to steal them. What's your hunch about what happened?"

I sipped my drink and looked at him down my nose. "Your Uruguayan pal probably talked curt and Waldo didn't listen good. Then the little guy thought maybe that Mauser might help his argument—and Waldo was too quick for him. I wouldn't say Waldo was a killer— not by intention. A blackmailer seldom is. Maybe he lost his temper and maybe he just held on to the little guy's neck too long. Then he had to take it on the lam. But he had another date, with more money coming up.

And he worked the neighborhood looking for the party. And accidentally he ran into a pal who was hostile enough and drunk enough to blow him down."

"There's a hell of a lot of coincidence in all this business," the big man said.

"It's the hot wind," I grinned. "Everybody's screwy tonight."

"For the five hundred you guarantee nothing? If I don't get my cover-up, you don't get your dough. Is that it?"

"That's it," I said, smiling at him.

"Screwy is right," he said, and drained his highball. "I'm taking you up on it."

"There are just two things," I said softly, leaning forward in my chair. "Waldo had a getaway car parked outside the cocktail bar where he was killed, unlocked with the motor running. The killer took it. There's always the chance of a kickback from that direction. You see, all Waldo's stuff must have been in that car."

"Including my bills, and your letters."

"Yeah. But the police are reasonable about things like that—unless you're good for a lot of publicity. If you're not, I think I can eat some stale dog downtown and get by. If you are—that's the second thing. What did you say your name was?"

The answer was a long time coming. When it came I didn't get as much kick out of it as I thought I would. All at once it was too logical.

"Frank C. Barsaly," he said.

After a while the Russian girl called me a taxi. When I left, the party across the street was doing all that a party could do. I noticed the walls of the house were still standing. That seemed a pity.

6

When I unlocked the glass entrance door of the Berglund I smelled policeman. I looked at my wrist watch. It was nearly 3 A.M. In the dark corner of the lobby a man dozed in a chair with a newspaper over his face. Large feet stretched out before him. A corner of the paper lifted an inch, dropped again. The man made no other movement.

I went on along the hall to the elevator and rode up to my floor. I soft-footed along the hallway, unlocked my door, pushed it wide and reached in for the light switch.

A chain switch tinkled and light glared from a standing lamp by the easy chair, beyond the card table on which my chessmen were still scattered.

Copernik sat there with a stiff unpleasant grin on his face. The short dark man, Ybarra, sat across the room from him, on my left, silent, half smiling as usual.

Copernik showed more of his big yellow horse teeth and said: "Hi. Long time no see. Been out with the girls?"

I shut the door and took my hat off and wiped the back of my neck slowly, over and over again. Copernik went on grinning. Ybarra looked at nothing with his soft dark eyes.

"Take a seat, pal," Copernik drawled. "Make yourself to home. We got pow-wow to make. Boy, do I hate this night sleuthing. Did you know you were low on hooch?"

"I could have guessed it," I said. I leaned against the wall.

Copernik kept on grinning. "I always did hate private dicks," he said, "but I never had a chance to twist one like I got tonight."

He reached down lazily beside his chair and picked up a printed bolero jacket, tossed it on the card table.

He reached down again and put a wide-brimmed hat beside it.

"I bet you look cuter than all hell with these on," he said.

I took hold of a straight chair, twisted it around and straddled it, leaned my folded arms on the chair and looked at Copernik.

He got up very slowly—with an elaborate slowness, walked across the room and stood in front of me smoothing his coat down. Then he lifted his open right hand and hit me across the face with it—hard. It stung but I didn't move.

Ybarra looked at the wall, looked at the floor, looked at nothing.

"Shame on you, pal," Copernik said lazily. "The way you was taking care of this nice exclusive merchandise. Wadded down behind your old shirts. You punk peepers always did make me sick."

He stood there over me for a moment. I didn't move or speak. I looked into his glazed drinker's eyes. He doubled a fist at his side, then shrugged and turned and went back to the chair.

"O.K.," he said. "The rest will keep. Where did you get these things?"

"They belong to a lady."

"Do tell. They belong to a lady. Ain't you the light-hearted bastard! I'll tell you what lady they belong to. They belong to the lady a guy named Waldo asked about in a bar across the street—about two minutes before he got shot kind of dead. Or would that have slipped your mind?"

I didn't say anything.

"You was curious about her yourself," Copernik sneered on. "But you were smart, pal. You fooled me."

"That wouldn't make me smart," I said.

His face twisted suddenly and he started to get up. Ybarra laughed, suddenly and softly, almost under his breath. Copernik's eyes swung on him, hung there. Then he faced me again, bland-eyed.

"The guinea likes you," he said. "He thinks you're good."

The smile left Ybarra's face, but no expression took its place. No expression at all.

Copernik said: "You knew who the dame was all the time. You knew who Waldo was and where he lived. Right across the hall a floor below you. You knew this Waldo person had bumped a guy off and started to lam, only this broad came into his plans somewhere and he was anxious to meet up with her before he went away. Only he never got the chance. A heist guy from back East named Al Tessilore took care of that by taking care of Waldo. So you met the gal and hid her clothes and sent her on her way and kept your trap glued. That's the way guys like you make your beans. Am I right?"

"Yeah," I said. "Except that I only knew these things very recently. Who was Waldo?"

Copernik bared his teeth at me. Red spots burned high on his sallow cheeks. Ybarra, looking down at the floor, said very softly: "Waldo Ratigan. We got him from Washington by teletype. He was a two-bit porch climber with a few small terms on him. He drove a car in a bank stick-up job in Detroit. He turned the gang in later and got a nolle prosse. One of the gang was this Al Tessilore. He hasn't talked a word, but we think the meeting across the street was purely accidental."

Ybarra spoke in the soft quiet modulated voice of a man for whom sounds have a meaning. I said: "Thanks, Ybarra. Can I smoke—or would Copernik kick it out of my mouth?"

Ybarra smiled suddenly. "You may smoke, sure," he said.

"The guinea likes you all right," Copernik jeered. "You never know what a guinea will like, do you?"

I lit a cigarette. Ybarra looked at Copernik and said very softly: "The word guinea—you overwork it. I don't like it so well applied to me."

"The hell with what you like, guinea."

Ybarra smiled a little more. "You are making a mistake," he said. He took a pocket nail file out and began to use it, looking down.

Copernik blared: "I smelled something rotten on you from the start, Marlowe. So when we make these two mugs, Ybarra and me think we'll drift over and dabble a few more words with you. I bring one of Waldo's morgue photos—nice work, the light just right in his eyes, his tie all straight and a white handkerchief showing just right in his pocket. Nice work. So on the way up, just as a matter of routine, we rout out the manager here and let him lamp it. And he knows the guy. He's here as A. B. Hummel, Apartment Thirty-one. So we go in there and find a stiff. Then we go round and round with that. Nobody knows him yet, but he's got some swell finger bruises under that strap and I hear they fit Waldo's fingers very nicely."

"That's something," I said. "I thought maybe I murdered him."

Copernik stared at me a long time. His face had stopped grinning and was just a hard brutal face now. "Yeah. We got something else even," he said. "We got Waldo's getaway car—and what Waldo had in it to take with him."

I blew cigarette smoke jerkily. The wind pounded the shut windows. The air in the room was foul.

"Oh, we're bright boys," Copernik sneered. "We never figured you with that much guts. Take a look at this."

He plunged his bony hand into his coat pocket and drew something up slowly over the edge of the card table, drew it along the green top and left it there stretched out, gleaming. A string of white pearls with a clasp like a two-bladed propeller. They shimmered softly in the thick smoky air.

Lola Barsaly's pearls. The pearls the flier had given her. The guy who was dead, the guy she still loved.

I stared at them, but I didn't move. After a long moment Copernik said almost gravely: "Nice, ain't they? Would you feel like telling us a story about now, Mis-ter Marlowe?"

I stood up and pushed the chair from under me, walked slowly across the room and stood looking down at the pearls. The largest was perhaps a third of an inch across. They were pure white, iridescent, with a mellow softness. I lifted them slowly off the card table from beside her clothes. They felt heavy, smooth, fine.

"Nice," I said. "A lot of the trouble was about these. Yeah, I'll talk now. They must be worth a lot of money."

Ybarra laughed behind me. It was a very gentle laugh. "About a hundred dollars," he said. "They're good phonies—but they're phony."

I lifted the pearls again. Copernik's glassy eyes gloated at me. "How do you tell?" I asked.

"I know pearls," Ybarra said. "These are good stuff, the kind women very often have made on purpose, as a kind of insurance. But they are slick like glass. Real pearls are gritty between the edges of the teeth. Try."

I put two or three of them between my teeth and moved my teeth back and forth, then sideways. Not quite biting them. The beads were hard and slick.

"Yes. They are very good," Ybarra said. "Several even have little waves and flat spots, as real pearls might have."

"Would they cost fifteen grand—if they were real?" I asked.

"Sí. Probably. That's hard to say. It depends on a lot of things."

"This Waldo wasn't so bad," I said.

Copernik stood up quickly, but I didn't see him swing. I was still looking down at the pearls. His fist caught me on the side of the face, against the molars. I tasted blood at once. I staggered back and made it look like a worse blow than it was.

"Sit down and talk, you bastard!" Copernik almost whispered.

I sat down and used a handkerchief to pat my cheek. I licked at the cut inside my mouth. Then I got up again and went over and picked up the cigarette he had knocked out of my mouth. I crushed it out in a tray and sat down again.

Ybarra filed at his nails and held one up against the lamp. There were beads of sweat on Copernik's eyebrows, at the inner ends.

"You found the beads in Waldo's car," I said, looking at Ybarra. "Find any papers?"

He shook his head without looking up.

"I'd believe you," I said. "Here it is. I never saw Waldo until he stepped into the cocktail bar tonight and asked about the girl. I knew nothing I didn't tell. When I got home and stepped out of the elevator this girl, in the printed bolero jacket and the wide hat and the blue silk crêpe dress—all as he had described them—was waiting for the elevator, here on my floor. And she looked like a nice girl."

Copernik laughed jeeringly. It didn't make any difference to me. I had him cold. All he had to do was know that. He was going to know it now, very soon.

"I knew what she was up against as a police witness," I said. "And I suspected there was something else to it. But I didn't suspect for a minute that there was anything wrong with her. She was just a nice girl in a jam—and she didn't even know she was in a jam. I got her in here. She pulled a gun on me. But she didn't mean to use it."

Copernik sat up very suddenly and he began to lick

his lips. His face had a stony look now. A look like wet gray stone. He didn't make a sound.

"Waldo had been her chauffeur," I went on. "His name was then Joseph Coates. Her name is Mrs. Frank C. Barsaly. Her husband is a big hydroelectric engineer. Some guy gave her the pearls once and she told her husband they were just store pearls. Waldo got wise somehow there was a romance behind them and when Barsaly came home from South America and fired him, because he was too good-looking, he lifted the pearls."

Ybarra lifted his head suddenly and his teeth flashed. "You mean he didn't know they were phony?"

"I thought he fenced the real ones and had imitations fixed up," I said.

Ybarra nodded. "It's possible."

"He lifted something else," I said. "Some stuff from Barsaly's briefcase that showed he was keeping a woman—out in Brentwood. He was blackmailing wife and husband both, without either knowing about the other. Get it so far?"

"I get it," Copernik said harshly, between his tight lips. His face was still wet gray stone. "Get the hell on with it."

"Waldo wasn't afraid of them," I said. "He didn't conceal where he lived. That was foolish, but it saved a lot of finagling, if he was willing to risk it. The girl came down here tonight with five grand to buy back her pearls. She didn't find Waldo. She came here to look for him and walked up a floor before she went back down. A woman's idea of being cagey. So I met her. So I brought her in here. So she was in that dressing room when Al Tessilore visited me to rub out a witness." I pointed to the dressing-room door. "So she came out with her little gun and stuck it in his back and saved my life," I said.

Copernik didn't move. There was something horrible

in his face now. Ybarra slipped his nail file into a small leather case and slowly tucked it into his pocket.

"Is that all?" he said gently.

I nodded. "Except that she told me where Waldo's apartment was and I went in there and looked for the pearls. I found the dead man. In his pocket I found new car keys in a case from a Packard agency. And down on the street I found the Packard and took it to where it came from. Barsaly's kept woman. Barsaly had sent a friend from the Spezzia Club down to buy something and he had tried to buy it with his gun instead of the money Barsaly gave him. And Waldo beat him to the punch."

"Is that all?" Ybarra said softly.

"That's all," I said licking the torn place on the inside of my cheek.

Ybarra said slowly: "What do you want?"

Copernik's face convulsed and he slapped his long hard thigh. "This guy's good," he jeered. "He falls for a stray broad and breaks every law in the book and you ask him what does he want? I'll give him what he wants, guinea!"

Ybarra turned his head slowly and looked at him. "I don't think you will," he said. "I think you'll give him a clean bill of health and anything else he wants. He's giving you a lesson in police work."

Copernik didn't move or make a sound for a long minute. None of us moved. Then Copernik leaned forward and his coat fell open. The butt of his service gun looked out of his underarm holster.

"So what do you want?" he asked me.

"What's on the card table there. The jacket and hat and the phony pearls. And some names kept away from the papers. Is that too much?"

"Yeah—it's too much," Copernik said almost gently. He swayed sideways and his gun jumped neatly into his hand. He rested his forearm on his thigh and pointed the gun at my stomach.

"I like better that you get a slug in the guts resisting arrest," he said. "I like that better, because of a report I made out on Al Tessilore's arrest and how I made the pinch. Because of some photos of me that are in the morning sheets going out about now. I like it better that you don't live long enough to laugh about that baby."

My mouth felt suddenly hot and dry. Far off I heard the wind booming. It seemed like the sound of guns.

Ybarra moved his feet on the floor and said coldly: "You've got a couple of cases all solved, policeman. All you do for it is leave some junk here and keep some names from the papers. Which means from the D.A. If he gets them anyway, too bad for you."

Copernik said: "I like the other way." The blue gun in his hand was like a rock. "And God help you, if you don't back me up on it."

Ybarra said: "If the woman is brought out into the open, you'll be a liar on a police report and a chisler on your own partner. In a week they won't even speak your name at Headquarters. The taste of it would make them sick."

The hammer clicked back on Copernik's gun and I watched his big finger slide in farther around the trigger.

Ybarra stood up. The gun jumped at him. He said: "We'll see how yellow a guinea is. I'm telling you to put that gun up, Sam."

He started to move. He moved four even steps. Copernik was a man without a breath of movement, a stone man.

Ybarra took one more step and quite suddenly the gun began to shake.

Ybarra spoke evenly: "Put it up, Sam. If you keep your head everything lies the way it is. If you don't— you're gone."

He took one more step. Copernik's mouth opened wide and made a gasping sound and then he sagged in the chair as if he had been hit on the head. His eyelids dropped.

Ybarra jerked the gun out of his hand with a movement so quick it was no movement at all. He stepped back quickly, held the gun low at his side.

"It's the hot wind, Sam. Let's forget it," he said in the same even, almost dainty voice.

Copernik's shoulders sagged lower and he put his face in his hands. "O.K.," he said between his fingers.

Ybarra went softly across the room and opened the door. He looked at me with lazy, half-closed eyes. "I'd do a lot for a woman who saved my life, too," he said. "I'm eating this dish, but as a cop you can't expect me to like it."

I said: "The little man in the bed is called Leon Valesanos. He was a croupier at the Spezzia Club."

"Thanks," Ybarra said. "Let's go, Sam."

Copernik got up heavily and walked across the room and out of the open door and out of my sight. Ybarra stepped through the door after him and started to close it.

I said: "Wait a minute."

He turned his head slowly, his left hand on the door, the blue gun hanging down close to his right side.

"I'm not in this for money," I said. "The Barsalys live at Two-twelve Fremont Place. You can take the pearls to her. If Barsaly's name stays out of the paper, I get five *C's*. It goes to the Police Fund. I'm not so damn smart as you think. It just happened that way— and you had a heel for a partner."

Ybarra looked across the room at the pearls on the card table. His eyes glistened. "You take them," he said. "The five hundred's O.K. I think the fund has it coming."

He shut the door quietly and in a moment I heard the elevator doors clang.

7

I opened a window and stuck my head out into the wind and watched the squad car tool off down the block. The wind blew in hard and I let it blow. A picture fell off the wall and two chessmen rolled off the card table. The material of Lola Barsaly's bolero jacket lifted and shook.

I went out to the kitchenette and drank some Scotch and went back into the living room and called her—late as it was.

She answered the phone herself, very quickly, with no sleep in her voice.

"Marlowe," I said. "O.K. your end?"

"Yes . . . yes," she said. "I'm alone."

"I found something," I said. "Or rather the police did. But your dark boy gypped you. I have a string of pearls. They're not real. He sold the real ones, I guess, and made you up a string of ringers, with your clasp."

She was silent for a long time. Then, a little faintly: "The police found them?"

"In Waldo's car. But they're not telling. We have a deal. Look at the papers in the morning and you'll be able to figure out why."

"There doesn't seem to be anything more to say," she said. "Can I have the clasp?"

"Yes. Can you meet me tomorrow at four in the Club Esquire bar?"

"You're really rather sweet," she said in a dragged out voice. "I can. Frank is still at his meeting."

"Those meetings—they take it out of a guy," I said. We said good-bye.

I called a West Los Angeles number. He was still there, with the Russian girl.

"You can send me a check for five hundred in the

morning," I told him. "Made out to the Police Relief Fund, if you want to. Because that's where it's going."

Copernik made the third page of the morning papers with two hotos and a nice half-column. The little brown man in Apartment 31 didn't make the paper at all. The Apartment House Association has a good lobby too.

I went out after breakfast and the wind was all gone. It was soft, cool, a little foggy. The sky was close and comfortable and gray. I rode down to the boulevard and picked out the best jewelry store on it and laid a string of pearls on a black velvet mat under a daylight-blue lamp. A man in a wing collar and striped trousers looked down at them languidly.

"How good?" I asked.

"I'm sorry, sir. We don't make appraisals. I can give you the name of an appraiser."

"Don't kid me," I said. "They're Dutch."

He focused the light a little and leaned down and toyed with a few inches of the string.

"I want a string just like them, fitted to that clasp, and in a hurry," I added.

"How, like them?" He didn't look up. "And they're not Dutch. They're Bohemian."

"O.K., can you duplicate them?"

He shook his head and pushed the velvet pad away as if it soiled him. "In three months, perhaps. We don't blow glass like that in this country. If you wanted them matched—three months at least. And this house would not do that sort of thing at all."

"It must be swell to be that snooty," I said. I put a card under his black sleeve. "Give me a name that will —and not in three months—and maybe not exactly like them."

He shrugged, went away with the card, came back in five minutes and handed it back to me. There was something written on the back.

The old Levantine had a shop on Melrose, a junk

shop with everything in the window from a folding baby carriage to a French horn, from a mother-of-pearl lorgnette in a faded plush case to one of those .44 Special Single Action six-shooters they still make for Western peace officers whose grandfathers were tough.

The old Levantine wore a skull cap and two pairs of glasses and a full beard. He studied my pearls, shook his head sadly, and said: "For twenty dollars, almost so good. Not so good, you understand. Not so good glass."

"How like will they look?"

He spread his firm strong hands. "I am telling you the truth," he said. "They would not fool a baby."

"Make them up," I said. "With this clasp. And I want the others back, too, of course."

"Yah. Two o'clock," he said.

Leon Valesanos, the little brown man from Uruguay, made the afternoon papers. He had been found hanging in an unnamed apartment. The police were investigating.

At four o'clock I walked into the long cool bar of the Club Esquire and prowled along the row of booths until I found one where a woman sat alone. She wore a hat like a shallow soup plate with a very wide edge, a brown tailor-made suit with a severe mannish shirt and tie.

I sat down beside her and slipped a parcel along the seat. "You don't open that," I said. "In fact you can slip it into the incinerator as is, if you want to."

She looked at me with dark tired eyes. Her fingers twisted a thin glass that smelled of peppermint. "Thanks." Her face was very pale.

I ordered a highball and the waiter went away. "Read the papers?"

"Yes."

"You understand now about this fellow Copernik who stole your act? That's why they won't change the story or bring you into it."

"It doesn't matter now," she said. "Thank you, all the same. Please—please show them to me."

I pulled the string of pearls out of the loosely wrapped tissue paper in my pocket and slid them across to her. The silver propeller clasp winked in the light of the wall bracket. The little diamond winked. The pearls were as dull as white soap. They didn't even match in size.

"You were right," she said tonelessly. "They are not my pearls."

The waiter came with my drink and she put her bag on them deftly. When he was gone she fingered them slowly once more, dropped them into the bag and gave me a dry mirthless smile.

I stood there a moment with a hand hard on the table.

"As you said—I'll keep the clasp."

I said slowly: "You don't know anything about me. You saved my life last night and we had a moment, but it was just a moment. You still don't know anything about me. There's a detective downtown named Ybarra, a Mexican of the nice sort, who was on the job when the pearls were found in Waldo's suitcase. That is in case you would like to make sure—"

She said: "Don't be silly. It's all finished. It was a memory. I'm too young to nurse memories. It may be for the best. I loved Stan Phillips—but he's gone—long gone."

I stared at her, didn't say anything.

She added quietly: "This morning my husband told me something I hadn't known. We are to separate. So I have very little to laugh about today."

"I'm sorry," I said lamely. "There's nothing to say. I may see you sometime. Maybe not. I don't move much in your circle. Good luck."

I stood up. We looked at each other for a moment. "You haven't touched your drink," she said.

"You drink it. That peppermint stuff will just make you sick."

I stood there a moment with a hand on the table.

"If anybody ever bothers you," I said, "let me know."

I went out of the bar without looking back at her, got into my car and drove west on Sunset and down all the way to the Coast Highway. Everywhere along the way gardens were full of withered and blackened leaves and flowers which the hot wind had burned.

But the ocean looked cool and languid and just the same as ever. I drove on almost to Malibu and then parked and went and sat on a big rock that was inside somebody's wire fence. It was about half-tide and coming in. The air smelled of kelp. I watched the water for a while and then I pulled a string of Bohemian glass imitation pearls out of my pocket and cut the knot at one end and slipped the pearls off one by one.

When I had them all loose in my left hand I held them like that for a while and thought. There wasn't really anything to think about. I was sure.

"To the memory of Mr. Stan Phillips," I said aloud. "Just another four-flusher."

I flipped her pearls out into the water one by one at the floating seagulls.

They made little splashes and the seagulls rose off the water and swooped at the splashes.